Wings Above the Diamantina

In this series:

The Sands of Windee
Winds of Evil
Mr Jelly's Business
The Bone is Pointed
Bushranger of the Skies
Death of a Swagman
The Devil's Steps
An Author Bites the Dust
The Widows of Broome
Man of Two Tribes
The Battling Prophet
The Mystery of Swordfish Reef
The Bachelors of Broken Hill
The Will of the Tribe
Murder Must Wait
The New Shoe
Bony and the White Savage
The Lake Frome Monster
Venom House
Wings Above the Diamantina

ARTHUR W. UPFIELD

Wings Above the Diamantina

ANGUS & ROBERTSON PUBLISHERS

NOTE
All characters in this book are entirely fictitious, and no reference is intended to any living person.

ANGUS & ROBERTSON PUBLISHERS

Unit 4, Eden Park,
31 Waterloo Road, North Ryde,
NSW, Australia 2113
and
16 Golden Square, London
W1R 4BN, United Kingdom

First published 1936
This Arkon paperback edition first published in Australia by Angus & Robertson Publishers and in the United Kingdom by Angus & Robertson (UK) Ltd in 1985

National Library of Australia
Cataloguing-in-publication data.

Upfield, Arthur W. (Arthur William), 1888-1964.
Wings above the Diamantina.
First published: Sydney: Angus & Robertson, 1936.
ISBN 0 207 15076 1.
I. Title.
A823'.2

Printed in Great Britain by
Richard Clay (The Chaucer Press) Ltd,
Bungay, Suffolk

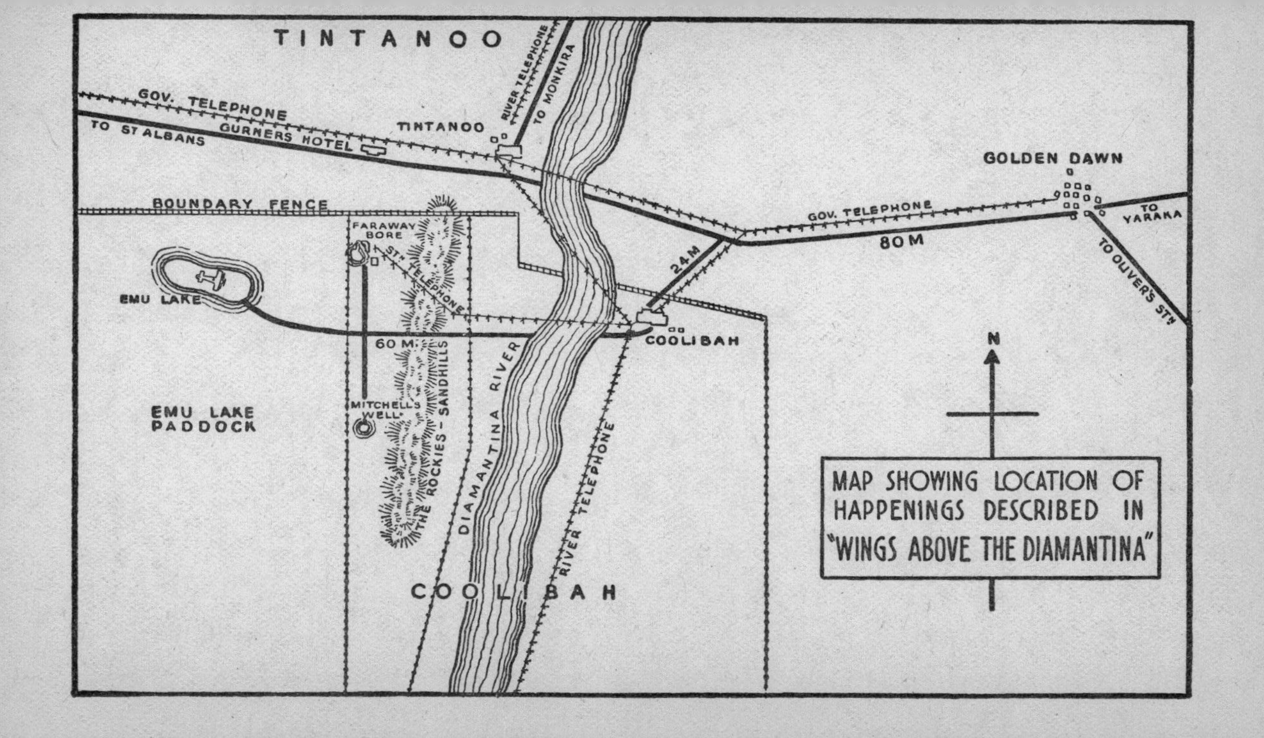
TINTANOO
GOV. TELEPHONE
TO ST ALBANS
GURNERS HOTEL
TINTANOO
RIVER TELEPHONE
TO MONKIRA
GOLDEN DAWN
TO YARAKA
TO OLIVER'S STN
GOV. TELEPHONE
80 M
24 M
BOUNDARY FENCE
FARAWAY BORE
STN TELEPHONE
EMU LAKE
60 M
COOLIBAH
MITCHELL'S WELL
THE ROCKIES - SANDHILLS
DIAMANTINA RIVER
RIVER TELEPHONE
EMU LAKE PADDOCK
COOLIBAH
N
MAP SHOWING LOCATION OF HAPPENINGS DESCRIBED IN "WINGS ABOVE THE DIAMANTINA"

CONTENTS

CONTENTS

CHAPTER I

THE DERELICT AEROPLANE

BECAUSE the day was still and cool and invigorating, Elizabeth elected to accompany her father on a tour of the fifteen hundred square miles of country called Coolibah. The sample of late October weather in the far west of Queensland had nothing to do with Nettlefold's decision to make this tour of the great cattle station of which he had been the manager for thirty-two years. With him such a tour came within the ambit of routine work, but on this occasion he wished to inspect a mob of store cattle before they were handed over to the drovers who were to take them to Bourke for the Sydney market; and, further, he wanted to inspect the condition of the feed in a huge paddock, named Emu Lake, which had been resting for two years.

"I am glad you came, Elizabeth," he said, while the comfortable car took them ever westward of the great Diamantina River.

"I am, too," the girl replied quickly. "The house is always very quiet when you're away, and heaven knows it's quiet enough when you are home." Elizabeth smiled. "And then when you are away something always happens to the radio."

Her beautiful face gave the lie direct to those who say that the Queensland climate ruins feminine complexions.

Her hair was deep brown, and so, too, were her large eyes. The colouring of her face was fresh, and only her lips were touched with rouge.

"This is the fourth time you have come with me since we took to cars," he pointed out after a little silence.

"The fifth time," she corrected him.

Laughter narrowed his eyes and rounded his brick-red face.

"Well, a car is not so slow and boring as the buckboard used to be. I remember the first occasion you came out with me. You were only five years old, and, although we joined forces against your mother, it was a hard tussle to get her to let you go."

"That was the time the river came down while we were outback, and we had to camp for two weeks waiting for it to subside enough to make the crossing back to the house. I remember most distinctly poor mother running out of the house to meet us. I think that my earliest memory is of her anxious face that day."

"She had cause to be anxious. There was no telephone from the homestead out to the stockmen's huts in those days, and no telephone from the stations up north by which we could have ample notice of a coming flood. Before you were born your mother often came with me and used to enjoy the camping out. We were great pals, your mother and I."

The girl's hand for a moment caressed his coated arm. Then she said softly: "And now we are pals aren't we?"

"Yes, Elizabeth, we are pals, good pals," he agreed, and then relapsed into silence.

They were twenty miles west of the maze of intertwining empty channels of the Diamantina, and thirty-five miles from Coolibah homestead. Ahead of them ranged massive sand-dunes, orange-coloured and bare of herbage save for scanty cotton-bush. Here and there beyond the sand crests of the range reared the vivid foliage of bloodwood trees, while beyond them rose a great brown cloud of dust.

"That'll be Ted Sharp with the cattle," Nettlefold said, with reference to the dust cloud.

"How many are we sending away this time?" asked the girl.

"Eight hundred—I am hoping. It will depend."

The track led them round a spur of sand running upward for forty odd feet to the summit of a dune. It then led them in and among the sandhills, following hard and wind-swept claypans, on which the wheels of vehicles left imprints barely visible. The Rockies, Elizabeth had called them the first time she had induced her father to stop here for lunch and permit her to scramble up one and then slide down its steep face with shrieks of laughter and boots filled hard with the fine grains.

Then, as suddenly as they had passed into the seeming barrier, the car shot out on to a wide treeless plain, a grey plain which was fringed along its far side with dark timber. Before them milled a slow-moving mass of cattle, moving like a wheel, and driven by four horsemen. A fifth horseman, leading a spare saddled horse, came cantering to meet them. When they stopped he brought his animals close to the car. Off came his wide-brimmed felt hat to reveal straight brown hair and the line across his forehead below which the sun and the wind had stained his face. Above the line the milk-white skin made a startling contrast.

"Morning, Mr Nettlefold! Morning, Miss Elizabeth!" he shouted, before dismounting to lead the horses closer.

To the girl he added with easy deference: "I thought you would have gone to Golden Dawn and had a flip or two with those flying fellows. All the boys were going to ask for time off to go up and look-see the bush from above if this muster hadn't been ordered."

"Somehow I just couldn't be bothered," she said, smiling, and not unmindful of his lithe grace in the saddle. "Anyway, the eggs in the incubator were due to hatch yesterday, and while they were hatching I could not be away from home."

"A good hatching?" he asked, with raised brows.

"Yes. Ninety-one out of the hundred."

"How do they weigh up, Ted?" interrupted Nettlefold, his thoughts running on more important things than chickens.

"Fair. Ought to average eight hundred pounds dressed. There's eight hundred and nineteen in the muster. Will you look 'em over?"

"May as well, now that you've brought the spare hack. Who have you got with you beside Ned Hamlin and Shut-eye?"

"Bill Sikes and Fred the Dogger."

Nettlefold nodded and then, telling Elizabeth he would not be long, he swung into the saddle of the spare hack and rode away stiffly towards the milling cattle. Ted Sharp waved his hat to the girl. Elizabeth smiled and waved back. He was the most cheerful, life-loving man she had ever known.

With the smile still playing about her lips she watched them ride towards the cattle: her father stiffly, his head stockman with the swinging grace of one who spends the daylight hours on the back of a horse. Sharp pointed out something relative to the cattle, and the horses began to canter in a wide arc.

Ted Sharp had arrived from nowhere in particular eleven years before, and even now he was not much more than thirty. When he came to Coolibah Elizabeth had been a tomboy of fourteen, and her mother had been dead four years. From early childhood she could ride, but with the coming of Ted Sharp her horses and her riding improved beyond measure. He was a born horse-breaker, beside being a first-rate cattleman, and it was not long before he was promoted boss stockman. He appeared to be a born boss stockman, too, for he never had the slightest trouble with the men.

Presently her father and he came riding slowly back to the car. They were in earnest conversation, and she guessed without hesitation the subject of discussion. She could not possibly be wrong, because when two men meet anywhere in cattle country they talk cattle.

"We're all going to Golden Dawn to-morrow, Miss Eliz'-beth," the boss stockman called out while distance still separated them. "Mr Nettlefold says we can go. Hope to see you there, too. You must command your father to take you."

"I never command my father to do anything," she corrected him, her serious expression belied by laughing eyes.

The big, bluff manager of Coolibah regarded her with obvious pride. Everything about her—the grey tailor-made costume, the modish hat which did not conceal the golden sheen of her hair—combined to place his daughter on an equal footing with the smartest city women.

"No, you never command, Elizabeth," he said slowly. "But somehow I always obey."

Giving Sharp the reins of the horse, he walked to the car and climbed in behind the wheel. There, having settled his big, strong body, he proceeded to cut chips from a large plug of black tobacco, the kind which has long gone out of fashion among bushmen.

"Tell Sanders that I have arranged credit for him at Quilpie, Cunnamulla and Bourke," he directed. "Ask him to let me know by wire when he has trucked these beasts because there may be enough fats in Bottom Bend for him to lift in January to take to Cockburn for Adelaide. We're due for a dry time after this run of good seasons, and I don't want to be caught overstocked."

"All right! There'll be fats enough in Bottom Bend, I'll bet."

"There should be, provided we don't get an overdose of windstorms to blow away all the feed. Well, we'll get on. Want to get back home to-night. So long!"

"So long, Mr Nettlefold! *Au revoir*, Miss Eliz'beth."

Having given the manager a quick salute, the boss stockman was less hasty with the daughter. She eyed him coolly, but her look only made his smile broaden. She laughed at him when the car began to move, and returned his salute with a white-gloved hand.

Twenty minutes later they were across the plain and among the stunted bloodwoods and the mulgas. Here in this imitation forest grew no ground feed of bush and grass, but it provided good top feed in dry times.

A few miles of scrub, and then their way lay across a wide area of broken sand country criss-crossed by water gutters that appeared to follow no uniform direction. It was barren save for far-spaced, thirst-tortured coolibah trees, and here and there patches of tussock-grass. An amazing place, this. It was the studio of the Wind King who had chiselled the sand hummocks into fantastic shapes, a veritable hell when the hot westerlies blew in November and March.

Sixty miles from home they boiled the billy for lunch, the car halted in the shadow cast blackly on the glaring ground by three healthy bloodwoods. The girl set up the low canvas table beside the running board. She busied herself with cut sandwiches and little cakes and crockery ware which her father never thought of bringing when he travelled by himself. Alone, his tucker box furnished with a tin pannikin and a butcher's killing knife, bread and cold meat, tea and sugar, sufficed him. His wife, and, after her, his daughter, had failed to alter the habits of his youth when he served as a stockman, and later as a boss stockman.

"Ah! By the look of things we are going to do ourselves well to-day," he said cheerfully.

"Of course," she agreed emphatically, smiling up at him. "You would not expect me to be satisfied with a thick slice of bread and an equally thick slice of salt meat, would you?"

"Hardly. What's sauce for the old gander would be sandstone for the young goose. However, I am not sure that elegant living is good for a man. I have noticed lately a touch of indigestion. I never had that when I lived on damper and salt meat and jet-black tea."

"Probably not, Dad; but you now have a touch of indigestion because you once lived on those things," she countered swiftly. "Pour out my tea, please, before it becomes ink-black."

Nettlefold was happy because his daughter was with him, and she was happy because he was so. Elizabeth was not the bush lover that her father was. The bush had "got" him in its alluring toils, but she had resisted it and, having resisted, escaped it. Paradoxically, she found no love for the bush, and yet hated the city.

The meal eaten, he gallantly lit her cigarette, and, with his pipe alight, began to pack away the luncheon things. She watched him, her eyes guarded with lowered lids, and told herself how fine was this simple, generous father of hers. It was understood that when she was out on the run with him she was his guest, staying at his country house, as he put it, and as his guest she was not to do any of the chares.

Then on again, through the gate into the great Emu Lake paddock, a fenced area eighteen miles square. The stock having been excluded for two years, the grasses lay beneath the sun like turned oats. Patches of healthy scrub encumbered the undulating grasslands like dark, rocky islands. Here in this paddock sheltered for two years, the kangaroos were numerous; and, on nearing a bore-head, the travellers were greeted by a vast flock of galah parrots.

Every twenty-four hours seven hundred thousand gallons of water hotly gushed from the bore-head to run away for miles along the channel scooped to carry it. Years before, when the bore first had been sunk to tap the artesian reservoir, the flow was nearly eleven hundred thousand gallons every twenty-four hours.

Day and night, year in and year out, the stream spouted hot from the iron casing to run down the channel now edged with the snow-white soda suds. Not within half a mile of the bore could cattle drink the water, so hot and so loaded with alkalies was it.

Nettlefold drove the car beside the channel for some distance before turning to the north along an old and faint track. About ten minutes after leaving the bore stream they emerged from dense scrub and were on the dry, perfectly flat bottom of a shallow ground depression from which the paddock was named. It was edged, this waterless lake, with a shore of white, cement-hard claypan lying like a bridal ribbon at the foot of swamp gums crowned with brilliant green foliage. The girl uttered a sharp exclamation, and her father unconsciously braked the car to a halt.

In the centre of the lake, and facing towards them, rested a small low-winged monoplane varnished a bright red.

CHAPTER II

AERIAL FLOTSAM

"THAT'S strange!" Nettlefold said softly, still sitting in the halted car and gazing across the flat surface of the lake. In area the lake was some two miles long and about one mile wide. On it grew widely spaced tussock-grass which, because of its spring lushness, the kangaroos had eaten down to within an inch of the ground. Had Emu Lake been filled with water—as it had been after the deluge of 1908—it would have been a veritable bush jewel. Now the colouring of the lake itself was drab. Without the water it was like a ring from which the jewel had fallen, leaving the mere setting.

"I believe there is somebody in the plane," Elizabeth said sharply. "Isn't that someone in the front seat?"

"If there is, then your eyes are better than mine," her father replied. "The pilot must have made a forced landing. We'll drive round a bit and then cross to it."

Nettlefold had to take care when negotiating the steep yet low bank to reach the ribbon of claypan, and then, because the machine was a little to the left, he drove the car along the firm level claypan strip until opposite the aeroplane, when he turned sharply out on to the lake bed.

The heavy car bumped over the tussock-grass butts, the open spaces between them covered with deep sand, and so eventually drew to within a few yards of the spick and span red-varnished monoplane.

Slightly above their level, a girl occupied the front seat. Her pose was perfectly natural. Her head was tilted forward as though she were interested in something lying on her lap. She was quite passive, as though absorbed by an exciting book. No one could be seen in the pilot's cockpit.

"Good afternoon!" called Nettlefold.

The occupant of the monoplane offered no acknowledgment of the salute. She continued impassively to gaze down at her lap. She made no movement when he called again.

"It certainly is strange, Dad," Elizabeth said uneasily.

"I agree with you. Wait here."

John Nettlefold's voice had acquired a metallic note. Alighting from the car, he walked towards the plane until his head became level with the edge of the front cockpit. He was then able to observe that the girl's eyes were almost closed. She was not reading. She was asleep—or dead. . . .

"Good afternoon!" he called for the third time.

Still she made no response. He gently pinched the lobe of her left ear. It was warm to the touch, but his act failed to arouse her.

"Come, come! Wake up!" he said loudly, and this time he shook her, finding her body flexible with life. He failed, however, to awaken her.

Nor, he assured himself, was the rear cockpit occupied, although here were the controls of the plane.

"Is she dead?" asked Elizabeth from the car.

"No, but there is something peculiar about her. Come here, and have a look." Then, when she had joined him: "She looks exactly as though she is asleep, but if she is I can't wake her. Where, I wonder, is the pilot?"

"Walked away for assistance, I suppose. The plane appears to be quite undamaged. Ought we not to lift her out? She may be merely in a faint."

"Wait . . . one moment! Don't move about!"

Nettlefold's bush-acquired instincts now came into play. His gaze was directed to the ground in the vicinity of the machine. As mentioned, the grass butts were widely spaced, and between each cropped butt the lake surface was composed of fine reddish sand. Their own boot and shoe prints from the car were plainly discernible, but there were no other tracks left by a human being. The pilot had not jumped from the machine to the ground on their side. Neither had the girl.

Having walked round to the far side of the machine, the cattleman discovered that neither the girl nor the pilot had dropped to the ground on that side. When he rejoined Elizabeth he had made a complete circuit, and he at once proceeded to make a second, this time one of greater circumference.

"There wasn't a pilot," he said when he again joined his daughter. "That girl must have piloted the aeroplane herself. No one has left it after it landed here."

"But if she controlled the machine she would be in the rear cockpit, wouldn't she?" queried Elizabeth.

"Doubtless she was. She must have climbed forward to the front cockpit after she landed the machine. That no one has left the machine is certain. No one could have left it without leaving tracks."

With compressed lips, Nettlefold stepped back the better to view the crimson varnished aeroplane from gleaming propeller to tail tip. It was either a new machine or had been recently varnished. Along the fuselage in white was painted the cipher, V.H-U, followed by the registration letters.

It was indeed an extraordinary place in which to encounter a flying machine. They were hundreds of miles off any established air route, and to Nettlefold's knowledge no squatter within the far-flung boundaries of the district possessed an aeroplane. He was, of course, aware that adventure-seeking people were beginning to fly round and across Australia, but hitherto they had kept to well-defined routes. Here they were about one hundred and twenty miles from the nearest township, Golden Dawn, and Emu Lake did not lie on any line from town to town, or from station homestead to homestead.

"Let's get her out, Dad," urged Elizabeth. "If she has fainted we must bring her round."

Placing his foot in the step cut in the side of the fuselage he hauled himself up and astride the plane as though mounting into the saddle. He settled his weight securely on the narrow division between the two cockpits and behind the motionless girl. His hands slipped beneath her arms, and then he cried out to Elizabeth: "Why, she is strapped into her seat!"

"They all do that, you know," she reminded him.

"Maybe they do, but why should this young lady strap herself into her seat if she got into it after she landed the machine from the rear seat controls?"

"The plane may have what they call dual controls."

"Well, there are no gadgets in the front cockpit," he objected.

"Never mind, Dad. Lift her out and down to me. The mysteries can be cleared up after we have discovered what is the matter with her."

It proved no mean task to lift the girl out of the cockpit. She remained absolutely passive during the operation of getting her down to the waiting Elizabeth. She was well developed, and her weight proved Elizabeth's strength when she took the unconscious girl and laid her on the ground beside the aeroplane. When her father joined her, she was looking intently at the rigid face.

"She's rather pretty, isn't she?"

"Yes," Nettlefold agreed. "Do you think she is in a faint?"

"I don't know. I doubt it. It doesn't look like a faint. Will you bring me some water from the car, please?"

Elizabeth, while waiting for the water, continued to study the immobile features. The lips were parted just a little, and the breast rose and fell regularly. The girl appeared to be sleeping, and yet it was a strange sleep, because as a rule the face of a sleeping person registers some kind of expression. It was strange, too, because it was a sleep from which no ordinary methods could wake her. She was wearing a blue serge skirt and a light-blue jersey over a silk blouse. Her shoes and stockings were of good quality. She was wearing no jewellery.

When her father brought the canvas waterbag and a cup, Elizabeth seated herself beside the still figure and lifted the head into her lap. The filled cup she set against the curved lips, but the unconscious girl made not the slightest effort to drink. With her handkerchief, Elizabeth sponged her forehead and the backs of her hands, but to all her treatment the aeroplane girl failed to respond.

"I can't understand it," Elizabeth said at last. "It frightens me."

Now on his knees beside his daughter, the station manager used the tip of a little finger to raise the girl's left eyelid. He uttered an exclamation and raised the other. The girl was now staring at him with sinister fixity, her eyelids remaining in the position to which he had raised them. They were large and blue, dark-blue, and in them was the unmistakable expression of wild entreaty. Involuntarily, he said:

"It is all right! Really, it is. We are going to be your friends."

"What! Is she awake?" Elizabeth demanded sharply. Quickly she lifted the girl's head and then, finding the angle difficult, she squirmed her body round so that she, too, was able to look into the blue eyes. "Why, she is conscious!"

For a moment they regarded the staring eyes, in their hearts both horror and a great pity. Not once did the eyelids blink. The helpless girl uttered no sound, made no smallest movement save very slightly to move her eyes. Except for the poignant expression in them, her face might have been cast in plaster of Paris.

"Can't you speak?" said Elizabeth, barely above a whisper.

Obtaining no response, she took up the cup of water and again pressed its edge against the immobile lips. There was no movement, no effort made to drink.

"Oh! You poor thing! Whatever is the matter?"

"Part her lips and see if she will drink when you drop the water into her mouth," Nettlefold suggested.

Elizabeth accepted the suggestion, and they presently saw that the helpless girl swallowed. Her eyes were now misty, and from them welled great tears which Elizabeth sponged away with the handkerchief.

"Won't you try to talk?" she pleaded softly. "Can't you talk? Can you close your eyelids? Try—just try to do that. No?" To her father, she said: "I can't understand it. She seems perfectly conscious, and yet she is so helpless that she cannot even raise or lower her eyelids. I am positive that she can hear us and understand us."

"Yes, I think so, too," he agreed instantly. "Well, the only thing to do is to get her home as quickly as possible. Then we must call Dr Knowles. He should know what is the matter with her. We'll be moving. We can do nothing here."

"All right. You take her. I'll get into the back seat of the car, and you can hand her in to me," Elizabeth directed. To the girl, she said: "I am going to close your eyes because of the sunlight. Have no fear—Dad and I will look after you and find your friends. And Dr Knowles is really clever."

Throughout the entire homeward journey, Elizabeth supported the helpless girl against her body, exhibiting stoical endurance. She took the shocks that her careful father was unable to avoid.

Ted Smart and his men, with the cattle, had disappeared from the grey plain, and for mile after mile the car hummed eastward to one of the most extraordinary rivers in Australia. At this time no water was running down the Diamantina's multitudinous channels. Here the river had no main channel to distinguish it from the veritable maze of streams which intertwine between the countless banks. Westward from the Coolibah homestead, the channels which form the river are fifteen miles across, and when the great floods come sliding down from the far northern hills only the tops of the coolibah trees are left visible.

When crossing the river the track was a seemingly endless switchback, and here the greatest trial was put upon

Elizabeth coming after the long journey from Emu Lake. Narrow channels and wide channels; narrow banks and wide banks: the car was constantly being forced up and down like a ship passing over sea waves. Long before they arrived there could be seen the large white-painted homestead, men's quarters and outhouses, all with red roofs gleaming beneath the sun. The conglomeration of buildings appeared and disappeared endlessly until at last the travellers reached the easternmost flat to speed smoothly for half a mile before reaching the horse-paddock gate. From the gate it was a quick run up a stiff gradient to the house which, with the many other buildings, was built on comparatively high land. Before the car stopped outside the gate of the garden fronting the south veranda, a woman came running to meet them.

She was tall and angular, strong and exceedingly plain. She was dressed in stiff white linen, reminding one of a hospital nurse. Mrs Hetty Brown, the deserted wife of a stockman, was the Coolibah housekeeper.

"Oh, Mr Nettlefold! Miss Elizabeth! Whatever do you think?" she cried. Her light-grey eyes were slightly protuberant, and now they were wide open with excitement. "Just after you left this morning Sergeant Cox rang up to say that last night someone stole an aeroplane at Golden Dawn. He said he would have rung through before but there was something the matter with the line. He wanted to know if we had seen or heard the aeroplane. It belongs to. . . . Why, Miss Elizabeth, who is that?"

"It is a young lady whom we found in peculiar circumstances, Hetty, and we have to get her to bed," the manager informed her. "Where will you have her, Elizabeth?"

"In my bed for the present—Hetty, come round to the

other side and assist Mr Nettleford. My arms are useless with cramp."

"Dear me! Whatever has happened to her?" Hetty cried.

"We don't know yet. There now. Hold her while I move aside. Take her weight. Gently, now! Got her, Dad?"

"Yes, I have her."

Despite his growing years, John Nettlefold was still a powerful man. He lifted the helpless girl and bore her along the garden path, up the several veranda steps and through the open house door as a lesser man might carry a child. At Elizabeth's command, Hetty assisted her from the car, and then was ordered to run on and prepare her bed for the stranger. Grimacing with agony, Elizabeth followed slowly, moving her limbs to hasten returning circulation, and was just in time to meet her father coming from her room.

"I'll get in touch with Knowles and Cox right away," he said. "How's the cramp?"

"It's going," she stated calmly. "It was stupid of us not to have thought of looking in the plane for her belongings."

"Yes, we should have done that," he hastened to agree. "Anyway, either Cox or I will have to got out to it to-morrow, so our omission is unimportant."

She smiled at him, then smiled at something which flashed into her mind.

"Do you know," she said, "I think I am at last going to justify my life here at Coolibah."

"What do you mean?"

"Some day I will tell you," she replied swiftly, and was gone.

CHAPTER III

A FLYING DOCTOR

WHEN going "inside," people at Coolibah followed the track winding away to the north-east from the homestead. Having travelled that track for twenty-four miles, they arrived at the Golden Dawn-St Alban track. Here there was a roughly made sign-post pointing south-west to Coolibah, north-west to Tintanoo Station and St Albans, east to Golden Dawn. About noon every Wednesday, the Golden Dawn-St Albans mail coach reached the road junction, and the mailman alighted to place the Coolibah mail in the letter-box fashioned from a petrol case and nailed securely to a tree. At noon the following day, on his return journey to Golden Dawn, he collected the Coolibah outward mail from the same box.

In addition to the twenty-four miles from the homestead to the track junction, the person desiring to go "inside" had to travel eighty miles to Golden Dawn, and a farther hundred and ten miles to the railhead at Yaraka. And from there the long rail journey to Brisbane began. It is not precisely a journey which can be undertaken from a country town to the city on a Bank holiday, and consequently people in the far west of Queensland do not often visit Brisbane.

Beside the track to Coolibah ran the telephone line which at the road junction was transferred to the poles carrying the Tintanoo and St Albans lines. When John Nettlefold rang Golden Dawn he was answered by the girl in the small exchange situated within the post office building. She connected him with the police-station. It was exactly six o'clock, and Sergeant Cox was dining with his wife and son. To answer the call, the sergeant had to pass from the kitchen through the house to the office, which occupied one of the front rooms.

"Well?" he growled. "What is it?"

"Nettlefold speaking, Sergeant. I understand that an aeroplane belonging to the visiting 'flying circus' was stolen last night."

"Ah—yes, Mr Nettlefold. Know anything about it?"

"Was the machine a monoplane type varnished a bright red?"

"Yes. Have you seen it? Has it come down on your place?"

"It has," announced Nettlefold from Coolibah.

"Have you got the fellow who stole it?" grimly demanded Cox.

"I don't think so."

"You don't . . . you don't *think* so! Surely, Mr Nettlefold, you know definitely if you have or have not apprehended the thief?"

The station manager's prevarication acted like wind on sea. The policeman's large red face took to itself a deeper colour. The short iron-grey hair appeared to stand more stiffly on end, and the iron-grey eyes to become mere pinpoints. The iron-grey moustache bristled. Place Sergeant Cox in khaki, and on him put a Sam Browne belt and a pith helmet, and you would see the popular conception of an army general on Indian service.

"No, I cannot say definitely whether I have the thief," replied Nettlefold easily, quite unabashed by the sergeant's asperity. "Listen carefully."

He related the bare details of all that had happened at Emu Lake, and then he asked for particulars of the theft.

"It's queer, Mr Nettlefold, to say the least," Cox said, as though he addressed John Nettlefold, Esq., J.P., when sitting on the bench. "This aeroplane circus—that is what Captain Loveacre, who is in charge, calls it—has been here three days. There is a twin-engined de Haviland passenger machine for taking up trippers, and there's that red monoplane which the captain flies himself, the big one being flown by his two assistant pilots. We have got no proper aerodrome here, as you know, but the surrounding plain makes a fair landing ground.

"As usual, last night the two machines were anchored just back of the hotel; and, at one-forty-two this morning, everyone was awakened by the roar of a motor engine. Captain Loveacre states that when he woke he recognized the sound of the engine as that of his monoplane, but before he or any one else could get out to it it had left the ground and flown off eastward."

"So you do not know the sex of the thief, Sergeant?"

"No. Is the girl you speak of very ill?"

"We can't make her out at all," answered Nettlefold. "Look here! It is now only a minute past six. Do you think you could get Knowles to fly here this evening to have a look at her? There are two hours of daylight yet, remember."

"Oh—he'll agree to go," Cox said, with airy assurance. "He'd start if he had to make a night landing on those river channels. What I can't understand about him is that he's still alive. The more drunk he is the better he flies. I might come with him."

"Do. We can put you both up. I could then take you out to Emu Lake early in the morning. Tell Knowles that he can land with reasonable safety on the white claypan country half a mile north of this homestead. I'll be there in the car, and in case it's dark when he arrives I'll have the boys light fires along the edges of the enclosing scrub. Will you ring me when you know what he will do?"

"I will. But he'll go all right," Cox further assured the station manager. "If he breaks my neck . . . well, I'll be the most unlucky man in Queensland."

"You're game, anyway. I wouldn't trust my life to Knowles . . . off the ground."

Cox chuckled and replaced the instrument, to walk thoughtfully back to the kitchen.

"Pack me a bag, Vi," he commanded his wife. "I'm going to Coolibah Station."

"For how long?"

"I don't know. Only a night, I think."

"Have they found the stolen aeroplane, Dad?" asked his son, a fair-haired, blue-eyed boy of fifteen years.

"Yes, Jack," Cox replied, nodding. "It is at a place called Emu Lake at the back of Coolibah. Pass the bread. I may just as well finish my dinner while your mother's hunting up those pink-striped visiting pyjamas of mine."

"Who stole it, Dad?" pleaded the boy.

"We don't rightly know, son, but you can trust your father to find out."

The red face was now less red. The stern lines about the iron jaw were much less hard. Sergeant Cox led a double life, one of which was known only to his wife and son. He was softly human when with them in their home.

"I won't be home to-night to show you how to do your home lessons, so you've got to get right down to them yourself and work out those sums the best you know how."

"All right, Dad. I'll do 'em goodo."

"Of course he will, Pops," added Mrs Cox, then entering the kitchen. "Who is going to drive you to Coolibah? Driving your own car?"

"I am going with Dr Knowles."

"What! With that cranky fool! Oh, Pops!"

"Pops" grinned, rose from the table, kissed his wife and put on his hat with habitual care to achieve the right angle. He was dressed in civilian clothes, and yet with the addition of the felt hat he no longer was "Pops," but Sergeant Cox.

"If Dr Knowles crashes the machine when I am with him," he said sternly, "I will arrest him on the D and D charge."

"But you might be killed, Pops."

"Dad'll be all right, Mum. Why, Dr Knowles can fly underneath the telephone wires," Jack pointed out.

"I shall not be killed," Cox said. "Dr Knowles might crash, but I will live to arrest him and keep him in our lock-up. I'll be back for the bag later on. And don't forget, son, what I told you last night about those square roots."

Again leaving the kitchen, Sergeant Cox strode along the passage to the open front door, passed across the veranda, down the steps and so to the front gate in the wicket fence. Above the gate on a narrow wooden arch were the words, POLICE-STATION, and on the fly gauze covering the window frame of the left hand room was the word OFFICE.

Across the hundred-yards-wide unmetalled track stood

the store, a low, rambling, wooden building badly infested with termites and badly in need of paint. When he emerged from the Government premises it was to turn left to stride along the main street of Golden Dawn.

Once Golden Dawn had been a thriving mining town, and still the poppet heads of the mine half a mile to the north stood cutting clearly into the sky like the gibbet outside a medieval town. Cox passed vacant building sites on either side of the dusty street, sites from which the buildings long since had been purchased and removed for the iron and wood.

Golden Dawn now had a forsaken appearance: it was like a homeless old man who dreamed ever of better days. In the middle of the street wandered the town dairyman's cows, while the dairyman himself was within the too-commodious hotel. Across each vacant allotment could be seen the flat gibber plain stretching to blue-black hills lying to the north and east, and to the flat horizon line to westward and to southward. Outside the hotel stood Mounted Constable Lovitt.

"Who's inside?" asked Cox.

Lovitt began a list of names, but Cox cut him short.

"Is Dr Knowles in there?"

"No, Sergeant."

"Captain Loveacre, then?"

"No. He went along to Dr Knowles half an hour ago."

"I am flying with Dr Knowles to Coolibah this evening. Might be away for a couple of days," Cox said in his most official manner. "The crowd staying in seems to be thinning out a lot, so you won't have much work. It is a good thing that neither Ned Hamlin nor Larry the Lizard are in town. Keep in touch with the office as much as possible. I may want you on the phone."

"Very well, Sergeant."

Cox glared at the constable and turned to walk away, but relented and faced him.

"The monoplane has been found on Coolibah by Mr Nettlefold," he said. "He found a strange woman in it. I understand that she is injured. Circumstances peculiar. Know any woman around here who can fly an aeroplane?"

"No, I don't, Sergeant. There isn't one."

"I don't know of one, either. Who is still in town of importance?"

"Only Mr Kane, of Tintanoo. The Greysons have gone. So have the Olivers, of Windy Creek."

"All right!"

Sergeant Cox walked on along the street which incongruously enough was bordered with well-kept sidewalks and veteran pepper-trees, evidences of Golden Dawn's departed prosperity. At last he came to a gate in a white-painted fence beyond which stood a large wooden house with a wide veranda. When he knocked on the open door it appeared to be a mere act of courtesy; for, on hearing voices in the room to the left, he did not wait for the doctor's housekeeper to answer his knock but walked right in.

"Good evening, Doctor! Evening, Captain!" he greeted the two men at table. Dinner, evidently, was just over.

"Hullo, Cox! Looking for Captain Loveacre?" inquired one, a medium built man with dark eyes and short moustache.

"Both of you, as a matter of fact."

The second man, also of medium height, but clean shaven, stood up.

"Have you news about my bus?" he asked eagerly.

"Yes. It is all right as far as is known. No, thanks! I've just had dinner. I'll take a cigarette."

Seating himself, Sergeant Cox related the incidents concerning the discovery of the stolen aeroplane.

"Mr Nettlefold says that the young woman found in it strapped in the front cockpit is suffering from a form of paralysis," he continued. "The Coolibah manager thinks she did not steal the machine. It has made a good landing, and as far as he can see it is quite undamaged."

"Rather an extraordinary business," said the doctor. "If the girl did not steal the machine, where is the pilot? No trace of him?"

"None—if there was a pilot with the girl. What about having a look at her to-night?"

Dr Knowles laughed shortly and pounced on the whisky decanter.

"I am not sufficiently drunk to fly and set down in the dark in a strange place."

"Then you had better get drunk enough without wasting time," Cox said in the exact tones he used when ordering a reveller off to bed. "Half a mile north of the Coolibah homestead is a stretch of level claypan country good enough to land on. We can make it before dark. Mr Nettlefold will be waiting with a car."

"How far is it?" asked Knowles, again tipping the decanter.

"One hundred miles, as near as dammit. We've got an hour and a half of daylight left us."

"All right! What about you, Loveacre?"

"Is it a prepared ground?" asked the famous airman, who had been forced to air-circusing for his daily bread.

"No."

"But I could land the de Haviland on this Emu Lake without being cramped, couldn't I?"

"Yes," chipped in the doctor, again tipping the decanter. "I've never been there, but I have heard Nettlefold talk about it. He says it is the best natural 'drome in western Queensland. Hi! Mrs Chambers!"

"Aren't you drunk enough yet?" Cox asked with frozen calm.

"Just about, Sergeant. Oh, Mrs Chambers! Bring me my black bag, please. I shall be away all night."

"Well, when you come back don't have to be carried in again like a squashed tomato," grumpily returned the old housekeeper. " Flying about in the dead of night."

"Now, now! Get my bag, and don't take the door frame with you. I told you before not to go in and out of door frames frontways."

Loveacre chuckled, and the doctor once more tipped the decanter. Sergeant Cox glared. Then he stood up and took the decanter from the flying doctor and placed it inside the sideboard cupboard.

"We'll be going," he snapped.

Dr Knowles stood up, swaying slightly.

"You are a good scout, Sergeant, but you are damned rude. I'll make you as sick as a dog for that." His voice was perfectly clear. Turning to the captain, he said: "Come along with us to my plane, and I'll loan you a decent map of the country."

The doctor's pale face now was tinged with colour. His dark eyes gleamed brilliantly. He visibly staggered on his way to the door, but his articulation was perfect when he again called to Mrs Chambers. He was talking to her in the hall, and solemnly assuring her that he had left her the house in his will, when the airman touched Cox's arm.

"Good in the air?" he asked doubtfully.

The sergeant nodded, his body as stiff as a gun barrel.

"Better drunk than sober," he replied. "He has had three crashes these last two years, but he was stone sober on each occasion. You will be flying to Emu Lake to-morrow?"

"Yes, I'll go with the boys in the de Haviland, and fly my own machine back. That landing ground you will come down on to-night—how big is it?"

"I don't know. I'll get Mr Nettlefold to ring you up later. He can give you all the information you require."

"Good man! I'll be at the pub. I'm thundering glad that machine wasn't damaged. I am not too well off, and the insurance would not cover the complete loss."

"Well, come on. The doctor is ready. Might I ask you not to discuss the frills in reference to your monoplane being found?"

"Certainly, Sergeant."

At the street gate, Cox parted from the doctor and the airman to hurry back to his house for his bag. The sun was low in the western sky. The air was motionless and painted a deep gold where in it hung the dust raised by the dairyman's cows and the two separate mobs of goats being driven to yards on the outskirts of the town.

On passing opposite the post office, he noted that the main door was shut, and that at the door of the telephone exchange room a girl stood talking with a tall, finely built man. The man was John Kane, owner of Tintanoo, and the girl was Berle Saunders, the day telephone operator. Coming along the street was her brother, who was employed by the department as night operator.

Cox looked straight ahead after that one eagle glance. Miss Berle Saunders was a most presentable young woman and one, moreover, able to look after herself even with a suitor like Mr John Kane.

Having given his final orders to Mounted Constable Lovitt, Cox kissed his wife, renewed his order to his son regarding the square roots, and made his way with his suitcase to the hangar where Dr Knowles housed his black-painted monoplane. The colour was a touch of the doctor's irony.

On his arrival he found the aeroplane standing outside the hangar, the engine already being warmed up by the doctor, who occupied the pilot's seat. He had not troubled to put on either coat or helmet, but he wore goggles.

"The doctor says he will hedge-hop to Coolibah, so it won't be cold," shouted Captain Loveacre.

"All right! But I'm wearing my overcoat, all the same," stated Cox, putting on his heavy uniform coat. The captain indicated the grim head of the doctor, to be seen above the cockpit and behind the low windscreen.

"He's a corker," he cried. "Directly he climbed in he became sober."

"*Apparently* sober," the sergeant corrected. "So long! He's ready." He climbed into the passenger's seat, and then he turned to shout above the engine roar: "Do I put on the parachute?"

"Never use one," said the doctor. "If we crash, we crash. Anyway, we don't go high enough for a parachute to be any use."

He revved the engine to a prolonged roar for ten to fifteen seconds. When the roar died down, Captain Loveacre whipped away the wheel chocks. The engine voiced its power, and the machine began its race across the gibber plain before rising.

It was not the first time that Sergeant Cox had been off the ground, but it was the first time that he had left Mother Earth in the company of Dr Knowles. Looking down over the cockpit edge he saw Golden Dawn laid out for his inspection. There in the middle of the street stood the white-dressed figure of the exchange operator, still beside John Kane. Outside the police-station stood his wife and son waving to him, and he waved down to them. They and the town slipped away from beneath him, the machine sank nearer to the plain and then flew directly towards the sun.

To Sergeant Cox this air journey was by no means boring. The earth did not appear flat and featureless. It was too near to be either. He could even see the rabbits dashing to their burrows to escape the huge "eagle." He could distinguish the track, faint though it lay across the gibber plain, and he could observe the shadows cast by the old-man saltbush growing along the bottom of a deep water-gutter.

When they met a truck coming from Tintanoo or St Albans, the doctor deliberately dived at it, almost spinning his wheels on the driver's cabin roof. When they arrived over the scrub, the brown track lay like a narrow ribbon winding across the dark-green carpet, and now Dr Knowles set out to show just what he could do with an aeroplane —or to show just how mad he was. He followed the road, and when coming to an exceptionally high creek gum or bloodwood tree, he made the topmost leaves brush the dust off the wheels. Only when the sun went down did he fly higher, keeping steadily in its golden light until forced up to three thousand feet.

Presently the sun set even at that altitude, and then the ground was sinking into the shadows of night. The world came to be like an old copper penny lying on silver tinsel paper. Then, far ahead, two motor lights winked out to greet them.

Dr Knowles put down his ship as lightly as a feather and taxied to the waiting car. Shutting off his engine, he turned round to regard Sergeant Cox with bright, twinkling eyes.

"Good!" said Cox steadily. "I have a good mind to learn to fly. Lots more fun than driving a car."

CHAPTER IV

GUESTS AT COOLIBAH

ELIZABETH NETTLEFOLD waited on the east veranda before the hall door to welcome her guests. She was gowned in a semi-evening frock of biscuit-coloured voile, and in the deepening twilight she appeared extremely attractive.

"I am so glad you came, Doctor," she said, taking Knowles's hand. "Good evening, Sergeant Cox! Did you have a good flight?"

Dr Knowles turned to face both the sergeant and Elizabeth.

"I tried to make him sick, Miss Nettlefold," he told her with mockery in his voice. "After what he's been through nothing would upset him; not even a hurricane in the North Sea on a fishing trawler."

"I've lived before my time," Cox complained in his official voice. "I should not have been born until the year nineteen-eighty, and then I would have graduated as an air cop."

"You were born in a lucky year, Sergeant Cox," Elizabeth affirmed, giving Knowles a reproachful look. "Come in, please. Will you see the girl now, Doctor?"

"Yes! Oh yes! I'll examine her now. Cox can see her afterwards."

He went off with Elizabeth, her father conducting the policeman to his own room, which he was pleased to call his study and which opened on to the western end of the south veranda. Elizabeth led the doctor along the cool, dimly-lit corridor to pause outside a door with her hand on the handle. The smile of welcome had vanished, replaced in her dark eyes by one of pleading.

"It is the most terrible thing I have ever seen," she cried softly. "The poor girl cannot move a muscle. She can't even raise or lower her eyelids. Promise me something before we go in."

"What do you want me to promise?"

He stood looking down at her, his cheeks criss-crossed with fine blue lines caused by excess. His eyes were blood-shot, and the fingers which stroked the small black moustache markedly trembled. He was still good looking despite his thirty-eight years and hard living. His cultured English voice was the only thing about him which did not reflect his mode of life.

"What is it you want me to promise?" he repeated when she continued to stare up at him. With a start, she collected herself.

"Promise me that you won't order her off to a hospital," she replied earnestly. "Hetty and I will nurse her very, very carefully. We will do everything you say, and Dad says he will spare no reasonable expense."

"But the girl is nothing to you, is she? Do you know her?"

"We have never seen her before, Doctor, but nursing her will give me something to do. You couldn't understand, but . . . but she will give me an interest in life. You will not order her away, will you?"

"Not unless it would be for her own good," he compromised. "Come! Take me to her."

"A moment! You will not permit Sergeant Cox to have her moved to the hospital at Winton, will you? Promise me that."

A faint smile crept into the man's dark eyes.

"I'll promise you that," he told her, to add with a flash of humour: "Cox owes me a debt."

They found Hetty seated in a chair beside the bed, at her side an electric reading lamp which sent its shaded radiance to the edge of the small occasional table. The woman rose when they approached.

"This is Mrs Hetty Brown, my co-nurse."

Knowles nodded and passed to the bed. He raised the lamp-shade so that its light fell on the patient's face. And then he stepped back with a sharp ejaculation to stare down at the immobile features. His eyes grew big with amazement.

Astonished, herself, Elizabeth asked:

"Do you know her, Doctor?"

She had to repeat her question before he was able to master himself enough to answer.

"No," he said sharply, and bent over the helpless girl. Elizabeth noticed that no longer were his hands trembling, and when he spoke his voice again was steady.

"Well, young lady, you appear to be in a peculiar fix," he drawled. "If you are conscious and can hear what I'm saying, don't be afraid. They say that I am the best doctor in western Queensland, but, as I do not agree, you need not believe it."

Presently he raised the patient's eyelids and gazed steadily into the large, blue, intelligent and pleading orbs. He smiled at her, and the watching Elizabeth saw his expression soften, become one of infinite pity. She had heard a great deal about the flying doctor and his wild life. She had often seen him and conversed with him, and she had never thought he could be anything but reckless and cynical.

"I believe that if you could speak, you would tell us a lot of interesting things," he went on. "But never mind that now. You must not worry. You will regain the use of all your muscles quite suddenly, and the less you worry and fret the sooner that will be. Ah! I can see that you hear and understand me. Now I will partly lower your eyelids so that you will be able to note your surroundings."

For a little while he sat at the foot of the bed in a most unprofessional attitude whilst he regarded the pale face, almost beautiful in its impassiveness. Elizabeth and Hetty watched him, but they could not guess what passed through his mind. It seemed that he had utterly forgotten them.

"What do you think of her?" Elizabeth asked presently.

"What? Oh, what this young lady needs is quiet and careful attention. Yes, and a little amusement to stop her thinking about herself. I think we will have her up and about in no time. I will come to see her again during the late evening, and meanwhile I will ask my colleague to drop in and see her. *Au revoir*, young lady. Remember now, no worry! Hetty will read you a book and talk to you, and to-morrow, perhaps, Miss Nettlefold will have the radio brought in."

Standing up, he then reached forward and took one of her palsied hands, which lay so still on the white coverlet.

"*Au revoir!*" he again said softly.

When in the corridor with Elizabeth, with the door closed behind them, he asked:

"Have you discovered any clue about her? Any laundry marks or initials on her linen?"

"Yes. Several articles have the initials M.M. worked on them with silk. That is all."

"Hum! She is rather lovely, don't you think? Not more than twenty-five. Perhaps not twenty."

"What is the matter with her, Doctor?"

"Candidly, I do not know yet," he confessed. "Has she eaten?"

"No. She can swallow, but she cannot move her jaw."

"All that she can do is to swallow and slightly, very slightly, move her eyes," he said slowly, as though to himself. "No, I do not understand. I might in the morning when I have examined her again. What liquids have you given her?"

"Milk."

"Good! Don't, however, give her too much. Give her cocoa and beef tea. I will draw up a diet list before I leave. To-night give her a teaspoonful of brandy in coffee. Who will be with her during the night?"

"I will from ten o'clock."

"Oh! I believe you will make an excellent nurse, Miss Nettlefold. I will look in before going to bed. Now we will permit Sergeant Cox to pay his official visit—as my medical colleague."

"Why as your colleague?"

"Because I am not going to have my patient frightened by a policeman."

She took him along to the study where they found Cox taking notes from what the cattleman was telling him.

"Well, do you know her?" asked the sergeant.

"No. I have never seen her before," Knowles answered, and Elizabeth looked at him intently.

"May I have a look at her?"

"You may," Knowles assented, a little curtly. Then, when the sergeant stood up, he added: "My patient is suffering from a form of muscular paralysis. She is conscious and her mind is clear, but she is quite unable to articulate. I don't care a sixpence who stole the aeroplane. All that concerns me is that she's my patient, and I will not have her frightened or worried, you understand. She is powerless to run away and escape from you. I told her that my colleague would visit her, just to look at her. It is no use your putting questions to her, but by all means ascertain if you can identify her."

Sergeant Cox glared at the doctor, and Knowles strolled across to a wall cabinet where he could see a decanter, glasses and a soda bottle.

"I won't excite her," Cox promised readily. "Do you think she could have stolen the aeroplane?"

"No . . . emphatically."

"Is there any basis for your opinion?"

"So far there is nothing definite on which I could base any opinion," Knowles replied, turning with a filled tumbler in his hand. "In her present condition it would, of course, be quite impossible for her to have flown the machine. I have never before seen a case even remotely like it. The general paralysis of all consciously controlled muscles may have been produced by physical injury, mental shock, or—" and he made a distinct pause: "or drugs. I can find no external physical injury, but I will examine her again tomorrow. I can conceive no mental shock of sufficient strength to produce such a result. Therefore I incline to the hypothesis that she has been drugged."

Cox pulled savagely at his grey moustache. Elizabeth stared with peculiar intensity at the doctor. Her father frowned down at his polished slippers, and began a hunt for tobacco plug and clasp knife.

"If the poor thing has been drugged, Doctor, will not the drug wear out of her system in time?" Elizabeth asked.

"Drugs are so varied in their effects," Knowles replied. "If the patient has been drugged the drug *may* slowly lose its hold upon her. I stress the word 'may'."

"And if it does not?" put in Cox.

"Then she will inevitably die despite all our efforts to save her. The paralysis of the consciously controlled processes will have a grave effect on those that are involuntary."

"Go along and find out if you know her, Cox," urged Nettlefold.

The sergeant nodded and followed Elizabeth.

"Pardon me, Nettlefold," said Knowles, "for helping myself to your whisky. Ah . . . but I was perishing."

"Whatever you do, don't perish, or let me perish either," the big bluff manager returned warmly. "Three fingers is my usual measure."

The doctor turned again to the wall cabinet. Glass tinkled against glass, and the hiss of aerated water splashing into liquid were the only sounds to break the little silence which lasted until the doctor seated himself, having handed his host a glass.

"It is quite a mystery, isn't it?" he queried.

"Too deep for me," Nettlefold admitted. "An aeroplane is stolen at Golden Dawn, and it is then found undamaged one hundred and eighty-four miles away. In it is a drugged girl. The pilot is missing, and there are no tracks showing that he left the machine after he landed it."

"Your résumé contains several facts but one assumption.

You assume that the girl is drugged. That is not proven yet."

"Then it is possible that she is suffering the effects of some physical injury?"

"Yes. There is that possibility."

The door opened to admit the sergeant. He was alone, and before he spoke they knew he had been unable to identify the patient.

"I do not know her," he said. "I have been in control of this district for twenty-four years, and I am positive that she has never lived in it. I could swear that she was not in Golden Dawn yesterday. I was among the small crowd watching the air circus and seeing people taking trips in the de Haviland. You are quite sure, Mr Nettlefold, that you saw no tracks of the pilot leaving the aeroplane?"

"Quite!" replied the cattleman with conviction.

"Then he must have jumped out before the machine landed—if there was a pilot other than that girl."

"In that case, would not the machine have crashed?" Nettlefold asked the doctor.

Cox looked steadily at Knowles.

"My machine would go into a fatal spin immediately I left the controls," he said. "Captain Loveacre's monoplane, however, might not. There was the affair during the war when a German flier was shot dead when over the lines, and his machine made a perfect landing several miles behind our front. Better ask Loveacre how his monoplane behaves."

Yes. And, by the way, I told him, Mr Nettlefold, that you would supply him with information how to get to Emu Lake. May I ring him up?"

Dr Knowles again permitted himself to become the needle

attracted by the magnet of the wall cabinet. There was something terrible in his steady drinking as well as in the extraordinary effects it appeared to have on him. The potent spirit attacked his legs and arms, but failed utterly to cloud his mind or thicken his speech. Before leaving the cabinet he refilled the glass to take with him to one of the lounge chairs, and into that he dropped to lean back his head to rest on the cushion and to stare up at the coloured lamp-shade.

It was obvious that he did not hear, whilst the others were too much engrossed by the telephone to note Elizabeth's quiet entry. She stood now just inside the door she had quietly closed, and there she continued to stand.

She saw and heard her father speaking into the telephone. She saw Cox crouching forward across the large writing-table. And then she saw the white, upturned face of Dr Knowles. He was staring at the lamp-shade, and the light fell directly on his face. It was devoid of expression, a cold white mask beneath the glaring electric light. The little silky black moustache and the fine black hair but emphasized the whiteness of the skin, an unnatural whiteness, considering that the man spent hours in the air every week.

He was a clever doctor, she knew. She knew, too, that his medical studies had been interrupted by fifteen months in the Royal Air Force during the war. For a period of that time—how long she did not know—he and the owner of Tintanoo had been pilots in the same squadron. But, while John Kane often spoke of those days, Dr Knowles always avoided the subject of army flying.

Her father having called good night, and the telephone receiver having been replaced on its hooks, she stepped forward and suggested supper. Not till then was Knowles aware of her presence, when he flung himself to his feet so precipitately as to indicate annoyance.

"I am ready to eat—anything," he said, smiling to conceal his confusion.

"And the flight has sharpened my appetite instead of blunting it," added Cox.

"Then come along. I have to go on night duty at ten o'clock," Elizabeth told them.

She led them to a cold supper set out in the dining-room. Her father carved from a great round of beef, the quality of which is never found on offer in a butcher's shop. Everything was in keeping with the furniture, solid and homely, easy and comfortably luxurious.

Beneath the conversation was an undercurrent of excitement, of expectancy. They could discuss nothing save the helpless young woman lying on Elizabeth's bed, although the sergeant did make several attempts. Through the open windows came the subdued and methodical reports of the petrol engine running the station dynamo. From farther afield drifted the notes of an accordion. The night was silent and peaceful and warm. They each sensed rather than knew positively that drama had come to Coolibah.

CHAPTER V

THE VIGIL

ELIZABETH relieved the housekeeper at ten o'clock, leaving the men to depart for Nettlefold's study.

"I think she is sleeping, Miss Elizabeth," Hetty reported. "I closed her eyes and turned her on her side half an hour ago. You will find the spirit lamp and the supper things in your dressing-room. Now, what time will I relieve you? Remember, you have not slept since last night."

They stood just outside the bedroom, the door almost shut. The corridor was lit by one electric bulb midway along it. The electric power had to be conserved, so that it had been decided to light an oil lamp, placed on a small table opposite Elizabeth's bedroom door after all had gone to bed.

"Mr Nettlefold and Sergeant Cox will be leaving for Emu Lake at six in the morning, Hetty," Elizabeth said. "If you will, please get up in time to see that they have a proper breakfast and take good lunches with them. After they have gone you can relieve me. I have explained everything to Dr Knowles, and he tells me he will be staying until to-morrow afternoon."

"What does he think? Oh, Miss Elizabeth, will the poor girl get better?"

"We hope so, Hetty."

"And Sergeant Cox!" Hetty's hands began to flutter like a bird's wings. "Has he found out who she is?"

Elizabeth shook her head.

"No. He hasn't found out yet. No one seems ever to have seen her before. Now, be off to bed, Hetty. You must be tired."

"Very well! Good night, Miss Elizabeth!"

Again within her room, Elizabeth passed across to the bed to make sure that her patient was lying comfortably. That was more difficult than it sounds, because the girl was unable to voice a complaint or even subconsciously to move her body. For a while Elizabeth listened to her regular breathing, to become convinced that she was sleeping.

The room was large and oblong in shape, the corridor wall taking one side and two pairs of french windows occupying spaces in the opposite side. The bed had its head to one of the shorter walls, while in the opposite one was the door leading to the dressing-room. As well as the small table beside the bed there was a larger one set against the corridor wall to the right of the door. On this table Elizabeth set the shaded electric lamp, and beside it she placed her chair so that she was able to face both the corridor door and the patient's bed, the dressing-room door then being partly at her back and the two windows on her left.

Before settling in her chair to await the doctor's promised visit, she crossed to the windows to close one pair and to draw the light curtains before both. Here, in western Queensland, there was absolutely no necessity to lock and bar windows and doors, and from one year's end to the other neither windows nor doors were ever locked at Coolibah.

Shortly after eleven, Dr Knowles came in without a

sound. He waved her back into her chair before closing the door, and, stepping across to the table, seated himself on the edge of it and scrutinized her closely.

About him there was a faint aroma of alcohol. His face was flushed, and before he sat down she noticed that he staggered ever so slightly. Yet when he spoke his voice was steady, clear, and low.

"You will have to guard against bed sores. Do you know how?" he asked.

"If by constantly moving the patient . . ."

"Exactly. During the night she must be moved from side to side, say every two hours. Most of us cannot sleep when lying on the left side, so you should be careful not to put your patient too far over that way. Throughout the day she may be allowed to lie on her back, but she must be constantly eased and half-turned to right or left, and maintained in those positions with pillows. Bed sores are the very devil to get rid of once they come, and our patient's absolute helplessness will be productive of them unless every care is taken. You are still determined to nurse her?"

"Yes! Oh yes!" was her quick reply.

"Why?"

The interrogative was snapped at her. For a second she was confused. Then:

"Perhaps the answer to this question will be my answer to yours," she suggested hesitantly. "Why do you fly about the country so recklessly?"

The dark brows drew closer together, and the white lids narrowed before the dark eyes. He was instantly on his guard, and Elizabeth knew it.

"I never fly recklessly," was his evasive answer.

"Answer my question, please, if you want yours answered," she persisted.

He smiled faintly.

"I believe I can correctly guess the answer you think I would make. No, I do not fly everywhere, and take what may be thought risks, because I am bored with life. In fact, if I had not found life most interesting, I should have departed from it years ago. How is it that life bores you?"

"I am not bored . . . *now*, Doctor. I *was* . . . terribly. Dad is always happy to live here in the bush. So was my mother. I should be, too, but I am not. I have never been truly happy here after I gave up my studies to come home and look after Dad. You see, I don't do anything. Managing Hetty who manages the house is not doing anything, really. I cannot be bothered with the garden, and horses and car driving no longer interest me. If my mother was living or I had sisters . . ."

Knowles was staring at her—not rudely—merely as though he saw her clearly for the first time.

"After a while you will find nursing boring, too," he warned her.

"Oh no, I won't!" she hastened to assure him. "It will give me something to do—something to think about. Do you know that for the last three years I have done nothing but read novels? I keep all the men supplied with reading matter."

"There are plenty of people who wish they could do just that, Miss Nettlefold," he pointed out, and then began to scribble with a fountain pen on a writing-pad. When he had finished he went on: "I have drawn up a diet list for the time being. Follow it strictly. I may alter it later. As the patient is sleeping, I will look in at daybreak, and then, during the morning, we will make another and a more careful examination of her."

"You will let her stay with us?"

"Until you relax in your duties or"—and he smiled for the first time—"or I find out that you think you know more about it than I do. Now, no temper, please! I think she will be better off here in your care than in the hospital at Winton, but should you tire say so instantly, and I will remove her to Winton. She has no claims on you, remember."

"Yes, she has," Elizabeth said, a little fiercely. "She has conquered my boredom, and if only you knew what that means——"

"Believe me, I know what boredom is," he said, quietly cutting in. "There is only one thing worse than boredom, and that is memory. Boredom can be banished, but memory cannot be obliterated. Now, I'll be off. If the patient wakes during the night—but no! Feed her with coffee containing a teaspoonful of brandy to the cup at one o'clock and at four o'clock. If you should see any change in her, call me at once. Good night . . . Nurse!"

They rose together.

"Good night, Doctor!"

Having smiled at her for the second time, he spent a few seconds beside the bed feeling the patient's pulse, and then left. From the table in the corridor he picked up the newly opened bottle of whisky and the glass he had placed there before entering the room, and departed for his own.

A few minutes after the doctor had gone, Elizabeth heard her father conducting the sergeant to his room; then heard the sergeant's door quietly closed, and a moment later heard her father close his. The petrol engine running the electric light had long been stopped, and the accordion player now was fast asleep. The house was silent, and the world of the bush surrounding the homestead was silent, too.

She tried to read, but, after a determined effort to be interested in the antics of alleged bohemians in Sydney, she put down the book and relaxed. The little clock on the table announced the hour of midnight. One of the stockman's dogs chained beyond the men's quarters began to bark—not frenziedly, but methodically—as though tantalized by the nearness of a rabbit. The animal was too far away to be a disturbing influence.

She began to go over all the incidents of the afternoon. It was so stupid of them not to have searched the red monoplane for the girl's belongings: her hat and coat and vanitv bag, without which no woman dare leave her home. It was excusable stupidity, of course. Who would not have been astonished first when finding the machine, and then by the discovery of the helpless girl in it? Her very plight, which had so cried out for compassion, had swept aside all thought to look for articles proving her identity, especially when Emu Lake was on Coolibah and someone would have to come out for the aeroplane the next day.

The military-minded Sergeant Cox had failed dismally to conceal his disapproval of their omission. What a straight-backed man he was to be sure! Elizabeth wondered if he ever bent mentally and physically, even in his own home. She could find in him nothing soft or humanly weak, and yet there was much good spoken of him. Even Ned Hamlin, who invariably got himself locked up when he went to Golden Dawn, did not seem to dislike the sergeant particularly.

Well, the affair had certainly banished boredom. Why she should ever have been bored both vexed and surprised her. The Greyson girls were never bored, but then numbers were in their favour. They could go to tennis and golf and bridge parties. Elizabeth liked tennis, but she was an indifferent golfer and bridge she hated.

Perhaps it was in her mental make-up, that poignant dissatisfaction with life and its gifts! Why could she not face life with the insouciance of Ted Sharp? Ted Sharp, who rode like a devil, worked like a horse, and who was as staunch as a rock! No, that was a bad simile. What was the time?

Half-past twelve. She found herself sleepy, and again made a determined effort to become interested in her book. Apparently it did master her attention, for time slipped by and the little clock struck its elfin bell once.

Stifling a yawn, she rose and stepped to the bed, where she tenderly moved the patient over to her other side, making sure that the under-arm was free and naturally easy. She experienced a little thrill of pride when intent listening told her that the patient still slept, that the movement had not disturbed her.

Within the dressing-room, now her bedroom, she lit the spirit lamp and set the saucepan containing milk above the blue flame, and by the time she had undressed and flung about her a dressing-gown, it was time to brew the coffee.

Elizabeth realized quite abruptly that, tired though she was, she yet was feeling a sweetly contented happiness. The old gnawing but ever-present dissatisfaction with life no longer existed. She had lived on board the ship of life like a sailor; now she was the first mate! She might never have been the sailor had not Hetty become the Coolibah housekeeper before Elizabeth's return from the university, or if Hetty had then retired to the position of an ordinary servant. But Hetty had kept her important position with

Elizabeth's unspoken sanction . . . and Elizabeth had become just a member of the crew.

Taking a cup of the coffee to the small occasional table at the head of the bed she carefully measured into it a teaspoonful of the brandy. And, as she gave it to the patient, spoonful by spoonful, she talked softly to her.

Having drunk her own coffee and eaten the sandwiches provided by Hetty, Elizabeth felt much more mentally alert. For an hour she read, now and then listening to be assured that the patient slept. Persistently the distant dog maintained its half-hearted barks, and it began to get on her nerves. It would have to be moved farther away. Why could it not bark furiously, with reason, instead of that eternal half-bark, half-yap?

The night wore on, and towards four o'clock she again found herself being mastered by the desire to sleep. More coffee was indicated for herself; anyway, it was nearly time to give some to the patient. Rising, she raised her arms above her head and stretched herself before walking into the dressing-room.

Beside the table on which were the coffee things was a full-length pedestal mirror. It faced the bedroom door, then partly open, and, having brewed the coffee, she heard a slight movement, and turned. The mirror revealed the figure of a man standing with his back to the dressing-room door in front of the small table beside the bed and on that side of it nearest the door opening on the corridor.

Although she could not see the man's face she was sure that it was Knowles. He was fully dressed in a dark suit like that worn by the doctor earlier in the night. Evidently Dr Knowles was paying his promised early morning visit, although as yet daylight was not visible in the sky beyond the window. Unperturbed, Elizabeth placed the coffee jug and cups on a tray, and on taking the tray into the bedroom was in time to see the corridor door closing behind the visitor.

Half-expecting to find on the small table a bottle of medicine, she set the tray down on the larger table and crossed to the bed table. But there was no bottle, no note, nothing in addition to the tumbler of water, a teaspoon and the opened bottle of brandy.

Hallucination! A waking dream! A vision due to want of sleep! She opened the corridor door and peeped out to see—as she expected—no one in the corridor. The burning lamp on the table standing opposite the door clearing revealed the extremities of the corridor. There was no one there, and if it had not been a vision—if it had been Dr Knowles—there had been ample time for him to reach his bedroom.

Of course there was a perfectly natural explanation, she told herself, while she attended her patient. Unable to sleep, the doctor had stepped in to look at the girl, and, finding the nurse in the dressing-room, he had left without speaking. Or he might have wanted a drink, and had come in to take some of the brandy. The brandy! Setting the cup of coffee down on the small table, she picked up the bottle of brandy, turned, and held it between her eyes and the table lamp. Ah! Most certainly the doctor had not taken any of the spirit. The bottle was quite full. Then a little icy shaft sped up her back and caused her scalp to tingle.

What if. . . . Quickly she carried the bottle to the table lamp. The liquid reached almost to the bottom of the cork —in fact, it would reach the cork if the cork was driven into the neck as it had originally been by the bottlers. And yet she had taken one teaspoonful of the brandy from the bottle, and Hetty had taken another.

It was most strange. Surely Dr Knowles would not put anything into the brandy without informing her? He might have done so, not thinking it of sufficient importance to bother her, or to call her. But then it might not have been the doctor at all!

Again the icy shaft swept up her back to tingle her scalp. Suppose. . . . Well, suppose the man had been an enemy? It seemed impossible, but then . . .

Thoughtfully, she returned to the bed and gave her patient the coffee without adding the teaspoonful of brandy. She was half-inclined to call Dr Knowles, but he might think her nervous or incapable of nursing his patient. No, it were better to wait until the morning, and then, when the doctor came in, casually to mention it.

Presently a cock crowed, and when she drew aside the window curtains she found the new day arrived. As she stepped out on to the veranda to inhale the clear, cool air, she heard the bright screeches of a flock of galah parrots among the gums bordering the creek which carried floodwater down to the river channels.

It was five o'clock when she heard Hetty talking with Ruth, the fat and happy aboriginal cook. Hetty was up and supervising the breakfasts and lunches for Nettlefold and Sergeant Cox. She expected Dr Knowles, but he did not appear, and at six o'clock, almost to the minute, she heard them leave in her father's car for Emu Lake.

Shortly after they had gone, Hetty came in to say that she had set out Elizabeth's breakfast in the morning-room.

"You must be so tired!" cried Hetty in her dove-like voice.

"Thank you, Hetty. I will run along and have something

to eat," Elizabeth said. "The patient is all right. If the doctor should call while I am breakfasting, please tell him where I am."

She was engaged with bacon and eggs when she first heard the low humming of distant aeroplane engines. Steadily the hum rose in pitch until, aeroplanes still being a novelty, she left the room and walked the length of the corridor to step out on to the east veranda, and from there to walk down to the short metalled strip of road.

And there all silvered by the rising sun sailed the big passenger-carrying biplane belonging to the air circus. It was coming to fly directly over the house and so low was it that she clearly saw a man's head thrust out of a window and then his hand waving a handkerchief to her. Waving up to him she watched the machine until it disappeared beyond the house roof, humming on its way to Emu Lake.

"Captain Loveacre must have made an early start, Miss Nettlefold," called Dr Knowles from the veranda. Arrayed in a black silk dressing-gown trimmed with silver facings, he was smoking a cigarette. "Good morning!" he added.

"Good morning, Doctor!" she returned, the thrill of that man-made bird still in her blood.

"How is the patient this morning?"

"I have seen no change in her. I suppose you wondered where I was when you peeped in?"

"Peeped in, Miss Nettlefold? But Hetty said you were at breakfast."

He spoke nonchalantly, and into her mind swept the suggestion of evil which before day broke had touched her heart with an icy finger.

"Oh! I mean before daylight, you know," she told him coolly.

By now she had joined him on the veranda, and she noted the perplexity in his eyes.

"But I did not go into the patient's room before day broke," he said evenly, and yet evidently puzzled. "I trust you did not fall asleep and dream that I did."

"No, I was not sleeping," she told him with conviction, and then explained how she had seen a person whom she thought to be the doctor, standing at the little table beside the bed.

Knowles laughed shortly.

"So you *did* fall asleep!"

"But I did not," Elizabeth protested.

"But I did not visit the patient's room after we were talking last night until just now, when I found Hetty in charge."

Elizabeth regarded him with troubled eyes. She recalled the mystery concerning the brandy. Knowles became serious.

"You are quite sure that you saw me, or someone like me, in the room last night? What time was it?"

"Just after four o'clock," she replied. "Yes, I am sure a man was in the room when I looked into the mirror, and that he was closing the door after him as I walked into the bedroom. He did something to the brandy. I am sure of that, too."

"Took some, you mean?" the doctor demanded sharply.

"No, he put something into the bottle. There is more in it now than when I took out the teaspoonful at one o'clock."

"Come! Did you give her any of the brandy at four o'clock as I ordered?

"No. After what I had seen I was doubtful what to do."

"That's good. When in doubt do nothing, as Bonaparte used to say. Let's have a look at that brandy."

Throwing away his cigarette, he hurried before her to the patient's room. There he snatched up the bottle of brandy and gazed at it earnestly.

"How much have you taken out of this bottle, Miss Nettlefold?" he asked.

"One teaspoonful, Doctor."

"What about you, Hetty?"

"Oh, Doctor! Only one teaspoonful, Doctor!" fluttered Hetty.

"Well, more than two teaspoonfuls have been put back, or I have never opened a bottle of spirits in my life," he said slowly.

CHAPTER VI

ELIZABETH IS DETERMINED

IT was like a sand cloud that comes from the west, rolling over the ground with very little wind behind it, to plunge the brilliant noon-day world into utter darkness. Weary from her all-night vigil, Elizabeth lay down on the bed in the dressing-room only to find that, despite the urgent need for sleep, sleep could not master her aching brain.

Carrying the bottle of brandy, Dr Knowles had led her to the morning-room, where, at his request, she had brought the other two half-bottles of brandy supplied, with the open bottle, by the hotel at Golden Dawn. In each of the unopened bottles the vacant space between the bottom of the cork and the spirit was approximately one inch, but the spirit in the opened bottle—when two teaspoonfuls had been taken out for the patient—reached the bottom of the cork before it could be pushed right to its original position.

"Something wrong, evidently," the doctor had said. "But what it is we shall have to discover through analysis. Now to bed, or I shall be having two patients at Coolibah on my hands."

Now convinced that it was not Dr Knowles she had seen standing before the bed table, alarmed by the sinister import provided by the opened bottle of brandy, Elizabeth tossed and turned and suffered the dull brain ache resultant from want of habitual sleep.

Yes, it was as though the sun had been obliterated by a sand cloud, this sudden terrible suspicion. Here at Coolibah, which had gone on and on for eighty years with nothing to disturb its serenity save floods and storms, droughts and the cattle tick, the shadow fell of some black conspiracy of evil men . . .

Poison! Suppose the night visitor to the sickroom had poured poison into the brandy bottle? The doctor had not voiced his grave suspicions, but she had been able clearly to see and understand them. Who was that man? She reviewed in turn the station hands and could recall not one whose back resembled that of the man she had seen. He had stood in the shadow, and she could not say definitely what kind of clothes he was wearing excepting that they were of dark material.

Without warning, slumber overtook her, and she was awakened by Hetty who set down a cup of tea on the table at the head of her bed.

"I hate to wake you, Miss Elizabeth, but it is six o'clock in the evening," Hetty exclaimed. "Oh, Miss Elizabeth! Such news! Such happenings on Coolibah!"

So long and so soundly had she slept that Elizabeth awoke mentally alert and refreshed.

"What has happened, Hetty?" she asked, sweeping back the clothes and swinging her legs over the side of the bed. "Six o'clock! Why did you not call me earlier?"

"Mr Nettlefold said I was not to. He and Sergeant Cox came in an hour ago. Someone has burned the aeroplane out at Emu Lake."

"Burned it!"

"Yes, Miss Elizabeth, burned it. When your father and the sergeant reached Emu Lake early this morning they found the big plane landed there and the men all looking at the remains of the small one."

Elizabeth accepted the proferred cup of tea.

"Do they think it was done on purpose?" she inquired, frowning.

"I don't know! I suppose so! And then about midday they phoned the doctor from Golden Dawn to say that Mrs Nixon was going to have her baby, and he had to leave right off in his aeroplane. Wouldn't stay for lunch. He set off to walk to the plane with that opened bottle of brandy in one side pocket and a half-filled bottle of whisky in the other. Oh, dear! He drinks terribly. Does he ever stop? And flying an aeroplane, too!"

"The patient. Is she . . .?"

"Just the same, Miss Elizabeth! Doctor left you a note about her, and I fed her every two hours as I was told."

"Have my father and the sergeant had dinner?"

"The sergeant left for Golden Dawn without waiting for dinner. He wanted to ask you a number of questions, but Mr Nettlefold forbade him to have you wakened. They brought Ted Sharp in with them, and he's taken Mr Cox to Golden Dawn."

"Give me a cigarette and a match, Hetty," Elizabeth ordered. "I used to cry my eyes out because everything was so hatefully quiet here. Well, life has bucked up with a vengeance."

"Oh, Miss Elizabeth! Do you think it wise to smoke before you have eaten?"

"No, I don't, but I'm doing it just the same."

While drawing at the cigarette, Elizabeth stared up at this fluttering woman. Eleven years had Hetty been at Coolibah, and for eleven years the homestead had run like a well-oiled machine. Beneath the nervous exterior was the calm placidity of the born organizer. Elizabeth, for the first time, realized to the full her stability and loyalty. A little impulsively, she said:

"You know, Hetty, I don't know how I would get on without you. Where is Father?"

"He was in the study five minutes ago, Miss Elizabeth."

"Then run along and tell him that I will be ready for dinner in half an hour, there's a dear."

Hetty nodded and smiled, and vanished into the bedroom, and two minutes later Elizabeth, arrayed in her bath gown and carrying a towel, entered the patient's room on her way to the shower.

The room was illuminated by the soft golden light of the westering sun. A cool evening breeze from the south teased the lace curtains ribbon-caught to the side of each of the open windows and, entering, stirred the scent of the roses in the bowl on the larger table. The only sounds were the petrol engine and the cries of birds.

"How are you?" Elizabeth softly asked, when she bent forward over the helpless girl. The patient's eyelids were raised half-way, and the dark blue eyes moved just a fraction, in them an expression of welcome. Hetty had been at work on the light-brown hair.

"I am glad Hetty did your hair so nicely," she said, smiling down at the pallid but beautiful mask. "I've been terribly lazy, you know. I have slept all day. But I will be with you all night, so you need not be a tiny bit uneasy. The doctor has had to go to Golden Dawn to attend a woman, but he will be back again to-morrow."

The blue eyes became hard in expression and then were filmed with mist.

"Now you mustn't fret," Elizabeth said. "I know you want to speak ever so much, but you must not fret because you cannot speak. Speech and everything else will come back to you presently. The doctor says it will, so you really must not worry. We will soon find out who you are, and then we can send for your relatives or friends."

Elizabeth smiled at her patient and patted her cheek before turning to take up from the table the envelope addressed to her. The note was from Knowles, and read:

Have to rush off to attend to Mrs Nixon. Carry on with the patient's diet according to my instructions in writing. I will fly back as soon as I am able. Regards!

Having bathed and dressed, Elizabeth found her father waiting for her in the dining-room. His first words were an inquiry after the patient.

"About the same, Dad," Elizabeth told him. "Is it correct that someone has burned the red aeroplane?"

"It is. I'll tell you about it while we eat. I am famished. Had a hard day and a devilish exciting one, too."

The young lubra, smartly dressed in a maid's uniform, of which she was obviously proud, came in with the dinner dishes, and not till she had gone out and they were engaged with knives and forks did the big man begin his explanations.

"We left here, the sergeant and I, about six this morning," he said. "We reached Emu Lake just before half-past eight. Captain Loveacre's big de Haviland passed us before we cleared the Rockies. When we got to the lake, there it was with the pilots standing about the ruins of that beautiful red monoplane. Parts of the wreckage were still hot. The petrol tank had exploded with terrific force, for the wreckage was strewn about almost all over the lake."

"Tracks?" breathed Elizabeth, the bush-bred.

Nettlefold shook his head and sighed.

"It beats me," he said gravely. "The sergeant told the airmen not to move about, and he and I circled the ruins. But not a blessed footprint could we discover. No one had approached that monoplane to fire it. No one could have done it without leaving tracks, as you know.

Still, Cox and I are white men having the white man's deficiencies. I drove across to Ned Hamlin's hut, and I was just in time to stop Ted setting off in his car with Ned and the two blacks. Shuteye and Bill Sikes went back with me, and we loosed 'em on a hunt for tracks. They found nothing of the kind, although they circled on the lake and all around it."

"Strange!" murmured Elizabeth. "Could the monoplane have caught fire through natural causes, do you think?"

"The captain said it was possible, but not probable. The weather yesterday was quite clear, as you know. There was no lightning last night or this morning." The cattleman smiled grimly, and then added: "For some time, I think, the sergeant suspected us of firing the machine."

That made Elizabeth laugh.

"How stupid of him!" she said. "What possible motive could we have had for doing anything so silly?"

"Ignorance of motive does not prevent suspicion," her father replied. "Our tracks were plainly to be seen, but there were no others. Therefore, we must have done it. That was his reasoning. However, the sergeant's suspicions faded when he read Dr Knowles's letter."

"Oh! Did Dr Knowles write him before he left?"

"Yes."

Nettlefold pinched his nether lip with sudden pensiveness

and regarded his daughter with penetrating eyes. She looked at him with ill-concealed impatience.

"Well, what did Dr Knowles write to Sergeant Cox?" she demanded.

"Quite a lot—about that man you saw in the sickroom, and who tampered with the brandy on the bed table. Elizabeth"—his voice became very grave—"Elizabeth, that poor girl will have to be taken to the hospital at Winton, where she can be properly looked after."

Then he saw his wife with brilliant clarity in his daughter's eyes when she flashed at him:

"Do you mean, Dad, that Hetty and I are not looking after her properly?"

"No, not in that respect," he was quick to assure her, "but you must realize that last night a probable assassin entered this house and poisoned the brandy which Knowles ordered to be given the patient."

"Are you sure that the brandy was poisoned?" she countered.

"No. We are not sure, yet. Knowles, however, states in his letter that when he examined the brandy before strong sunlight, he could easily detect a substance foreign to the spirit. Further, he stated that he was convinced that the brandy was poisoned, and that a most serious attempt had been made on the girl's life. He urged that someone sit up on guard all to-night in case another attempt be made."

"One of the men can be persuaded to do that, and we can leave the dogs off the chain," she suggested swiftly.

"Quite so," he agreed. "But we cannot turn this house into a fort."

"Oh, yes, we can. After last night no one is going to harm that girl, not if I have to sit beside her with a loaded rifle in my lap. Dr Knowles told me that the patient may remain here, that she is better off here than in Winton, and therefore you are going to give in to me and allow her to stay with us. Why, her coming has given me just the stimulus that I have so badly needed."

"Well, have it your own way, Elizabeth. You always do," her father said, with just that tinge of sulkiness betrayed by a woman-defeated man. "It's all so damned mysterious, and I hate mysteries."

"I don't. I love them," she said, smiling his reward. "I am going to fight for that poor girl to remain at Coolibah. She is better off here than anywhere. What does Sergeant Cox think of it all?"

"Candidly, I think Cox is well and truly bluffed. He hinted that the case looked too big for him to handle, and that he intended to advise his immediate superior to call for a detective from Brisbane."

"A lot of good that will do," Elizabeth burst out. "If those two blacks cannot pick up any tracks, how could a city policeman succeed?"

"Detectives are trained. . . . There's the telephone. Excuse me!"

He rose at once and departed for the study, and, frowning, Elizabeth continued the meal which their conversation had interrupted. She had read novels with plots far less fantastic than these happenings at Coolibah. The room, the house, life itself, appeared to have passed into a shadow making the real world distorted and fantastic. Down in Sydney and Melbourne there was a murder at least every week, and a hold-up or a smash-and-grab raid every night. One could accept a straightout murder, but helpless young women in abandoned aeroplanes and mysterious men slinking through the house poisoning brandy, belonged to the world of nightmare.

"That was Knowles," Nettlefold explained, returning. "He is leaving Golden Dawn at once, and he wants me to meet him at the landing ground. I'll have to hurry to finish dinner and get out there."

"Did he give any news? Anything about the brandy?"

"No. When I mentioned it, he shut me up."

"Oh! Well, I am glad he is coming to-night. I am glad, too, that Ted Sharp will be here. When should he be back?"

"Not before midnight."

Elizabeth regarded her father steadily. Then she said:

"Before you go, get the men to let all their dogs off the chains, will you?"

CHAPTER VII

SERGEANT COX'S VISITOR

SUMMER had come again, and Golden Dawn drowsed in the hot afternoon sunlight. The poppet-head of the mine danced in the heat waves rippling across the gibber plain, translucent waves which distorted the shapes of distant cows and flocks of goats. A hammer clanged on metal in the blacksmith's shop, where, instead of making a set of horse-shoes, the smith was straightening a truck axle. The striking hammer appeared to mark time for the school class singing "Waltzing Matilda" in the little wooden building at the far end of the town.

With both coat and waistcoat removed, Sergeant Cox was at work in his office. His shirt-sleeves were rolled up above his elbows, and his jaw methodically worked at a large chunk of chewing gum. Office work demanded gum in preference to a pipe or an occasional cigarette, and the work in hand called for so much mental attention that the humming of the car that entered Golden Dawn from Yaraka passed quite unnoticed.

The sergeant was expecting the arrival of detectives from Brisbane on the mail coach due in at five-thirty, and his pen was busy drawing up a full report concerning the derelict aeroplane found at Emu Lake. The present was a distinct lull, as it were, after the storm of activity consequent on the discovery of the monoplane and its helpless passenger.

Captain Loveacre had flown away with his fellow pilots in the de Haviland, and the members of the Air Accidents Investigation Committee had arrived, examined the wreckage, and had departed only that morning. Their findings, Cox had been informed, would be made known to the Commissioner, Colonel Spendor.

When a light step sounded on the veranda, Sergeant Cox frowned fiercely and continued to write. Filling in forms and making official returns were easy to a man long accustomed to such red tape, but he was finding the writing of an account of an investigation far more difficult. The coming of a visitor added to an irritation partially produced by the distracting tinkle of china in the kitchen where his wife was preparing afternoon tea. He kept his iron-grey head bent over his writing when the caller entered the office, and his pen continued its laborious scratching.

"Good afternoon, Sergeant!" greeted a low and cultured voice.

"Day!" snapped the sergeant, continuing to write.

"You appear to be very busy this afternoon," remarked the voice.

Had he heard that voice before? Cox decided that he had not. Some traveller, without doubt. Men of all types, cultured and coarse, tramped the outback and here was one seeking the usual ration order supplied by the government. With grim determination, he went on with the paragraph in hand, and then, having completed it, he raised his head to glare at the caller.

He saw, seated on the small iron safe, a man of medium height and build, dressed in a light-grey tweed. His tie matched his shirt, and so did the soft felt hat now resting on the edge of the writing-table. The visitor's face was turned downward to the busy fingers engaged in making a cigarette, and with no little astonishment the sergeant noted that the man's hair was fine and straight and black, and that his skin was dark brown. And then he was gazing into a pair of bright blue eyes regarding him with a smile.

"Well, what's your business?" Cox demanded, affronted by the caller's freedom. The fellow was obviously a half-caste. He struck a match and calmly lit the cigarette he had made. Cox flushed to a deep red. He was used to stock-men and half-castes treating him with more respect than this.

"I asked you your business with me," the sergeant rasped, his nether jaw protruding, his eyes blazing.

And then the soft and pleasing voice again:

"My dear Sergeant, my business is the same as your own. My name, given me in the long ago by an unthinking matron at a mission station, is Napoleon Bonaparte. Believe me, I have often considered seriously taking another name by deed poll, because no man—least of all myself—is worthy to be so honoured."

"Napoleon Bonaparte!"

The pen dropped from the sergeant's fingers. Slowly he stood up, his legs pushing back the chair. The glare now was drained from his eyes, but they remained as widely open.

"Not Detective-Inspector Napoleon Bonaparte!"

The caller bowed ever so slightly.

"I hold that rank in the Queensland Police Force," he admitted.

"Well, sir, I am surprised. I was not expecting any one from Brisbane until the mail arrives this evening. How did you get here, sir?"

"I hired a car at Yaraka. I should have been here two days ago, but I was finalizing a case out from Longreach. The Commissioner thought I would be the best man to clear up this little bush mystery of yours. Oh, by the way! Please do not employ the 'sir.' I am known to all my friends and colleagues as Bony. Just Bony. Even Colonel Spendor calls me Bony. He says: 'Where the hell have you been, Bony?' and 'Why the devil didn't you report, Bony, when I ordered you to?' Colonel Spendor is volcanic but likeable. He will die suddenly—as a soldier should—and we shall all miss him. I like a man who damns and blasts. There is no conceit and no sly treachery in his make-up."

"Well, sir—er, Bony—I am glad to meet you," barked Cox, still controlled by astonishment. Moving hurriedly round the table, he jerked a chair from the wall corner. "Have heard a lot about you, of course. The wife is boiling the billy, I think. Can I offer you a cup of tea?"

"I was hoping that you would," Bony assented smilingly. "The driver of my hired car is removing the alkaloids of the track with pots of beer, but I find that beer taken during the day gives me a headache. Do not, however, put your wife to any trouble."

"Not at all! Not at all! I shall ask her to bring a tray here, and we could then discuss this aeroplane business. Have you seen my report which, I take it, was forwarded to Headquarters?"

"Yes. Otherwise I might have been disinclined to come," Bony replied.

"Disinclined! But the Chief Inspector, C.I.B., allocates cases, doesn't he?"

"He does, Sergeant. He allocates cases to me, but sometimes I decline to accept them." Bony smiled and revealed his perfect teeth. "I have found it necessary on more than one occasion to refuse to stultify my brain with a common murder or a still more common theft. The Chief Inspector of my department does not see it in the same light, or from the same angle. Neither does the Commissioner, whose damns and blasts are frequent."

"Yes, yes, of course!" Cox gasped, his face now purple, the military soul of him seared by this devastating defiance of discipline and questioning of authority. "Just a moment! I'll see about the tea."

When the sergeant had gone, the blue eyes of Napoleon Bonaparte twinkled. His defiance of authority and lack of respect for superiors never failed to create horror, and that horror never failed to amuse him. Moving his chair forward so that he came to be seated at one end of the writing-table, facing where the sergeant would be sitting, his long brown fingers began rapidly to manufacture a little pile of cigarettes.

This slight and handsome man had carved for himself a remarkable career. Taken into a mission station when a small baby, there had grown in the matron's heart a warm affection for him. At her death, she left in trust for him the whole of her small estate. Early in youth, Napoleon Bonaparte revealed a quick intelligence and facility for assimilating knowledge. At a State school he won a scholarship taking him on to high school at Brisbane from which he graduated to the then new university, at which he obtained his Master of Arts degree.

Then occurred a grave disappointment in love that sent him back to the bush. For a year he ran wild among the natives of his mother's tribe, and during that year he learned as much bushcraft as he would have done had he never been to school and to the city. The murder of a little girl out from Burketown, in which case he did invaluable tracking and found for the police the murderer, was the beginning of a brilliant career in the police force. His successes were remarkable, because wise superiors employed him wholly on bush cases, at which his natural instincts, inherited from his aboriginal mother, added to his own natural mental astuteness, were given full scope.

For a little while low-pitched voices drifted to him from the kitchen, and presently the sergeant returned to lower his bulk into the official chair.

"The wife will be bringing the tea in a minute or two," he informed Bony. "As for this aeroplane case . . . well, I don't think it will—what did you say?—stultify your brain, although it has deadened mine thinking about it. I can manage drunks and disorderlies, and make the owners of cars and trucks comply with the regulations, and all that, but this business is right off my beat."

"What you say is most promising. By the way, since the aeroplane was found has it rained or blown dust?"

"No. The weather has been clear and hot."

"Excellent! I understand that the Air Accidents people have visited the wreckage. What did they have to say?"

"Nothing," Cox growled. "Said they would report to the Commissioner."

"Well, well! We must allow these civil servants to wield their own thunderbolts. Dignity, you know, must be maintained. I wonder, now! Did they tramp about in the vicinity of the burned plane trying to shoot kangaroos or otherwise enjoy themselves?"

"I believe not. They were there most of one day pottering among the ruins. No, they did no kangaroo hunting.

The only men who have tramped about much looking for tracks are the two station blacks, Shuteye and Bill Sikes."

"Oh! Another unfortunate, named this time after a famous person in literature. I do not think it right. Was this Bill Sikes so named because of any resemblance to the original cracksman?"

"Maybe. He's ugly enough in all conscience."

"What success did they achieve?"

"None—unless the fact that they could find no tracks does prove that no person left the machine after it landed, and no person approached it to destroy it."

"Well, that will all have to be checked, and, as the weather has been fine and still, it will be mere routine work."

"I have here statements made by several men on Coolibah and elsewhere."

At this moment Mrs Cox arrived with the afternoon tea. She was wearing an afternoon frock, hastily donned. Knowing as much about police matters as her husband, she had insisted on bringing the tea in order to be presented to the most remarkable member of the force, and the member of it least known to the public.

On his feet, Bony bowed acknowledgment of the introduction. Mrs Cox had called him "sir," and now she was staring at him.

"Tell me, Mrs Cox," Bony urged, "do I look like a commercial traveller?"

"No, sir."

"Or a tramp?"

"Of course not, sir."

"Or a criminal?"

"Criminals are hard to detect until they are found out, sir," she answered cautiously.

"Thank you, Mrs Cox. I was afraid your husband mistook me for a criminal, or a tramp, or a commercial traveller. And now will you render me a great kindness?"

"If I can, sir."

"Please call me Bony. Just Bony. You see, I hold an inspector's rank merely because my training and my mental gifts entitle me to an inspector's salary. But it is the salary, not the rank, I covert. I have a beautiful wife and three growing boys to educate, and I have to find a great deal of money. My boys and my wife, the Commissioner and your husband, all call me Bony. I would be happy were you to do so."

Mrs Cox wanted to laugh, though not altogether with merriment.

"Certainly, if you wish it, Bony," she managed to say.

"Thank you! And thank you for the tea. I am sure I shall appreciate it."

The sergeant's wife fled, and the sergeant fell to manipulating the tea service.

"Have you any children?" asked Bony.

"One. A boy of fifteen. Illness in his early years put him back a lot, but the new school teacher has done wonders with him."

"What are you going to make of him?"

"Not a policeman."

"Why not? The police force offers a fine career."

"I beg to differ," Cox growled, in his voice a hint of anger. "Look at me, shoved out here as a young man to keep order among a peaceful, law-abiding people. Pushed here out of the way. No chance of further promotion—no chance to use what little intelligence I may possess. My wife sacrificed city life for me, and now my son will sacrifice a decent career for me, too. What chance has a lad out here, bar life as a stockman? What chance have I, for that matter? I have asked for a transfer until I'm sick of asking."

Bony's eyelids drooped. He sensed the almost extinguished ambition in the other, and, gauging it by his own illimitable ambitions, he read the book of life plainly in this police office.

"Perhaps you will gain promotion out of this aeroplane case," he suggested softly.

"Oh, yeah?" Cox returned with a wry smile. "Pardon the Americanism, but I'll get nothing out of this case. Why, I had to call on the C.I.B. for assistance, or rather to ask them to take it over from me."

"Without doubt, in that you acted wisely," Bony said, again softly. "Remember, from the carcass of the lion came forth sweetness. We will collaborate, and I will see that you get all the credit possible. I will get none, because my superiors have become used to my successes. Have you previously had an important case?"

"No, worse luck."

"Then we must make this one a stepping-stone for your promotion out of Golden Dawn. Tell me all about it—from the beginning."

While Sergeant Cox related the facts in proper sequence, now and then assisted by the report he was writing when Bony arrived, the detective smoked cigarettes he took from the pile he had made and sipped several cups of tea, munching buttered scones between the cigarettes.

"Analysis showed that the brandy beside the girl's bed was doctored with approximately one quarter of an ounce of strychnine reduced to liquid form by boiling in vinegar," Cox wound up.

"You have a map of the district?"

"Yes. It is there on the wall."

They rose to stand before the large-scale map, and the sergeant pointed out the places he had mentioned.

"Thank you," Bony said, turning back to the table. "You have put the case in a manner both concise and clear. I understand that to date the people who have seen that girl are: yourself, this Dr Knowles, the Coolibah housekeeper, and Nettlefold and his daughter. And not one of you recognized her?"

Cox shook his head. "She is a complete stranger to us."

"At the time of the theft of the monoplane was there any one else in this district able to fly an aeroplane other than Loveacre and his companions and Dr Knowles?"

"Yes. There is Mr John Kane, the owner of a station north of Coolibah, called Tintanoo. He was in the Royal Air Force during the war, but as far as I know he hasn't piloted a machine since his return from France."

"Where was he the night that the machine was stolen?"

"Here in Golden Dawn."

"And the next night, when the machine was burned?"

"At his home at Tintanoo. You may be sure, Bony, I convinced myself that he could have had no hand in it. Besides, although he is a fast liver, he is otherwise well respected. Tons of money."

"Hum! It is obvious that there is more than one person concerned in this matter, unless, of course, it was possible for one person to burn the aeroplane—if it was destroyed by human action—and then travel nearly seventy miles to poison the brandy at about four o'clock. The latter fact gives us every excuse to assume that the machine was wilfully destroyed. Now this Dr Knowles! Tell me about him."

"He came here in 1920 from Brisbane where he had lived without practising from early in 1919. He, too, was in the Flying Corps. In fact, he and John Kane were for some time attached to the same squadron. They met again in Brisbane, and it was due to Kane that Knowles came to practise at Golden Dawn.

"Naturally we all welcomed the doctor. He has proved himself a good man. He doesn't get overmuch work, and yet his fees are reasonable. Private income, I think. Five years ago he bought his first aeroplane. We expected him to break his neck, but he soon showed that he can fly as well as he can doctor. He is, of course, known to us as the flying doctor, but he has no connexion with the Australian Aerial Medical Service, which is responsible for other flying doctors."

Sergeant Cox regarded Bony steadily when he paused.

"We can forgive a man much when he will fly anywhere in all weather to attend a case. We can overlook his heavy drinking, because I have never seen the man drunk in the ordinary sense. To use a common phrase, he drinks like a fish, and he sticks to spirits, too. The effect of alcohol on him is peculiar. It weakens him from the belt down while having no visible effect from the belt up. And the more he takes the better he flies. He has never given me any trouble. He has always behaved like the gentleman and the man he is."

"Dear me!" Bony exclaimed. "And how long has this drinking been going on?"

"Ever since he came here, to my knowledge," Cox affirmed.

"Where is he now—to-day?"

"In town. He came in this morning from Coolibah."

"Then I think we will go along and see him. By the way, would Mr Nettlefold be kind enough to put me up?"

"Yes, I am sure he would be only too pleased," Cox said warmly. "He's worried, of course, about that poisoner. He wanted to have the patient moved to Winton hospital, but Miss Nettlefold would not hear of it."

"Indeed!"

"Yes. Jolly fine girl that. About twenty-six years old. Came home from school to look after the old man when, I hear, she wanted to go in for science. Told me the other day—or at least didn't tell me, but let me guess—that she had been bored stiff with the dull life at Coolibah, and welcomed the job of nursing. She does the night shift, and the boss stockman out there roams around all night. You see, we half expect another attempt to be made on that girl's life."

Bony rose and took up his hat. Once again he stood before the wall map. Then, when he turned to Cox, he said: "I believe, Sergeant, that this case will interest me. I am particularly pleased that the weather has continued fine. Now for Dr Knowles. On our way I will call at the post office to dispatch a telegram to Colonel Spendor."

Together they walked to the post office, the only brick building in Golden Dawn. Outside, Sergeant Cox stopped to talk with Constable Lovitt, and Bony entered.

The postmaster was writing at a table beyond the counter. Through a glass-built partition could be seen the telephone exchange. The glass door was wide open, and through the doorway Bony noted the young woman who turned to observe him. Cold, appraising eyes of blue regarded him with what in a less attractive person would be a rude stare.

Bony's message, addressed to Police Commissioner, Brisbane, ran:

Delighted with prospects. Weather has been splendid. Have met exceptionally keen colleague in Sergeant Cox.

CHAPTER VIII

STINGRAYS AMONG FISHES

ON the majority of Australian sheep and cattle stations people are divided into three grades or classes; for, even among Australia's most democratic portion of her alleged democratic population, class distinctions are rigidly maintained. Heading this class trilogy on the average station is the owner, or the manager, and his family. They reside in what is termed "government house," the main residence on the property and the centre from which it is directed. On a great number of stations there is another and less pretentious building housing the apprentices or jackeroos, and the overseer or boss stockman. They are provided with a sitting-room and a dining-room. The "lower orders," comprising the station men and the tradesmen, inhabit a hut, and their dining-room adjoins the kitchen ruled by their own cook.

At Coolibah there was no separate establishment for jackeroos and the boss stockman. Normally Ted Sharp would have been a member of this middle class, and when Nettlefold asked him if he would live at "government house" for a few days, and carry out night guard while the aeroplane girl was a patient within it, he gladly agreed to the guard duty, but expressed a desire to live with the men.

"I work with them, and when on the run I eat with them,

and, as there are no jackeroos' quarters, I prefer to live with the men here," he said.

To this, however, Elizabeth would not listen, not that she was more democratic than others of her class, but because Ted Sharp was no ordinary bushman, and . . . well . . . just because . . .

"If you are good enough to keep guard over the house all night and every night," she told him firmly, "you are good enough to live with us. Don't argue, Ted, please."

"All right!" he agreed, sighing, but secretly pleased.

Thus he fell into a routine. All day he slept in a cool room at "government house"; he ate his meals with the manager and his daughter, and at night he roamed about the house or sat on the veranda outside the patient's room. Elizabeth never saw him after she went on duty, but she knew he was never far away, and consequently felt no anxiety.

But to accept a half-caste detective as an equal was quite another matter. When Hetty had awakened her to tell of the arrival of Dr Knowles and a detective, who was an Australian half-caste, and that this detective even then was with the doctor and her father in the latter's study, and, above all, that Mr Nettlefold had given orders that a room be prepared for this half-caste detective, Elizabeth felt that it was really too much.

In their turn both the station manager and the doctor had accepted Bony with cold reserve, but few men could withstand the appeal of this extraordinary personality. The slightly grandiloquent manner of speaking was countered by the twinkling blue eyes that always seemed to mock at their owner's love of grandiloquence. On his arrival he had requested time to bath and change before beginning with the business which had brought him, and, during that interval, Knowles had passed to the manager all that Cox had managed to tell him regarding Mr Napoleon Bonaparte, M.A.

Bony had re-appeared freshly shaved and wearing a dark blue suit, and now Dr Knowles lounged in one of the easy chairs with a tumbler held by one white hand. When the door opened to admit Elizabeth, the doctor rose with alacrity, and when Bony stood up and walked a few steps forward he presented the half-caste to the young mistress of Coolibah.

"Miss Nettlefold, this is Detective-Inspector Napoleon Bonaparte. He insists on being addressed merely as Bony. Bony, permit me to present you to Miss Nettlefold, the lady who has undertaken to nurse my patient."

"How do you do?" Elizabeth said coldly, across a space of twelve feet.

"I am charmed to meet a woman who so nobly gives herself to the nursing of a complete stranger," Bony said, bowing as she had never seen a man bow before. "Knowing that a policeman in the house is always upsetting, I will try to give as little trouble as possible."

The light shone directly on his face, and she was held by his blue eyes, by the force of intelligence gazing from them. She noted the delicate mould of his features, pure Nordic and with no trace of his aboriginal ancestry. That lay only in the colour of his skin. She meant to say that, as she was night nursing, his presence would in no way disturb her. What she did say was:

"How do you know that a policeman in the house is a disturbing influence?"

"Because my wife always says so when I have been home five minutes," he replied quickly. Then, perhaps, because she stood her ground, he advanced to her. "I would like to see your patient as early as possible while the daylight lasts. If you will introduce me as an acquaintance. . . . Then, when I am about to leave, I will stand before the little bedside table, and I would like you to go into the dressing-room and stand just where you were when you saw in the mirror the man with his back to you. As I move from the table to leave the room will you then kindly act precisely as you did that night and at the same speed?"

"If you wish it. Will you see the patient now?"

Bony nodded assent. "Thank you," he said. "Excuse me, Mr Nettlefold and Dr Knowles." Holding open the door for her to pass out, he followed her into the hall.

"A moment, Miss Nettlefold, before we go to the sick-room," he requested, and she turned calmly to look at him, her hostility towards his colour not yet vanquished. "I have one or two questions to ask you concerning this poor young woman. I understand you have closely examined her clothing and have found on several articles the initials M.M. Once we have identified your patient our task of unmasking the person who is conspiring against her life will be partly accomplished. Now tell me please, of what quality is the young woman's underwear?"

He saw the quickly-gathered frown, and he knew that in Elizabeth Nettlefold he was facing the same battle he had during his career so often faced and won.

"Well, really . . ." she began haughtily.

"I am forty-three years old, Miss Nettlefold, and I have been married twenty years," he cut in. "Believe me, the information I seek is for the purpose of establishing the patient's identity. Do her clothes lead you to assume that she is—well, high in social circles? Are they expensive, or are they cheap and of poor quality?"

"I should say that her clothes have been purchased at middle-class shops," she replied steadily.

"Thank you! You see how no man could answer my question, unless he happened to be a draper. A person's outside clothes are not always a true index to his or her social station. Now, if you please."

Conducting him along the corridor, Elizabeth was puzzled by his address, and hostile yet to the fact of his admittance to her home as an equal. Hetty rose from her chair beside the bed when they entered the room. She, too, appeared hostile because of her mistress's avowed attitude earlier in the evening. The sun was not yet set, and, added to the chugging petrol engine, was the incessant noise of the chattering galahs and parrots. Within the room it was cool and bright, and, now that the heat of the day was over, the curtains had been drawn aside to admit the breeze.

"You have a visitor, dear," Elizabeth said, bending over the bed. "He is trying to find out all about you, and he promises not to say long enough to bore you."

Then, straightening up, she turned to Bony with an expression on her vivid face which there was no mistaking. He understood that this visit was considered wholly unnecessary, but, bland and unperturbed, he stood at the foot of the bed, and from there smiled at the patient whose eyes he could see beneath the partly lowered lids. They moved slightly when he encountered their almost fixed stare.

To him her tragically helpless condition made its instant appeal. The immobility of her frame and features were not themselves terrible to him who had seen death all too often. Those aspects were not terrible to Dr Knowles for the same reason. They were made terrible by the living, intelligent eyes which so clearly revealed a soul anguished by the prison bars of the body. Her aspect appalled him, struck at his gentle nature and aroused all his sympathy for the weak and the defenceless.

Yet he kept all this from his eyes, smiling at her across the length of the bed. Not a doctor, he yet was sure that her condition could not possibly be due to natural causes. Mental shock, no! Bodily injury, no! Hypnotism, perhaps! Perhaps a drug, but what drug? His ready tongue now almost failed him.

"I am grieved to see you like this, Miss M.M.," he told her, obviously fighting for words. "I am sure now that you are the victim of a conspiracy, and perhaps you may find solace in the fact that not only are your nurses and the doctor concerned for your welfare. Men in all the Australian States are working night and day on your behalf to find out who you are and where you come from, and to hurry to your bed-side those whom you love. I wonder, now!"

Moving round to the side of the bed opposite the two nurses, he took up the limp hands and carefully examined them. Elizabeth and Hetty watched him, the former ready to intervene. Then gently he laid them down on the white coverlet.

"You have beautiful hair," he said softly. "It reminds me of one whom I knew when I was a boy. Now I must leave you. Retain your courage and never let go the rock of hope." Bending still lower, he gazed directly into her eyes, to say: "You will get well again, believe me. You need not be doubtful that I shall find out all about you, and then you will be able again to work at a typewriter in an office." Seeing the flash of interest leap into the blue eyes, his own began to twinkle, and he said more cheerily: "You see, I am beginning to find out things about you already. I am an expert at finding answers to riddles. *Au revoir!*"

Standing up he regarded Elizabeth with a faint trace of triumph. Her eyes were wide, and involuntarily they directed their gaze at the white hands on the coverlet. Then he made a sign, and, recognizing her cue, she stepped to the dressing-room. Passing round the bed, the detective paused in front of the little table on which was a half-bottle of brandy, medicine bottles and a tumbler. Then with hastened action he moved to the door, silently opened it and passed out, then as silently closed it and backed swiftly down the corridor to the hall separating the study from the dining-room. He had reached the hall, and was waiting for Elizabeth to appear when a cold voice behind him drawled:

"Stand quite still, you!"

Bony stood still.

"If you move a fraction of an inch I'll shoot!"

At that instant Elizabeth emerged from the bedroom to stand for a space looking along the corridor at Bony and the man behind him. Then her eyes widened, and she called out:

"Ted Sharp! What are you doing? Put that pistol away!"

Bony ventured a half-turn to observe the man who had jabbed the barrel of a weapon rather smartly into his back.

"I should have been annoyed had you shot me," he said, chuckling. "You are, I presume, Mr Edward Sharp."

"This is Inspector Bonaparte, Ted," Elizabeth explained a little breathlessly.

"Oh! New rabbit inspector?"

His levity appeared to annoy Elizabeth, for she snapped out:

"No, of course not. Mr Bonaparte is a dectective-inspector just arrived from Brisbane."

"You don't say!" Ted Sharp's eyes grew big, and over his mahogany-tinted face spread a rueful smile. "Now, if I had plugged you——"

"As I said, I should have been annoyed," Bony interjected smilingly. "And then there is the carpet."

Elizabeth wanted to laugh but she remembered his colour. It was irritating, too, to find Ted so easily familiar with the man.

"I thought you were up to no good, backing along like you did," explained the boss stockman, frankly examining the dectective.

"With Miss Nettlefold's assistance, I was carrying out a little experiment," Bony informed him lightly. "I was determining if it were possible for a man to leave the sick-room and reach this hall, which is nearer than that giving exit to the east veranda, before Miss Nettlefold could reach the bedroom door and look out into the corridor."

"Apparently he could," suggested Sharp.

"Yes, he could. In fact, he *did*!"

"But why this experiment, Mr Bonaparte?" asked Elizabeth.

"Until we made the experiment we could not be sure that that man did come along to this hall after leaving the room."

"I don't think I understand," she told Bony, frowning.

"Pardon! The man you saw, you thought at the time to be Dr Knowles," Bony explained. Then he smiled, saying, "I merely wished to demonstrate to myself that it really was *not* the doctor."

"Oh!" Elizabeth exclaimed, with rising indignation.

"And now that I am reasonably sure that a man who was not a stranger to this house, did visit the sick-room and tamper with the brandy, I can permit my liking and admiration for Dr Knowles full sway. Dear me, what a man! I notice that the sick-room has two pairs of french windows. Were they opened on the night that the brandy was poisoned?"

The girl's indignation subsided before the warm magnetism of Bony's personality. For the first time she forgot his colour. For the first time her hostility was forgotten, too.

"Why, yes!" she replied. "One pair was kept open all that night. However, the curtains were drawn before both pairs of windows."

"Then, without doubt, the intruder watched you from outside the open window. He accepted the opportunity you gave him when you retired to the dressing-room. Having reached the bed-side table, knowing the plan of the house, he went out through the door because that was to him the nearest exit. Had he known nothing of the interior of the building he would have retreated by the way he had come. You did not notice if he wore a mask?"

Elizabeth shook her head.

"I saw him with his back to me. When I looked again he was outside the door and closing it," she said.

"Hum! Well, the matter turning out as it did, it was as well you did not confront him."

The aboriginal maid appeared to make an anxious sign

to her mistress. Elizabeth suggested dinner, and Ted Sharp volunteered to call the doctor and Nettlefold.

"This house, I observe, has two halls. That is unusual," Bony remarked, when Ted Sharp was standing just within the study door.

"Well, you see, this west part of the house was built long after the eastern portion," Elizabeth explained. "Originally the house faced to the east. Then when the addition was built on the centre passage was continued back here, and this hall was planned. As you see, it opens on to the south veranda, which is always comparatively cool and shaded. Now the kitchen and domestic quarters are in a detached building to the north, and connected by a covered passage."

"Ah! Thank you. And, of course, the hall door was not locked that night?"

"It was never locked, Mr Bonaparte."

The men joined them, and the doctor took Elizabeth in. Nettlefold occupied the seat at the head of the table, with Elizabeth on his left and Bony on his right. Ted Sharp sat next to the detective, and the doctor sat beside their hostess.

"I understand that in an army mess it is considered bad form to discuss army matters," Bony said to them all, after the soup. "But here and now I am compelled to err by the urgency of this business which has brought me here. On the map you marked for me, Mr Nettlefold, you showed the position of a hut beside a bore called Faraway Bore. How far is that from Emu Lake?"

"Roughly eight miles," replied the cattleman. "It is north of the main station track off which one turns along the Emu Lake paddock fence. From here it would be sixty-four miles."

"Thank you! Ned Hamlin and two blacks, Shuteye and Bill Sikes are living there at present?"

"Yes."

"Are there any spare hacks and gear at this Faraway Bore hut?"

"Plenty of horses. We keep extra saddles here."

"It would make rather a good headquarters," said Bony. "Would you lend me a horse and gear, and the services of those two blacks?"

"Why, yes, with pleasure."

Bony glanced across at his hostess.

"Pardon my persistence in talking shop, Miss Nettlefold, but I have decided to ask your father a great favour." To the manager he went on: "This continued calm weather indicates a severe disturbance. It might come at any hour, and it is of grave importance that certain work be done out there before it does. The favour I ask of you is to take me to Faraway Bore to-night."

"To-night? Well—certainly, if you wish it."

"Surely you have done enough travelling for one day, Mr—er—Bony!" Elizabeth exclaimed, her former hostility now forgotten.

"Yes—a hundred and ten miles by car after leaving the train, and then a hundred and four miles by plane," added Knowles. "Dash it, man! It is sixty-four miles over a rough track—fifteen of them like a switchback railway over the river channels."

"Notwithstanding, if Mr Nettlefold will . . ."

"Oh, I'll take you; the manager agreed. "I can make the return journey comfortably before midnight. You will be staying, Doctor, of course."

"Thank you! I want to keep the patient under observation," Knowles replied.

"Then, Bony, we will get away after dinner. Ted will be on guard with his two dogs."

"Ah! By the way, Miss Nettlefold," Bony said, regarding her across the damask, "how did the homestead dogs behave that night you saw the intruder?"

"One barked half-heartedly all night through."

"That strengthens the theory that the intruder was well acquainted with the interior plan of this house. The dog knew the poisoner; had he been a stranger the dog's bark would have been more than half-hearted, and it would, without doubt, have been joined by the others. It seems probable that the man works here, or is a visitor. No, I cannot suspect you now, Doctor."

"*Did* you suspect me?" Knowles asked blandly.

Bony smiled.

"I did, my dear Doctor, I did! Quite without reason, too. Sergeant Cox informs me that the population of his district numbers on the average about two hundred. I regard all these people—including those present—as fish in my net. Among these fish is a stingray—probably two stingrays. To discover the stingrays, it is essential to examine all the fish. You will admit, Doctor, that it was quite possible for you to enter the sick-room, having waited beyond the window curtains for the opportunity presented by Miss Nettlefold's temporary absence in her dressing-room. Miss Nettlefold and I carried out a little experiment just to prove that the intruder could have reached the nearer end of the corridor before she looked out from the room. It is a fact which, although it does not wholly exonerate you, does at least support your innocence. I am made happy by it after the cool manner you coaxed your choked engine to life with about thirty seconds to spare."

"Oh! That's the first time we have heard about a failing engine," Nettlefold said.

"It was only a piece of fluff or grit in the petrol system," the doctor explained, faintly annoyed. "Happened over dense mulga timber. It would, of course!"

"I do not intend flattery, Doctor, when I say that I cannot but admire coolness in the face of death," Bony said distinctly. "I am glad to say that I shall not suspect you again."

Knowles laughed.

"Whom do you suspect, then? Tell us, now, have you formed any theories about this case?"

"Several," Bony admitted. "There are obvious facts supporting some of them. The unfortunate young woman is not known in this district. I incline to the thought that she was not in the district when the aeroplane was stolen, and that it was stolen with the express purpose of bringing about her destruction. It is reasonable to assume that the person who did steal the machine is one having intimate knowledge of the district, and that having the person of the young woman on his hands outside the district, he stole the machine, flew it to where she was, took her up in it out to Emu Lake paddock, which he knew was resting, and, therefore, was not likely to be visited by stockmen, and there jumped by parachute, leaving the victim in the machine to crash and hoping that the crash would fire the machine. In the resultant debris would be found the charred remains of the supposed thief."

Bony ceased to speak while the maid cleared away the dessert and served coffee. Elizabeth provided cigarettes, and announced her intention of remaining at table. The afterglow of the departed sun poured into the room.

"Go on, please," she urged, when the maid withdrew.

"Well, from information received, as the constable says in court, the young woman was discovered in the abandoned aeroplane at twenty minutes to two in the afternoon," Bony proceeded. "By extraordinary chance the machine made a perfect landing on Emu Lake. Captain Loveacre states that this monoplane was easy to fly, and could conceivably remain in the air for a period without control. As it came to rest on the middle of the lake, the pilot had either shut off the ignition or the fuel supply ran out almost immediately after he had jumped from it.

"Then, you, Mr and Miss Nettlefold, leave the machine with the helpless young woman at about two-thirty, and you arrive here at about five minutes to six, having called nowhere and seen no one *en route*. At six o'clock Mr Nettlefold rings up Sergeant Cox. At four o'clock the following morning a serious attempt is made to poison the patient's medicinal brandy.

"Now, Coolibah Station is not a town or even a large city to be crossed and re-crossed in an hour or so. And yet swift action follows the failure to crash the machine and kill the young woman. The telephone system I will have to discuss with you later, Mr Nettlefold. There may be a leakage in it somewhere. On the other hand, you may have been observed removing the victim of the conspiracy from the aeroplane—which is why I am so anxious to look at the country out there before a rainstorm or a windstorm obliterates valuable evidence. You, Miss Nettlefold, told Sergeant Cox that on the night the brandy was poisoned you did not hear the sound of a car, near or distant, so that the intruder arrived on foot and departed on foot—unless he was then at Coolibah!"

Bony leaned forward across the table.

"We shall have done a great deal when we have identified

the unfortunate victim of this terrible outrage," he said.

"A description of her has been circulated throughout Australia. Her initials are double M, and she is employed in an office as a typist, or at her home doing typewriting work."

"How do you know that?" was the chorus.

"By the fact that the balls of both forefingers and the outer edges of both thumbs are distinctly flattened by the keys of a typewriter."

CHAPTER IX

EXAMINING THE FISH

WHEN the little party at Coolibah rose from dinner, Nettlefold passed out to see to his car preparatory to the long journey to the hut at Faraway Bore; Dr Knowles and Elizabeth went out through the french windows and made for the patient's bedroom.

Bony was in a happy mood. Adroitly he shepherded the boss stockman into a corner of the dining-room where there were two chairs flanking a small occasional table of Queensland oak.

"I understand, Mr Sharp, that you have been on Coolibah for eleven years," began the detective when they were seated. "Without doubt your position here enables you to have a clearer insight into the characters of the men than Mr Nettlefold could have. You are closer to them than he is, although some of them have been here longer than you. Is there one among them who possibly could have entered the sick-room and poisoned the brandy?"

Ted Sharp was looking steadily at the toes of his shoes, and for some seconds he offered no reply. His physical attitude remained flexible, but yet Bony sensed a mental tautness suddenly created by his question. It was as though the man at last realized why he had been manoeuvred into that corner of the room.

"Sergeant Cox asked me that," he said, without looking

up. "I can't think that any man here would do such a thing. They are all good fellows. They may be a bit wild, you know, when they're in town, but at heart they're all right. Of course, it is hard to say what a man will do if the price is high enough."

"You mean if he is offered enough money?"

Sharp nodded.

"Well, is there a man here who would poison a helpless woman's medicinal brandy if he were offered a thousand pounds?"

"No." The answer came with a prolonged exhalation of breath. "No, I don't think so. Poisoning is a filthy thing to do."

"Yes, I agree. It is far worse than killing with a gun. I am told that on the night the aeroplane was destroyed by fire you were out at Faraway Bore with Ned Hamlin and the two blacks, Bill Sikes and Shuteye. How far would that hut be from Emu Lake, as the crow is alleged to fly?"

"About eight miles. A little under, if anything."

The boss stockman had lost interest in his shoes, and now was regarding the detective between narrowed eyelids. Suavely Bony went on with the inquisition.

"And then north of Faraway Bore, on the main Golden Dawn-St Albans road, there is a wayside hotel known as Gurner's Hotel. As the crow flies, what is the distance between those two points?"

"I should say about sixteen miles."

"Ah! The hotel being in Tintanoo country, how far north of the bore is the boundary fence between the two stations?"

"Four miles."

"Thank you, Mr Sharp." The boss stockman moved as though to get up, but Bony waved him back into his chair. "Tell me, is there a track from the bore to Gurner's Hotel?"

"Yes. But it's rough and seldom used. There is no gate in the boundary fence where that track passes through to Tintanoo. We unhook and re-hitch the wires."

Bony lit another cigarette. He was, apparently, watching the maid clearing the table when he put his next question.

"Now, that night—the night Captain Loveacre's monoplane was destroyed—you were at Faraway Bore. Where did you sleep?"

"At Faraway Bore, of course," Sharp answered with a trace of impatience.

"Yes, yes! But did you sleep inside or outside the hut?"

"Outside. It was a fairly quiet night and warm."

"Pardon my seeming persistence, but just *where* did you sleep?"

"Oh—this side of the hut. There was a soft nor'-east wind that night."

"On the side farthest from Emu Lake?"

Sharp nodded. "That's so."

"Hum! Well, well! And yet you heard no explosion? I should imagine that the explosion of the aeroplane's petrol tanks would make a fairly loud concussion."

"No. We heard nothing. It was eight miles away, remember."

"Still, it was possible for you to have heard the explosion, and had you done so we might have been able to establish the time. The man, Hamlin, and the blacks—where did they sleep?"

"Ned slept inside the hut, and the two blacks camped in a tent close by."

"Are you a heavy sleeper?" Bony asked next. The question caused the boss stockman to chuckle.

"No. I have been too much with cattle on the track to

be anything but a light sleeper. You want to realize that eight miles is eight miles."

"Oh, I realize that all right. Bear with me, Mr Sharp. Now, tell me about the people at Gurner's Hotel. What kind of a man is Gurner?"

"Gurner's all right—in his way," Sharp replied more easily. "He considers himself a cut above us working-men. It has been said of him that he's not above taking more from a man's cheque than he has legal right to do, but I wouldn't like you to think I believed it. I've never handed a cheque over his bar with instructions to be told when it was cut out. Many of the men prefer the hotel at Golden Dawn, but there are no police near Gurner's, you understand."

"Of course," assented the detective-inspector. "That would be an important advantage."

Bony fell silent. Sharp moved impatiently in his chair. After a long pause Bony went on:

"Have you seen the young woman found in the plane?"

"Yes, I looked in on her to see if I knew her or not."

"She's in a bad state, Mr Sharp. I have never been in charge of an investigation where my sympathy for the victim has been stronger than in this case. Believe me, I am thankful for your co-operation. People, you know, are invariably reserved when in the presence of a detective, especially if he is engaged in a murder case. It is so difficult to understand the horror in the mind of the average citizen at the very thought of being publicly connected with such a crime as a witness. Where were you the night before the aeroplane was destroyed, the night it was stolen?"

"I was at Faraway Bore—or rather, I was there part of the time. What's the idea of putting all these questions to me? Do you suspect me of having stolen or destroyed the aeroplane?"

Bony smiled.

"Not that you *stole* the aeroplane, Mr Sharp," he replied. "Oh, no! But it is my business definitely to nail down, like butterflies on a sheet or cork, the exact position of everyone on those vital nights. All of you here—every one in the district—are as fish in my net, and I have to take up each one of you and examine you to ascertain which of you is the stingray."

Bony made this explanation with a purpose. It was done to permit Ted Sharp to depart from the truth—if he wished. It was Bony's favourite trap, this giving of time in certain circumstances.

"Where did you spend part of that night away from Faraway Bore?"

"I left the place about nine o'clock to visit Mitchell's Well. That's south of Faraway Bore. The weather had been quiet, and I wanted to see if the windmill had raised enough water into the receiving tanks to last the stock three days. You see, the next day we were shifting cattle for the drovers to take over. I got back about one in the morning."

"Ah yes! I remember seeing Mitchell's Well on the map. You heard no plane engines?"

"Not a whisper."

"And how did you go to Mitchell's Well? Horseback?"

"No. I did the job in my own runabout truck."

"Did you sleep that night in the same place as the night following?"

"Yes. The conditions were the same. Warm and quiet with a slight nor'-east wind cooling the temperature."

Mr Nettlefold came in at this point, and Bony rose to

meet him. Sharp got to his feet, relief evident on his weather-darkened face. The car was waiting, and the detective at once went to his room for one of his suitcases. He did not again see the boss stockman or Elizabeth, but Dr Knowles accompanied them to the car to see them off. Ten minutes later they were crossing the river.

The river! Surely the maddest, the most impossible river in the world, the Diamantina. It collects its mighty flood-waters from among the hills in north-central Queensland and rushes them down into the semi-desert of north-eastern South Australia. When this river runs, its width at Monkira is five miles. Here at Coolibah its width was fifteen miles, and at this time not a drop of water lay in the intertwining channels.

The beams of the car's headlights swept up and then became level when the machine rose to cross each succeeding channel bank, and they reached down to light the channel beds for the car to take them, hugging the narrow track. The flood of the previous year had deposited grass and herbage seed, and now along many of the channels cattle and horse-feed grew profusely. It was like a frozen sea, a sea frozen solid when in tempestuous anger; it was as though the car was a ship steaming over stationary waves.

"More than once in the old days, I have been returning from the back of the run to find fifteen miles of water barring me from home," Nettlefold told Bony. "Nowadays, when a flood collects at the head of the river, the intelligence is passed down from homestead to homestead. So we receive ample warning."

"I have been wondering why the Coolibah homestead

is built on the east side of the river when most of the run lies west of the river," Bony said lazily.

"Its present site was chosen chiefly for its elevation, and partly for the reason that it is many miles nearer to 'inside.' Again, Coolibah has about two hundred and fifty square miles of country east of the river. Tintanoo has no land on the east side, but its homestead, too, is built on a spur of high ground. Farther south, the river channels are thirty miles across."

Both men welcomed the easier travelling when beyond the river, and by the aid of the dashlamp the detective began to make his chain of cigarettes. He was now in possession of the telephone system connecting Coolibah with Golden Dawn and the outside world, but Nettlefold's reference to telephonic communication up and down the river made him ask:

"The line by which you receive warning of floods is a private line?"

"No. The stations maintain it and pay rent to the Postal Department."

"Then you can communicate with homesteads above and below you without doing so through the exchange at Golden Dawn?"

"Oh yes! In addition to that there is the usual private line connecting all the stockmen's huts with the homestead. I rang up Ned Hamlin before we left."

"I understand now. One line direct to Golden Dawn, another to the river homesteads, and a third to your own huts. I saw only one instrument in your study. The others——"

"Are in the office. I thought once of having all three in the study, but Elizabeth objected on the score that so many instruments would make the place like an office."

"Tintanoo being above you, what station is below you? Macedon, is it not?"

"Yes. The Chidlows are there, but we do not often see them. Their nearest town is Birdsville. We are better acquainted with John Kane."

"Ah—the ex-flying officer. Tell me about Mr Kane, will you?"

Nothing loath, for the manager enjoyed company when driving, Nettlefold complied with the detective's request for gossip.

"Old man Kane had two sons—John and Charles. I did not know Mrs Kane. She died before I came here. Before the war both boys were as wild as kangaroos, and early in 1914—when John was twenty-one and Charles twenty—the younger ran away with the Golden Dawn school teacher and married her.

"Old Kane promptly cut him out of his will. He was that kind of man, gruff and stern and hard. John, the elder son, was treated similarly when he defied the old man and joined the A.I.F., the father again making a will in favour of his nephews. Charles faded out of the picture for some time, and John obtained a transfer to the Royal Air Force and did good work until a German bullet fractured his leg.

"On his return to Queensland, John found that his brother and father were reconciled after a fashion, and, the war having broadened the old man's mind, he took John back again into favour, so that affairs stood as they were before Charles married the school teacher. Then, early in 1920, Charles and his wife were both killed in a car smash near Sydney, and shortly after that John quarrelled with the old man and went off up into the Cape York Peninsula with a missionary. He stayed there for about two years, not trying to convert the blacks, but for the purpose of studying them and their customs. In his way, John Kane is quite an anthropologist; better, in fact, than many who have learned all they know from textbooks—professors and such like. He was, I understand, always interested in aborigines. Anyway, he knows more about them than I do, or any one else in this district. He used to write a lot concerning them, and he is the author of an important book on their beliefs and legends.

"In 1923 he returned home when his father was desperately ill, and when the old fellow died the son naturally came in for the property. He never married, nor has he ever really settled down. The war might have spoiled him, but I think he was spoiled long before he went to the war.

"He drinks a good deal in patches. Goes the whole hog at times, and in between refuses to touch it. Erratic in other matters, too. He has house parties to which sometimes he invites a flash social crowd from Brisbane, and at others genuine anthropologists and people actively interested in the aborigines. When I add that he drives a car like a madman, sacks all his hands one day and re-employs them the next, runs his station efficiently, and yet wastes time, or, perhaps I should say spends his time in other pursuits, you will have some idea of the man's character. He's not a bad neighbour, although he does consider himself a cut above us. He's free with his money and supports all local charities.

"Yes, Kane is a peculiar man—tempermentally unstable. A few years back I heard that he contemplated selling a property his owns north of Tintanoo, a place called Garth. It is not a large property, but the country is first class and well watered. I got my agent to make him an offer, and he flatly refused to sell to me because a year before we had had a slight disagreement about some unbranded cattle Since then he has received several offers, but he has invariably refused to close because he thought they were made on my behalf."

"I should like to meet this Mr John Kane," Bony murmured. "He should be an interesting man. Do I understand that the wound received during the war stopped him flying?"

"I am not positively sure, but I think not. I think I heard once that he did a little flying afterwards, but the end of the war came before he could be sent again to France. He walks with a slight limp to this day. You must talk to Dr Knowles about him. He knows more about Kane's war career than I do."

"I will. By the way, Knowles isn't an Australian, is he?"

"No. He is a Sussex man. His early life is a mystery. Excellent fellow, it is a pity, though, that he drinks so hard."

"That is so," Bony readily agreed. "I wonder why he does it. In other ways he's not the drinking type."

The car's headlights picked up the sand barrier—called by Elizabeth the Rockies—silhouetting them against the seeming blackness of the sky beyond. Nettlefold explained how this range of pure, wind-blown sand extended roughly north-south for eighteen miles. Countless tons of sand had formed there during his period of managing Coolibah. It was due to the general overstocking of the runs and the lopping of the scrub for cattle in dry times, and in turn that was due to the stupid leasehold system of the pastoral areas of Australia, which gave the lessees no interest in preserving the land and its timber. With the bores failing and the denudation of the scrub, the face of Queensland was destined to be much altered by the end of another hundred years.

It did appear that the high walls of sand would block further progress, but the faint wheel tracks on the claypans twisted and turned to lead them through the barrier and on to the plain beyond. Here, where the ground was firm and level, the track ran straight away beyond the lamp beams, permitting fast driving.

The high speed was maintained for mile after mile, the car being stopped only when it was necessary to open gates, but it was well after nine o'clock when the headlights revealed the black and white picture of a wooden-walled, iron-roofed hut, several outhouses and a tent pitched beneath two pepper-trees which guarded the hut from the westerlies.

"Faraway Hut," said Nettlefold, braking the car to a stop several yards beyond the hut door. Three or four chained dogs barked a frantic welcome. Two men came round from the tent, and a third hastened from the hut carrying a hurricane lantern.

"Good night, boss!" chorused the first two.

"Evening, Mr Nettlefold," greeted the lantern-carrier. "The billy's boiling. Staying for a cup-er-tea?"

"Thanks, Ned, I will," the manager assented heartily. "This is Inspector Bonaparte, from Brisbane. If you call him Bony, he will be pleased."

"A policeman, eh?" snorted the lamp-carrier. Then with vocal modification: "Well, I suppose there could be better policemen than old Cox—and worse, too."

The dectective laughed, and the manager said:

"Bony will be staying for a few days, Ned. There is a box of stores on the carrier. Bony, this is Ned Hamlin."

"Good evening, Ned," Bony responded, getting out of the car. The lamplight fell full on his face and he knew he was being scrutinized. "No, I do not think that you will find me—from the layman's point of view—a worse policeman than Sergeant Cox. In confidence, I am not a real policeman."

"Ain't you?" exclaimed Ned. "Well, I am mighty glad to hear that. Ole Cox ain't a bad sort, but he gets officious like when me and Larry the Lizard goes into Golden Dawn. Come on in and have a drink-er-tea."

The stockman swung his lantern from a wire hook attached to a roof beam, and it illuminated an interior of a kind long familiar to Bony. Opposite the door and against the farther wall was the plain deal table, standing in fruit tins filled with water to defy the ants. The floor gave to the feet like a bitumen road on a hot day. It was composed of sand and beef fat. During the winter it was cement-hard. At one end of the oblong-shaped hut was the wide, open fireplace flanked with well-scoured saucepans and a frying pan. At the other end was Ned's stretcher bed, and in the opposite corner the two aborigines deposited the stretcher and roll of blankets loaned to Bony, and also his suitcase. The blacks then withdrew to hover about just beyond the door.

"You can come in, s'long as you don't spit on me floor," Ned said in invitation to them. They entered again to squat on their heels, each with his back hard against a door-post. Ned threw a handful of tea into the boiling billy, permitted the brew to boil for ten seconds, and then lifted the billy from the chimney chain with an iron hook.

"I want you fellers to give Bony a hand for a day or two," Nettlefold said, addressing the two blacks. They were dressed exactly alike in blue dungaree trousers and red shirts.

"Orl ri', boss! What do?" inquired one of them with enthusiasm.

"Bony will tell you in the morning."

"Too right he will!" interjected Ned Hamlin. Bony saw

a little rotund man with a fierce and unkept grey moustache, bushy grey eyebrows, and a grey thatch of hair which sprouted forward like the peak of a cloth cap. His light-blue eyes twinkled with humour when he said: "Hey, you, Shuteye! Stand up like a man and get interjuiced properly."

Shuteye revealed in his ample proportions the evidence of good living. His little black eyes beamed from the centres of rings of fat.

"He's the cleanest of the two," went on the remorseless Ned. "He's only got one shirt, but he washes that every night and then goes to sleep in it to dry it. Shuteye's gonna die young. I don't believe in being *that* clean. He ain't a bad worker, I'll say that for him. Now, you, Bill Sikes! Stand up."

Up jerked the other blackfellow, like a jack-in-the-box. He was taller than Shuteye, less fat and more powerful. His features were rugged enough to make Bony blink in amazement.

"Bill ain't exactly movin' picturish," explained Ned gravely. "He's got his good points, though, provided you keep your razor hidden and bar the door o' nights. His heart's handsomer than his dial. He's reliable, too, in a jam, and he knows how to track. Both him and Shuteye camps in the tent under the pepper-trees. And now, I reckon, the tea's properly draw'd."

"You funny feller like Jacky," Shuteye got in. They both chuckled and again slid down the door-posts to sit on their heels.

"We won't push the breeding cows into Emu Lake yet, Ned," Nettlefold said, now seated at the table and stirring sugar into his tin pannikin of tea. "There's no hurry, and Ted Sharp has work to do in at the homestead. I was thinking of sending you out some timber with which you could employ yourself repairing this hut. The stockyards, too, could do with overhauling."

"You've said it," Ned agreed. "If me and you and Shut-eye was to go outside and lean up against the north wall the whole place would fall down. Once the white ants start on a joint it's good night. Will you send out some tar as well?"

"Yes, I can spare a drum."

"Good! I don't wanter be like Mick the Murderer down Birdsville way. He got home one night after a razoo at the pub and brought a cuppler bottles of Blue Star Gin with him. Well, him and his mate, Paroo Dick, they gets to betting, and Paroo Dick bets a level quid that Mick the Murderer is so old and done for that he couldn't run a mile. 'You win,' says Mick the Murderer. 'But I'll bet you a level fiver that I'll blow down this ruddy place just to prove that me lungs is still sound.' 'Done,' says Paroo Dick. 'Have a go.'

"So Mick the Murderer he gets up and, like a fool, he tries to blow the hut down from the inside. He draws in his breath until his stomach busts his trouser-bottons and then his belt. Then he lets it go. Down comes the hut, and the iron roof crowns him and Paroo Dick, and give them discussion."

"Lovely!" cried the delighted Bony.

"Ain't that correct, Bill Sikes?" Ned demanded with sudden choler.

"Too right!" agreed the black, in the high-pitched voice so incongruent with his ferocious aspect. "I went by. I see the hut lying down. When I look under the roof there's old Mick the Murderer and Paroo Dick look like dead fellers."

"And didn't you drink all what was left of the Blue Star Gin before you dragged 'em out and revived 'em—with water?" cross-examined Ned.

"That's so. Blue Star no good to them fellers. They couldn't taste it nohow," argued Bill Sikes.

Bony caught the gleam in Nettlefold's eyes, and they burst into hearty chuckling.

"Still," said Ned, "the white ants ain't so bad here as they is up north. Why, up there a bloke gets into a habit of testing a chair every time he wants to sit down. Sometimes the chair just falls to bits in a kind of dust. One bloke he writ in his will that fifty quid was to be spent on lining his coffin with lead so's the white ants wouldn't get at him, but he might just as well have given it to his cobbers to drink his health. Them ants goes through chromium-plated steel, let alone lead."

Nettlefold did not dally after he had finished his tea and eaten with obvious relish a slice of brick-hard brownie. Bony went with him to the car.

"It was good of you to bring me out to-night," he said, when the manager was behind the steering-wheel and the engine was running. "I'll take the blacks across to the lake early in the morning, and should any serious developments occur at the homestead you might telephone to Ned and ask him to ride out to me."

"I will," Nettlefold agreed. "Don't hesitate to call on me for anything or any assistance you may want. Fortunately we'll be slack for a month or two."

"Thank you! Now that the police will be working inside to get on to a missing typist whose initials are double M, we might get word at any moment establishing her identity. *Au revoir!* I believe I find myself in excellent company."

"You do. Good night!"

The big car slid away on its return journey to the homestead, its headlights cutting into the black night like giant swords, its engine hum being slowly softened by increasing distance. Bony could hear Ned Hamlin telling the two blacks to be sure that the hen-house door was securely fastened.

On entering the hut, he found the stockman washing the supper utensils, and while he made up his bunk Ned talked volubly of the aeroplane mystery. Having made his bed for the night, the detective began to remove his collar.

Opposite him was Ned Hamlin's stretcher with its untidy blankets denoting that the bed had not been made for a week at least. One blanket was nearly touching the floor, and between its hem and the floor was to be seen a solitary unwinking eye staring at him with baleful hatred.

CHAPTER X

"EMBLEY" AND "'ARRIET"

RARELY did Bony carry a weapon on his person. The small but no less deadly automatic pistol which accompanied him on the job was generally pushed negligently among old garments in his suitcase. Sometimes he forgot to take the pistol with him, but he never forgot the old pair of drill trousers, two old shirts, the battered felt hat, and the elastic-sided riding boots.

At the moment he saw the unwinking eye looking balefully at him, the suitcase was pushed beneath the stretcher on which he was sitting. Now, with slow deliberation, while he stared back into the eye, he leaned forward and down, his left hand first feeling for the case and then, having found it, beginning to search blindly under the lid for the pistol.

Ned was talking cheerfully, but the detective no longer was heeding him. The position of the eye to the ground indicated a snake—a large snake—and, quite probably, a tiger snake. Tiger snakes are fighters when cornered, and Bony was offered no possible escape to the hut door if it chose to attack. Slowly and soundlessly he withdrew his hand from the suitcase, in it the pistol. Continuing to maintain deliberate movement, he regained upright position on the bed, slipped back the safety catch, and took steady aim at the still unwinking eye. He knew that if he did not kill the snake with his first shot—and like all normally civilized men he was not an infallible marksman—he would not do it with a second or third shot, because the snake would act too quickly.

"Hey! What's up? Whatcher doing?" Ned burst out. "Hey! Don't shoot! That'll be Embley or 'Arriet."

Bony hesitated. The stockman leaped the space between table and stretcher and pressed down the detective's wrist.

"Cripes! That was a narrer squeak," he rasped out.

"I don't like tiger snakes," Bony told him coldly. "Stay still while I kill that one. If you hop about like a bird it . . ."

"That ain't no snake, Bony," Ned said assuringly. "That's one of my goanners. It is either 'Arriet or Embley. They're both quiet enough if you knows 'ow to 'andle 'em. I told Shuteye and Bill to make sure that the 'en-house door was fast. Hey, you! You come outer that," he added to the solitary eye.

"Sure it isn't a snake?" Bony asked, still with grave doubt.

"Too right! You wait! Don't move!"

Ned slipped back to the table where he added some tea to a spoonful of tinned milk dropped into a pannikin. The warm tea and milk he poured out into a pie-dish, and then hastily rejoined Bony, who still sat motionless on his stretcher.

"Now, you watch," he implored, eagerness and pride evident in his voice. Then to the eye: "Now, *you*! You come outer that and drink up your tea."

Ned placed the dish on the ground between his and Bony's feet. The baleful eye winked for the first time. The blanket hem began to move, and from under it was thrust forth a narrow, snake-like head from the jaws of which flickered a long, fine, blue tongue. Then, inch by inch, the blanket hem was raised, and slowly there issued from concealment the long lizard body of an Australian goanna. It was of the Monarch species, one with powerful bulldog legs, thick strong neck, a thick tail, and a round body. Its under-throat and chest were of a sickly yellow, but its back was dark-green and patterned with black diamonds. Like the alligator it roughly resembles, it waddled across the floor of the hut with deceitful sluggishness. It came to stand with swelling neck at Bony's feet, its head slightly twisted to one side so that one eye might regard the detective with suspicion. Then, abruptly, it began to drink from the dish.

"Embley's seven feet six and a bit," Ned told Bony. "Ain't she a beaut? Lord, 'ere comes 'Arriet! Them two idjits have let 'em out instead of shuttin' 'em up. Hey, there! Shuteye! Bill Sikes!"

"What you want?" demanded Bill Sikes from the tent beneath the pepper-trees.

"Come here, you and Shuteye," Ned ordered angrily. "Here's 'Arriet and Embley. You've let 'em out. Come and take 'em back. You knows I can't 'andle 'em properly."

'Arriet, observing her friend taking supper, waddled with incredible speed to join her. Bony, now no longer fearing snakes, yet remained quite still. He was unaware precisely how tame these reptiles had been made, but they could not be excessively docile or Ned would not have called the blacks. More than once he had stayed a night with a lonely stockman who made a pet of a goanna, but these monsters presented quite a different picture. Embley, for instance, was again regarding him with cold suspicion while she swelled out her throat and stiffened her short legs. 'Arriet continued to drink the tea with obvious appreciation.

And then two dark figures appeared in the doorway.

Shuteye was arrayed only in his shirt, and Bill Sikes was as nude as his forebears.

"Grab 'em!" snapped Ned.

It was a command which could not well be obeyed smartly. The blacks moved forward cautiously. Foot by cautious foot they advanced on the suspicious Embley and the tea-drinking 'Arriet. Then Bill Sikes grunted a signal, and simultaneously making a little rush they each seized a tail and began to haul with persistent steadiness. Inch by inch they dragged the reptiles to the door, the captives clawing up the soft floor, the captors yelling with excitement. Out through the doorway they went. Ned rushed to the lamps, snatched down one, and followed them with shouted advice.

Bony seized the remaining lamp and rushed out after Ned. In the darkness, Shuteye and Bill Sikes were yelling their delighted laughter, and from their direction came the bumps and thumps of heavy bodies. Dust whirled past the rays of Bony's light.

"Stick to 'er!" ordered Bill Sikes.

"You bet! I stick like Jacky," panted Shuteye.

"Of course you stick to 'em, you pair of idjits," yelled Ned from within the fowl-house. "Cripes! They got out through an ant-eaten board. 'Ang on to 'em for a bit whiles I mends it. Waltz 'em some."

"You wants to hurry up," shouted Bill Sikes. "I ain't no alligator trainer. Not me!"

Directed by Ned's light, Bony ran to the fowl-house. He found it to be enclosed with a wire-netted yard which was roofed with netting as well. Inside the roughly constructed house Ned was frantically piling sand against the hole.

"That'll do for the present," he announced with whistling breath. "We'll get out and repair her from the other side. Them two can't hold them raging animals for ever."

When outside the netted yard, Ned shouted an all-clear, and into the lamp-light came the heaving forms of one be-shirted and one naked aboriginal hauling on sinuous reptiles struggling to go the opposite way and clawing up great clouds of sand dust in their determined efforts. Foot by foot the goannas were dragged to the fowl-yard. First, Shuteye had to drag his captive into the yard, then to swing it round so that it faced the house and he had his back to the doorway. When he let go, the monster shot forward, and he shot backward out through the doorway. It was then Bill Sikes's turn, and, having liberated his "animal," he jumped out and Ned shut the crazy door of the yard and secured it with fencing wire.

"You see," he cried, "we gets a bit of sport sometimes without going inside to the races."

"I believe you," cried the delighted Bony. "I think that I shall thoroughly enjoy my visit at Faraway Bore."

"Too right, you will," he was assured. "You need never have any fear of snakes around here when Embley and 'Arriet is in the offing. We lets 'em out in the daytime, and we can get 'em back 'ome with a dish of tea or a bit of liver cut up fine, but they's a different proposition after dark. Get a sugar bag, Bill, and a bit of string. We'll fill it with sand and lay it agen that hole they made. Just as well the boss is sending out timber and tar."

"Where are the fowls? Have you any?" asked Bony.

"Course. They're over there in their joint wot we built a month back. You see, we've only 'ad Embley a month, and 'Arriet less'n three weeks."

"And what do you intend doing with them?"

"Doin' with 'em?" echoed Ned. "Why, we races 'em. Every year on our birthday, which falls the same day, me and Larry the Lizard races our goanners to Gurner's pub wot's on the road to St Albans across on Tintanoo. Larry works on Tintanoo, you see. He thinks hisself the greatest goanner trainer in Australia, but back in 1880 my Australian Prince beat his Silver Star by nine lengths and a bit."

Ned waxed enthusiastic.

"Larry can train 'em all right," he went on, "and he's got the knack of picking 'em. This year, having Shuteye and Bill Sikes here with me, I'm hoping to get a runner wot'll put it acrost his reptile. Embley in there is a flier, and 'Arriet's got plenty of tow, but they ain't neither of 'em certainties."

Bill Sikes brought the bag and a shovel, and the hole in the fowl-house was effectively stopped. For a little while Bony had entirely forgotten that he was a detective-inspector. His speech had been less grandiloquent. The capture of the escaped goannas had brought to the surface of his strangely mixed personality a latent ebullience.

He was up at dawn, and the water in the billy was boiling with the tea in it when Ned Hamlin vented a soul-stirring yawn.

"What-cher-doing?" he demanded, when with half-opened eyes he began loading his ancient pipe with the black plug tobacco used by his boss. He swung his naked legs out over the edge of the stretcher revealing that he had slept only in his shirt. His moustache was ragged and his hair was raised to a mop. Bony saw that the "night" pipe was smoked empty, while the colour of the tobacco now going into the "day" pipe made him shudder.

"You want to give over them cigarettes," he was advised. "Real coffin-nails, they are. I wakes up every morning about three, smokes me night pipe, and then snoozes a bit more, and I don't hack and bark in the mornings."

Not till he had sipped half a pint of scalding black tea did Bony roll his first cigarette. By that time Ned had pulled on his trousers. He crossed to the billy, having snatched a pannikin from a nail in the wall, and the fumes of his tobacco floated in the still air beneath the roof.

"You gettin' an early start?" he asked, blinking his eyelids.

"Yes. The sky promises wind."

"But them blacks searched for tracks all around Emu Lake," Ned protested. "What they missed is nothink."

"Then that nothing may be of interest to me."

"You reckon someone fired the aeroplane?"

"I am uncertain about that. That's why I want to examine the ground before a windstorm wipes away the writing on the ground."

"Well, I reckon that aeroplane set fire to itself. No one could have got close enough to fire it without leaving tracks for that Shuteye and Bill Sikes to pick up. Howsomever, you know best. If you see a likely looking goanner, get them blacks to snare it and bring it 'ome. A cuppler days before the race at Gurner's pub, we'll give all the reptiles we've collected a trial gallop so's we can pick out the fastest. You go along and kick them two to life. Shuteye will go for the horses. It's his turn. I'll cook the breakfast."

"All right! Oh, by the way, how far is this Mitchell's Well from here?"

Hamlin blinked rapidly. His answer did not come as pat as it should have done considering the number of years he had been working at Coolibah.

"About fifteen miles, it'd be."

"Good track?"

"No, pretty rough. It crosses a lot of nasty water-gutters. Thinking of going there?"

"I may, yes. There is a windmill there, isn't there? Not a running bore?"

"That's right! A windmill, and when the wind ain't enough to work it there's a petrol engine wot works a pump."

"Who looks after it—the water-supply, I mean?" Bony asked carelessly.

"Oh, any one rides across now and then."

"Who went the last time?"

"I did."

"When?" Bony again asked, indifferently.

"Oh, a cuppler days before we mustered the cattle for the drovers."

"Sure?"

Again Ned blinked his eyelids, saying:

"Too right I'm sure."

When Bony asked him if he had heard the noise of a passing aeroplane, or the explosion that occurred at Emu Lake when the monoplane was destroyed, he shook his white-thatched head.

"Where did Ted Sharp go that night the aeroplane was stolen at Golden Dawn?"

"Eh?"

"You heard what I said, my dear Ned."

"Oh, Ted Sharp? He took a run across to Mitchell's Well."

"That's strange. A moment ago you said that *you* were the last to visit Mitchell's Well, and that you did so before the aeroplane was stolen."

The kindly face was troubled, and a child could have

seen that Ned was lying and that he was a poor liar. When Bony spoke again, his voice was low and friendly.

"Now look here, Ned. I am here to carry out an investigation. As you know, a young woman is lying very ill in at the homestead. I suspect foul play. What Ted Sharp did that night doubtless has no bearing whatever on my work here, but it is just possible it may have. I want the truth from you. Where did he go that night?"

"If I tell you, you won't tell the boss?"

Bony hesitated. Then slowly he said:

"No, if his absence had nothing to do with my case."

"Well, it hasn't, any'ow," Ned said, faintly triumphant. "As a matter of fact, he rang me up last night before you and the boss arrived asking me to say that he went across to Mitchell's Well if any one asked. You see, he took a short trip to Gurner's Hotel to get a bottle of whisky. The boss is dead nuts on any booze being brought on to the run, and he'd roar like hell if he knoo that Ted had gone to the pub."

"So that's it, is it? Why didn't he tell me that and have done with it? How long was he away?"

"He left about nine and he got back about one. You won't put him away, will you? He's a good sort, is Ted Sharp."

"No, Ned, I will not do that. And you need never let him know that you told me."

"You can rely on me for that, Bony. If all the ruddy Johns were like you, this blinkin' world would be worth livin' in."

Half an hour later a bunch of horses came streaking for the yards with a yelling Shuteye riding behind them in the swirling dust they raised. The sun came up, a blood-red, enormous disk to hang awhile above the line of distant scrub bordering the long narrow stretch of open broken country of low sand-dunes and claypans. The sun's rays stained light-red the ceaseless gush of water falling from the inverted L-shaped bore-head situated some six hundred yards north-east of the hut. Less than a quarter of a mile west of the ramshackle structure and its guarding pepper-trees ran, north-south, the Emu Lake fence, westward of which outstanding patches of scrub merged into a dark-green mass.

"You want good flash horse alonga me?" Shuteye asked, when he had yarded the hacks.

Bony smiled.

"Not to-day," he replied, a little regretfully. "We will want the quietest horses of the bunch for to-day's work."

Ned had one-pound slabs of grilled steak waiting for them, and he cut slices off a yeast loaf and filled the pannikins with tea. After breakfast three quiet horses—quiet for Queensland horses—were saddled, and to the saddles were strapped quart-pots and lunches. The three trackers walked the horses to the gate in the Emu Lake fence, and from there they rode towards the lake at a jog-trot.

A wise man, the detective elected to talk about cattle, horses, goannas, and the weather: of anything save the business of the day. No longer was he wearing a wretched collar and city clothes. Of the three Shuteye was the neatest.

Bony inhaled deeply. The hot sun already was striking on their backs. The sleeves of Bony's shirt were rolled above the elbows, and its neck was opened wide. He was feeling that delicious sensation of being wholly free, and he wanted badly to relax as he had done the previous evening, to make a waddy and, with his companions, go hunting.

The desire vanished when abruptly they left the scrub.

The light increased when the open dun-coloured plain of the dry lake stretched forward from the low sand-wall and the strip of white claypan. The body of Napoleon Bonaparte no longer commanded his attention. It was now his brain that thrilled, as his body had done, when through the windows of his blue eyes there was registered the expanse of flat, treeless land in the centre of which lay strange black and shapeless objects.

They rode at a walking pace across the kangaroo-eaten tussock-grass stubs, noting how they grew widely apart and how the bare ground was covered with fine sand.

From the saddle Bony surveyed the scene of desolation, the far-flung remains of a once beautiful man-made bird. The engine was a mere mass of metal junk. The steel framework of the fuselage was twisted beyond recognition of its original shape. The wreckage of the starboard wing had been thrown far by the exploding petrol-tank or tanks, while all about black patches of ground indicated where liquid fire had been thrown outward from the centre.

"I would scarcely have believed that exploding petrol would have such destructive force," Bony told his companions. Shuteye offered no comment. Bill Sikes grunted.

"Well, to work. I understand that you two have hunted for tracks all about this wreckage and all round the lake."

"Too right," they both assented.

"And yet it is quite probable that after the boss and Miss Elizabeth left with the unfortunate white woman a man came here and deliberately set fire to the monoplane," Bony persisted. Then he fell into Shuteye's manner of speaking. "You two blackfeller, you look-see alonga white feller's boot-tracks. You no thinkum white feller wise to blackfeller's dodges, eh? You no thinkum white feller do same as blackfeller when he run away with lubra, eh? You no thinkum p'haps white feller put blood on his feet and stick his feet in feathers till blood dries hard so's they not come off, and then he walk about without making no tracks, eh?"

Two pairs of black eyes opened wide, and two aboriginal brains were quickened by Bony's suggestion. Having been instructed to look for tracks made by a white man, they had not thought to look for possible evidence left behind by a white man using the blacks' methods of escaping detection.

"That white feller come long way on foot, and he go back long way on foot," said the detective. "Even feathered feet leave little smudge on soft sand. P'haps that feller drop cigarette end or a match. P'haps he scratch his head and drop some hairs. We find out, eh?"

"Too right," they said with hissing breath. With Bony they were now thrilled with the prospect of a man-hunt, and it wanted only imagination to turn them from terriers into bloodhounds.

CHAPTER XI

BUSINESS AND PLEASURE

CAPTAIN Loveacre's red monoplane had landed from the west, and then had run five hundred and seventeen yards before coming to a final halt to face the east. The tracks made by Nettlefold's car during its several visits, those made by the car conveying members of the Air Accidents Investigation Committee, and the boot imprints made by the people brought by those cars, had failed to blot out the broad tyre tracks indented by the monoplane's wheels.

Other than that, in their opinion, the aeroplane had made a perfect landing, the Air Accidents Investigation Committee had declined to indicate to Sergeant Cox its probable findings. Actually the red monoplane was outside the scope of its activities because no accident had occurred to the machine before it had made its landing. The fact that some time later it had been set fire to by some agency, human or otherwise, had nothing to do with them.

From the mere destruction of the machine, Bony had nothing on which to base a suspicion that some person had wilfully fired it. Like Cox and Nettlefold, he had not the expert experience of a fire assessor. Yet, from the mass of information he had already collected, he strongly suspected that natural causes had had nothing to do with it. Doubtless the expert members of the A.A.I.C. would, in their report, ask several pertinent questions, such as whether the machine had landed without a pilot at its controls as that German aeroplane mentioned by Dr Knowles had done. If this supposition turned out to be correct, then the pilot must have left the monoplane when in the air and landed by means of a parachute. If there had been no failure of the machine to cause that desertion, it would then appear that the pilot had deliberately left his passenger to crash with it, unless the young woman herself had piloted the machine and had landed it before crawling into the front seat to strap herself to it, and finally to succumb to the strange malady which since then had gripped her.

The affair of the red monoplane was made so obscure by both probabilities and possibilities that Bony was rightly attacking its weakest point; namely, definitely to establish whether the machine had been fired by natural causes or by some human being. If through human agency, then, through the movements of the person responsible, he might well get a line across the sea of mystery to the ship of truth.

It was useless to cogitate on the problem until he had established the causes of the fire. To do that he must with care read the pages of the Book of the Bush devoted to Emu Lake and its immediate vicinity. Loveacre had estimated on his arrival at Emu Lake that his machine had caught fire about five hours previously. He was quite positive that the fire had not occurred before sunset and after Nettlefold had left the lake—in which case the sun's rays might have been responsible.

The odds certainly were in favour of the theory that, during the night after the finding of the machine and its helpless passenger, some person had crossed through the bush from some point, done his work, and then returned to the point from which he had set out. In consequence he must have left some trace of his passage; and, because since that night the weather had been fine and calm, the traces he must inevitably have left still remained for Bony and his companions to find and read as a white man reads a newspaper.

The half-caste had raised himself to a position of eminence in the investigation of bush crime, because he brought to his work a keen mind, patience and super-sight. In him were housed the gifts and remarkably few vices of both races between which he stood half-way.

The accident of his birth had placed him in the unique position of being able to look dispassionately on both the white man and the black. As a proof of this, he knew that when Bill Sikes and Shuteye were instructed to look for the tracks of a man who could have destroyed the aeroplane they set off on their task with one idea in their minds—to find the imprints of a *white* man's boots on the ground. They looked for and hoped to discover a *white* man's tracks and had they crossed the boot tracks made by an aboriginal it is probable that they would not have mentioned it unless directly questioned. A white man's tracks they were set to find, and a white man's tracks would be all which would interest them.

Further, Bony knew, when the two blacks were commanded to look for tracks made by either black *or* white, they would search for the impressions made by boots or naked feet. And *only* that. Because it would not occur to them that the man whose tracks they were sent to discover might have adopted expert methods of leaving no traces, they would not have troubled to look for any indications revealing one of several methods.

Thus it was, Bony reasoned, that although the blacks had

not found a man's tracks the supposition that some person had visited the derelict aeroplane could not be put out of court. Rather the man who might have destroyed the machine—assuming that a man had done so—would know that determined men would search for his tracks, and he, therefore, would adopt measures to conceal his tracks or prevent his feet from making them.

To move about the interior of Australia without leaving plain signs for an expert native tracker to see is exceedingly difficult. To deceive or frustrate the expert white bushman is hard enough; to frustrate an aboriginal expert is almost beyond possibility—for a white man.

The detective noted with satisfaction how his two assistants brightened when he suggested that a possible incendiarist might have adopted the method of blood and feathers in an effort to leave no tracks. They knew now that the search had to be much wider than the hunt for mere boot tracks; and further that if the blood-and-feathers method of escaping detection had been used by a white man, he was yet bound to make serious mistakes, for he would not have the bushcraft possessed by the blackfellow. Their blood leaped to the thrill experienced by all stalkers whether of man or animal.

"We will track in a growing circle," Bony explained, to proceed then in the vernacular: "Aeroplane here. We spread out likum we muster cattle and walk about round and round farther and farther away. You go 'way back, Shuteye, till I say you stop, and you, Bill Sikes, you go 'way back beyond Shuteye."

"Orl right, Bony. Me track like Jacky," assented the eager Shuteye.

"Too right!" added the other. "Him clever feller put feathers on his feet, but Bill Sikes clever feller, too."

So forming a front, and separated from each other by about one hundred yards, they moved round the wreckage which acted as a pivot or the hub of a wheel of which they were spokes. To the hub and away from the hub had walked the possible incendiarist, and across the line of his double passage three pairs of eagle-keen eyes must pass their gaze. When a human spoke had made one revolution of the hub it moved outward to make another revolution, and so on and on until the three men were working in a wide circular movement round the hub and a mile from it.

They crossed the sand-dunes on which they could see the tracks of scorpions and centipedes. They crossed cement-hard claypans, which but faintly registered the hoof tips of their horses. They crossed grassy clearings, but after the lapse of time trodden grass would have regained its upright position. Once they passed over a large area of loose, sandy soil bearing tussock-grass and herbage.

They read all the little stories contained in the Book of the Bush: stories written by kangaroos and emus, rabbits and mice, bush rats and goannas and the tiny lizards that live by catching flies; the cockatoos and galahs, and the finches and the crows. Constantly did they dismount to pick up bird feathers in order to examine them for a smear of blood.

The sun poured down on them its hourly increasing heat but of it they were oblivious. Unconsciously they waved back from their eyes the countless small flies. Bony even forgot his cigarettes.

The day was windless. The willy-willies were out, marching drunkenly across the landscape from west to east, tall columns of revolving, heated air painted by the red sand swept upward into their vortex. Several passed quite close to the trackers, but they were disregarded. It was only the increasing determination of his horse to snatch morsels of grass and herbage that made the detective conscious of the passage of time, when he was astonished to see by the sun that it was after two o'clock. He called to his companions and dismounted in the shade cast by a leopard-wood tree.

"We'll have lunch. It's past two o'clock," he announced.

Off came the quart-pots, to be filled from the canvas waterbags slung against each horse's chest. Bill Sikes made a fire and superintended the quart-pots, while Shuteye secured the horses to trees by their neckropes. Again Bony glanced up at the sun, and now at his shadow. He knew that they were then east of Emu Lake and not so very far from the fence and Faraway Bore.

"That aeroplane caught fire itself, all right," Bill Sikes gave as his opinion.

"Until we have proof we must assume that someone fired it," countered the obstinate Bony. "He might have left feathers from his feet for one of those willy-willies to sweep up and carry away for miles. Have you seen them this summer before to-day?"

"Plenty," answered Shuteye, now seated on his boot-heels and busily rolling a cigarette.

Bony was experiencing disappointment, but he was far from giving up. There was yet the remainder of this day, and the next day and the day after that. Patience was his greatest gift. While the water in the quart-pots was heating they sat on their heels and smoked.

"The fellow who set fire to that aeroplane might have flown over it in another and dropped a bomb on it," he argued. "It is possible but not probable. Who has an aeroplane besides Dr Knowles?"

"No one else," replied Bill Sikes. "Them flying machines is too tricky for ord'nary fellers to fly around in. Ole Shuteye, here, couldn't fly one any'ow."

"No fear. Horse good enough for this feller. 'Way up there too close to bash up," and Shuteye laughed as readily as he always did, and revealed perfect teeth that nothing seemed to stain.

He and Bill Sikes continued to talk and laugh about the instability of aeroplanes, but Bony fell into pensive meditation. Had that poor helpless woman lying at Coolibah actually stolen the red monoplane? Recalling the picture of her lying so motionless on the bed, he could not bring himself to credit her with that feat. She was drugged. Knowles was positive; and if the doctor was right she could not have flown the aeroplane away from Golden Dawn. Besides, even if she had stolen it and flown it, she could not possibly have set fire to it.

Bony's mind clung to the idea that the machine had been destroyed through human agency. There was not a tittle of evidence to support what was, after all, mere supposition. They had no reason to believe that any one had approached the machine other than those whose visits were legitimate. And yet . . .

Long before, the question of motive had demanded an answer, and Bony thought he could supply it. The machine had been destroyed with fire, because fire was the easiest means to assure the removal of fingerprints. Dr Knowles had not worn gloves when he brought the detective to Coolibah. If the pilot of the stolen machine had not worn gloves, believing that his plan to crash the aeroplane would assuredly succeed, then his fingerprints would have been on the controls as well as on other parts of it.

However, all this was but creating theories, and Bony hated theories which had no basis of fact. If only he could find a clue proving that a man had stealthily visited the derelict machine!

He gave his assistants no rest after lunch had been eaten, and they took their stations and went on with the search. The sun continued its remorseless journey across the cobalt sky, and as remorselessly the three continued the hunt for a scent.

It was twenty minutes after lunch when, through the still air, came a cry of triumph. Bony saw Shuteye standing beside his horse and in the act of waving to him. Both he and Bill Sikes converged on the fat man, and Bony slipped eagerly to the ground when he saw that in his hands Shuteye was holding a stick.

"I see stick kicked up off ground," Shuteye explained with hissing breath.

Bony took the stick—a piece of mulga. Shuteye pointed to where it had been lying, and the history of the stick since it had been blown from the parent branch was plainly to be read. Having fallen to the ground, successive windstorms had blown sand grains against one side of it. The white ants, working upward, had attacked its underside, and now their peculiar cement adhered to the stick. The place where the stick had been lying for perhaps several weeks was marked by the depression as well as the termite cement within the depression. There was even the mark of the stick on the ground made by it when moved from its original position.

Shuteye, when picking it up, had been careful not to disturb the ground, and had a crow moved the stick in its search for termites, the imprints of its feet would have remained to betray its activity. There were no such signs.

Carefully and slowly, Bony examined the stick. It was about two feet in length, and weighed less than half a pound. His eyes appeared to magnify it for his brain to note every crevice and raised curve of the bark still fastened to the parent wood.

"Ah!" he said sharply, and the two blacks crowded close. From one jagged end he detached a silvery fibre about two inches in length. It was crinkled, like a gossamer strand from a spider's web. When Bony looked into the smiling faces of his assistants his blue eyes were blazing.

"There are no sheep on Coolibah, are there?" he asked softly.

They shook their heads.

"I see stick kicked alonga mark on ground," Shuteye burst out.

"Well, there are no sheep on Coolibah, and yet here, fastened to the end of this stick, is a fibre of wool," Bony pointed out. "How far away westward of this place are the nearest sheep—do you know?"

"West of Coolibah is Unesadoone. Big station, all cattle," Bill Sikes explained. "Mr Kane has a few sheep for killing on Tintanoo."

"Where are they kept?"

"Near homestead."

"The homestead is roughly north-east of here. You ever see willy-willies come from the north-east?"

"No fear," replied Bill Sikes. "Not this summer, any-'ow."

"Therefore," Bony continued, "this fibre wool could not have been brought here by a willy-willy. No ordinary wind would have carried it for so many miles. One of the countless trees would have caught it. Perhaps that feller he wear wool on his feet like blackfeller wear feathers, eh?"

"P'haps," they agreed.

"What other stations about here run sheep?"

"Windy Creek and Olarie Downs. Butcher at Golden Dawn runs sheep on the common," Bill Sikes replied.

"Ah! Well, so far so good," announced the satisfied Bony. Carefully he rolled the wool fibre within a cigarette paper and stowed it away in a pocket. A quick glance at the sun, a general survey of the scene, and he knew that they then were approximately north of Emu Lake.

"How far is the Coolibah-Tintanoo boundary fence?" he inquired.

" 'Bout half mile," answered Bill Sikes, and Shuteye instantly agreed.

"Well, if this stick was kicked aside by a man having wool glued to his feet he reached Emu Lake from the north, and, likely enough, he returned to the north. We will track on a zigzag course, with me taking middle position. You two keep your distance from me."

Less widely spaced, they advanced, having now a definite object for which to search—a wool fibre. Presently they came to fairly open country, and from the summit of a low whaleback of pure sand could be seen the wire boundary fence. Between the sand hummock and the fence Bill Sikes discovered a second wool fibre, caught in a butt of tussock-grass.

The second find of wool fibre, allied to the first, proved that some person had walked in wool from the Golden Dawn-St Albans road which ran east-west through Tintanoo Station, and, doubtless, had returned to the road. Bony knew that wool would leave impressions so slight—even on the softest sand—that the first zephyr would erase them. He had himself often used sheepskin boots, having the wool on the outside to enable him to investigate without leaving tracks behind him.

So the monoplane *had* been fired! That fact certainly provided firm ground on which to raise a structure of further theory.

Thought pictures were flickering through his brain when his body became taut. Between his lips issued a long low hiss, and the other stopped to look at him. He pointed to the west. A dark-brown mass, as solid-looking as a sand-dune, was rushing towards them, its upper edge about to blot out the sun.

"Grab your horses," shouted Bony.

They were given just time enough to lead their mounts to nearby trees and there tie them with the rope each animal had around its neck when the sun went out. Half a minute later the advancing wall of sand reached them, to sweep over them and to bury them in its suffocating embrace.

CHAPTER XII

THE SAND CLOUD

ON the morning of the day that Bony and his two assistants set out for Emu Lake, there landed at Golden Dawn a fast service plane which brought a Mr Cartwright, of the New Era Fire Insurance Company. The machine was piloted by Captain Loveacre.

While the pilot was supervising the re-fuelling of his ship from forty-gallon petrol drums stocked by the storekeeper, Cartwright sauntered to the police-station, where he met Sergeant Cox emerging from his office. The sergeant shrewdly noted the details of Cartwright's appearance: his age, which was about fifty; his large and flaccid face, with its bulbous nose; and the immaculate suit of grey flannel matched by a panama hat.

The stranger announced his name before proceeding to inform the controller of the Golden Dawn police district that he had been requested by the Air Accidents Investigation Committee to examine the aeroplane wreckage at Emu Lake in order to test certain theories formulated by the Committee.

Mr Cartwright did not add to this statement that he was a truly remarkable man. His disposition was too reserved to permit him to say that of one hundred fires he could accurately determine how ninety-nine had started, and that by examining the burned stock of, say, a drapery business, he could correctly estimate to within a pound or two the value of that stock before fire ruined it. It was rather foolish of a fire victim to swear that the value of his stock had been five thousand pounds when its actual value was only four thousand five hundred. It was foolish, too, to swear that he did not know how the fire had started, no matter how cunningly he might have short-circuited the electric lighting system, or rolled a piece of phosphorus within a bolt of curtain netting. On the other hand, if the fire victim was honest he received every pound of his insurance.

"From what I have been told, Sergeant," Mr Cartwright said, in his soft voice, "the aeroplane fire at this Emu Lake presents many interesting points. I understand that a young woman was found in the passenger seat, and that she is suffering from a kind of general paralysis. Is she any better?"

"Not the slightest," Cox replied. "What do the members of the A.A.I.C. think about that burning?"

"They are a little mystified about it. That is why they asked my firm to lend them my services. I am advised to get in touch with the officer in charge of the matter, Detective-Inspector Napoleon Bonaparte. Do you know where I can find him?"

"Yes. He went out to a place called Faraway Bore last night. I understand that to-day he intends examining Emu Lake for tracks, although two good trackers have already searched around the lake for tracks of any person who could have deliberately set fire to the machine. The inspector thinks that some person did destroy the aeroplane, and that in consequence he must have left tracks. He is anxious to clear up that point."

"Ah!" said Cartwright, stroking his chin. "A somewhat

unusual name, Napoleon Bonaparte."

Cox nodded unsmilingly. Then he said impressively:

"It belongs to an astonishing man. In his way, the inspector is just as great a genius in the investigation of bush crimes as the Emperor was in directing battles. Are you going to Emu Lake to-day?"

"Yes—when the machine is re-fuelled and we have lunched at the hotel."

Having chatted for a few minutes with the sergeant, Cartwright left the police-station. Within the hotel bar he found Captain Loveacre drinking beer, and called for a second "pot."

"Beer makes good men better," remarked the captain.

"Good beer," stipulated Cartwright.

"I meant good beer. Bad beer makes criminals of saints."

"Saints do not drink beer," Cartwright pointed out. Then to the landlord, he added: "As we are now better men, kindly refill the glasses."

Two men entered the bar, one of them to say with a faint trace of interest:

"Thought it was you, Loveacre!"

"Hullo, Dr Knowles! Cheerio, Mr Kane!" greeted the airman. "Our lunch is waiting, but we can just manage to sink another one. Meet Mr Cartwright, of the New Era Insurance, now on the business of that little red mono of mine."

The fire assessor shook hands. The doctor he summed up as a man who had been forced out to this cock-eyed place through over-indulgence in drink, but Kane puzzled and consequently interested him. Noting the details of his appearance, Cartwright saw a slight man of medium height, dressed in grey gabardine slacks, a coat that did not match, and an old felt hat. His teeth were large, and his brown eyes remained widely open in a stare of eternal surprise. The left corner of his mouth twitched, and the fire assessor observed that this twitch occurred regularly every ten seconds. In health he appeared to be robust, but, nevertheless, he was obviously a neurotic.

"The destruction of the captain's bus presents something of a mystery, does it not?" Kane put to Cartwright in a modulated and rather pleasant voice.

"It won't be a mystery after I have messed about the wreckage for an hour," the assessor boasted quietly.

"Seems probable that some bird deliberately set fire to it," remarked the doctor. "Anyway, Bony thinks so."

"Bony? Who's Bony?—Oh, you refer to that detective. Why does he think that?" inquired the squatter from Tintanoo.

"Couldn't say, I'm sure," said Knowles, with a surprising flash of impatience.

"What I am hoping is that he discovers the chap who did it," Loveacre contributed. "I'll bet a quid it didn't catch fire by itself. When I know who did it I am going to barge right into him. I always feel deep sympathy for the bloke who successfully robs a bank—or an insurance company, for that matter, Mr Cartwright—but I have none for the petty gent who snatches handbags and sets fire to a poor airman's skyjerker. Come on, Mr Cartwright! We must get lunch if we are to go out to the wreck to-day . . ."

He led the way to the hotel dining-room, followed by the insurance assessor. John Kane and the doctor remained in the bar. Cartwright noticed that the airman walked with something of the strut of a bird, while his face, too, was birdlike in its sharpness. Perhaps it was Loveacre's dark eyes, so brilliant and steady, that suggested the resemblance.

Kane and the doctor saw them off after lunch, the latter obligingly removing the chocks from the wheels when the two engines were ready to break into full-throated song. Knowles was all birdman while he watched the grey biplane slide skywards.

Captain Loveacre pushed his machine up to five thousand feet, at which height the assessor could observe that Golden Dawn lay almost in the centre of a roughly-circular gibber plain looking much like a worn patch on a dark green carpet. The St Albans road was an almost indistinguishable thread crossing the plain, but when it entered the scrub country it lay like a reddish-brown snake asleep on the same dark-green carpet. The fork presented by the junction of the Coolibah track was clearly discernible, and, through the telephone, the captain drew Cartwright's attention to it.

From then on Loveacre followed neither track, and presently, to the south, they could see the red roofs of Coolibah homestead. The empty river appeared like a skein of multicoloured wool, the channels winding in and out of the strands of green-topped coolibah trees. Here the river was twelve miles in width, presenting a twelve-mile deathtrap for airmen forced to land among its dry channels and whalebacked channel banks.

"We'd be on the rocks down there, all right," asserted Loveacre.

Westward of the river he put the ship down to two thousand feet, where he found, as expected, the west wind much less strong. On the green carpet to the south, Cartwright saw the sun-reflecting fans of a windmill. Then the long strip of reddish sand-dunes Elizabeth Nettlefold had named the Rockies attracted his attention. Far to the north, on the bordering grey plain from a dark blob of colour a grey column of dense dust rose upward, and began to slant to the north-east when apparently at their altitude. The captain, on seeing the dust column raised by a mob of mustered cattle on Tintanoo, put down his bus lower still and, at fifteen hundred feet, found the air comparatively quiet.

Here and there, like solitary red hairs sprouting from a blackfellow's bald head, the willy-willies conducted their drunken march. Several times the pilot had to deviate from his course to pass one. He had no mind to have his ship spun round like a top, and probably seriously damaged by an upwhirling vortex of hot air and sand.

It was a strange world to the fire insurance assessor, but even to him after a little while the landscape became boring. Westward of the grey plain were splashes of brown on a dun-coloured background—sand-dunes among scrub, and broken country on which no aeroplane could land without being destroyed.

Far ahead, right on the western edge of the world, appeared a diamond-shaped object dully reflecting the sunlight. This, the fire assessor was informed, was Faraway Hut, which was temporarily Bony's headquarters. When over it they would be able to pick out Emu Lake.

With renewed interest, Cartwright studied the distant hut, and wondered what caused the short splash of light in its vicinity. Later he discovered that it was the water gushing from Faraway Bore.

Beyond the hut evidently stretched another and far more extensive area of sand, for the horizon lay red beneath the sun.

It was, of course, an optical illusion which made that sand country move up and down as though the earth pulsated. It seemed to reach higher at the apex of every pulsation.

The ship, too, was rising now at a steep angle, and with increasing rapidity the distant sand country increased in area and in depth.

"Sandstorm coming!" Loveacre shouted into his telephone. "I can't put the ship down here without wrecking her." And then a minute or so later, when the air was stinging their faces and the altimeter registered nine thousand feet, he said: "Blow me if I understand it! It looks like a low-lying red fog, doesn't it? The air above it is clear enough. Ah, I've got it! It's a sand cloud. I've heard about 'em, but I've never seen one before."

A sandstorm without wind! Far westward, possibly near the eastern border of Western Australia, a storm of wind had raised sun-heated sand particles for many miles above the earth. And then in its freakishness, nature suddenly allowed the wind to drop from fifty to five miles per hour, and the heated sand particles had slowly fallen earthward to be cushioned by the earth-stored heat of the sun in so dense a mass as to appear, as Captain Loveacre said, like a fog.

Since the airman could not land on the broken country around Faraway Bore, the eternal gush of which had attracted the assessor's attention, the only obvious alternative was to turn back and land on the temporary 'drome north of Coolibah homestead. From other pilots he had heard of these rare sand clouds. He knew that in width they did not extend for more than a few miles. This was moving so slowly that if at great height he could not see its rearward edge, he could out-distance it and land at Coolibah with plenty of time in hand. He recalled the observation made by a pilot who had encountered a sand cloud: "Ride over it if you can. You can't fly through it, it's too thick. If you park under it you will have serious trouble with the carburettor and feed system for days afterwards, because no wrapping up of your engine will keep out the sand."

Down again at two thousand feet, the sand cloud now presented an inspiring sight. It had the face of a moving cliff four thousand feet high. The sunlight slanting sharply upon it brought into sharp relief bulging escarpments and inward sucking caverns. It was as though this enormous thing was living, that, as it advanced across the world, it was actually breathing. Cartwright saw that it was moving with dreadful inevitability towards the toy hut and the sparkling water gush at the head of a thin crystal channel. He could see a man the size of a pin's head walking near the hut, which he entered two seconds before it and the bore were blotted from sight. The place vanished, tramped on by this sand monster.

The full-throated roar of the aeroplane's engines deepened when the ship climbed to escape the living cliff of sand, while the cliff itself sank down as though pressed to earth by giant hands. Then it moved eastward beneath them, and there burst on their astonished gaze a great field of level sand limned by the sun in soft brown colours, in places stretched taut, in others rumpled like a badly laid carpet.

Loveacre went up to sixteen thousand feet before he flattened out. The cold air struck their faces with one continuous blow, and Cartwright's breath came in short gasps. During their up-rush the eastern edge of the world apparently defied the sand cloud, but now once again it was dwindling. Both to the north and to the south the red paving flowed beyond the horizon, but to the west lay the dark line of the real horizon beyond the rear edge of the cloud.

Knowing now that the sand cloud was but some sixty miles wide, Captain Loveacre decided to go down to warmer conditions. His engines were behaving well, and there was no danger of them both failing and thus forcing a disastrous landing in the bowels of that mass of floating sand.

"What do you think of it?" he asked the assessor.

"Terrific!" gasped Cartwright, when his breathing became less difficult. "What a sight! Why, it looks like solid ground!"

"Quicker than a quicksand, though. I pity all poor folk whom it will temporarily bury. That feller down there in the hut will be having a rough time of it, and so will that detective near Emu Lake. He will find no tracks, not even the tracks of an army tank—after this little lot has passed by."

The real world gradually emerged from the west, but it was not so dark in colour as it had been. It lay, a quickly-widening strip from the curved horizon, like a dead world painted one uniform colour by the brush of time. While the machine flew but a few hundred feet above the sand cloud in the seemingly still and utterly clear air, the two men could presently see the long, pointed writhing streamers of sand which formed the rear edge.

Then these streamers of light-red mist passed beneath them, and the earth below appeared without detail. The tree-tops were brown, all the small flats were brown—a brown tinged with red. The fliers saw at the same moment three tiny figures grouped below them, and Loveacre, having seen Emu Lake, brought his machine still lower.

Cartwright was glad of the increased warmth. He was about to say so when they began to skim the surface of the lake, shortly to stop beside the wreckage of the red monoplane.

CHAPTER XIII

BONY'S CRAMP

FOR Bony and his companions, sound continued, but sight did not. The storm had approached with a low humming, reminding the detective of a child's top at a distance. For a few moments the vast wall of sand towered above menacingly, threatening to bury them by toppling forward. Then its dark base swept upon them with a gentle hiss, and at once daylight vanished.

To cry out was impossible, for to open the mouth meant to draw into the lungs the choking sand particles. Even to talk was out of the question. After a period of staggering about in search of escape, Bony lay full length on the ground, and by pressing his mouth against his outstretched arms filtered the air a little.

Day was turned into blackest night. All about him, Bony heard a faint, persistent hissing sound, as though of escaping steam. It was caused by the incessant rain of sand particles falling like hard snowflakes.

Softly at first and then gradually submerging the faint hissing, there came to Bony's ears the low hum of motor engines, a humming which rose and fell rhythmically. Surely no one possibly could drive a car through this sand cloud! Ah—it was no car! It was an aeroplane. There could be no doubt about it. An aeroplane aloft in this sand cloud! It seemed almost impossible. Poor devils—lost, without doubt! It was only a matter of time when the sand would choke the engines, and then there must be a fatal crash.

For long minutes he lay still, breathing carefully through his nostrils. When he did move his head he felt the electric trickle of sand slide off his neck. It was his first experience of such a storm, but he had heard of this extremely rare phenomenon, and, provided he was not suffocated to death, the unpleasantness would be a small price to pay for the extraordinary nature of the experience.

Bony was still triumphant over the discovery of the fibres of wool. He now had definite proof that some person, wishing to prevent his passage through the bush being discovered, had used sheep's wool on his feet in place of feathers. Probably the person had worn slip-over boots of sheepskin with the wool on the outside. Bony himself had adopted this method more than once. The trouble taken to baffle possible trackers most certainly pointed to a deliberate act of incendiarism. Yes, this case was certainly yielding to his assault on it. Then there was that boss stockman. He certainly was a puzzle. A likeable enough fellow and evidently half in love with his employer's daughter. And yet there was his apparent failing for alcohol. There was something behind that trip to Gurner's Hotel for a bottle of whisky and Bony's old friend, intuition, warned him that all was not right in that quarter. Why had Ted Sharp deliberately told him a lie about having gone to Mitchell's Well? Why, when he could have admitted having gone to the hotel for whisky and then asked the detective not to divulge the fact to his employer? He must have known that his confidence would have been respected.

There was no necessity to tell a lie about so unimportant a point, and further to cover the lie by telephoning to Ned

Hamlin to endorse it. It was a thread that would have to be followed to the end. . . .

The aeroplane up aloft seemed to be constantly circling as though desperately searching for a landing ground. Time went on, and yet after all it was not long before the darkness lightened, despite his tightly-closed eyes. When he did open them and raised his head, Bony saw the world bathed in blood: it was like looking on it through crimson-coloured glasses. The sun was blood-red and of gigantic size. Its light was crimson. Above, the long streamers of sand were deep red against the lighter red of the clear sky westward of them. When the two blacks stood up they looked as though they had waded through a river of blood. The trees were drenched with blood.

The hum of the aeroplane engines became a thunderous roar, and, looking upward, Bony saw the machine, a large twin-engined biplane. It came sliding from above the sand streamers into the clear sky, a thing of superb grace and power.

And now, second by second, the light was changing in colour from crimson to yellow, from yellow to natural daylight. Bony waved to someone who waved from the plane, and then stood watching it flying to the south towards Emu Lake. It finally disappeared beyond the southern scrub.

"Cripes, Bony!" laughed the fat Shuteye. "You look like you bin sleep in a dog's kennel."

"You look as bad," chuckled Bony. "And so do you, Bill Sikes. Well, our tracking is at an end, and there is nothing more to do here. You can both go home. I will return after I have visited Emu Lake to see who was in that aeroplane. And not a word, mind, about finding those fibres of wool. Not even to Ned Hamlin. You understand?"

"Too right!" assented Bill Sikes, and was echoed by his mate.

Bony stood and watched them riding away, their horses hoofs kicking up the superfine dust laid by the storm. He wetted a handkerchief from the water-bag and sponged his own horse's dust-rimmed eyes and nostrils, and then, having taken a long drink, he mounted and rode at a jog-trot to Emu Lake.

The bush presented an extraordinary picture. On every projection provided by tree and shrub and grass and debris the red-brown sand lay like coloured snow. It thickened tree boughs and twigs, while the finer particles of sand dust clung to the leaves and grass stems. The few general colours of the bush were now overlaid by the uniform reddish-brown of sand. The air was motionless, and when, ahead of him, two crows settled in a leopard-wood tree, the slight vibrations set up by the birds so dislodged the settled sand that the tree seemed to shed some kind of vapour.

Bony experienced a pleasurable sense of elation when riding briskly southward to Emu Lake. The sun announced the time as being about three o'clock. His mind was busy creating theories and even fantasies based on the established fact that some person had taken every care not to leave his tracks when he had visited the red monoplane for the purpose of setting fire to it—he could have had no other object in mind.

To begin with, the theft of the aeroplane at Golden Dawn had not been actuated by the motive of gain—possession of the machine or its value in money. The drugging of the woman passenger implied that it had been stolen for the purpose of taking her somewhere from some place. The pilot had schemed either to land her in some selected spot, or to leave her to crash with the machine over country he knew was not being used for stock. There was a third supposition that might hold the water of plausibility. While journeying to some previously noted destination the engine might have ceased to function, and knowing that in the dark a forced landing was certain to be accompanied by grave danger, the pilot might have deserted the plane by parachute to save himself.

With Sergeant Cox, Bony keenly regretted the omission of John Nettlefold to search the machine before he and his daughter left with the drugged young woman. They might have found her handbag, or an article of clothing giving a clue to her identity. There certainly was something in or on the machine to have made its destruction so important. What was it the incendiarist had feared? If it was the discovery of something that could easily have been moved the destruction was senseless. He destroyed the plane because on it and its controls were his fingerprints.

Whose fingerprints? Those of the pilot, the person who had stolen the machine from Golden Dawn. Then the pilot was either a local resident or one well known to the police in a general way. More than likely a local resident, because, having heard that the machine was resting quite undamaged on Emu Lake, he had walked to it in the dark. That certainly indicated that he was a local resident and one, moreover, who new the country very well. Yes, if the girl herself was unknown to Cox and the Coolibah people, the pilot of the stolen aeroplane certainly was not. There must be living in the Golden Dawn district a man other than the doctor and Kane who possessed the requisite knowledge and experience expertly to handle an aeroplane.

It was a pretty problem, one that satisfied even Bony,

who was seldom satisfied. In this case there was only one disturbing element—the grave physical condition of the girl at Coolibah. Bony liked to spend plenty of time on an investigation but here the situation called for haste, because Knowles had said that if the cause of her singular condition were not cleared up, it might be impossible to find a cure in time to save her life.

It might be that only the clearing up of the matter of the stolen aeroplane would give the medico the information he needed. After all, it is difficult for any doctor to cure a complaint of that kind, when he has no idea of its cause.

So engrossed was Bony by these thoughts that the four-mile ride passed without the usual interest being taken in it. He failed to note that his horse left a trail of fine dust hanging in the air, and tracks of exceeding clarity on the ground. He failed to notice the rabbit that sped across the ground before him and flung up a trail of dust in miniature, much like that raised by a car speeding along a dry track. He had ridden down the low bank edging the lake before he realized that he had reached it.

Having secured the horse to a tree, he hurried with eager steps to the aeroplane, and the two men engaged among the debris of the burnt machine. So absorbed were they that his approach went unnoticed, until he said: "Good afternoon!"

Mr Cartwright and the airman straightened up and faced round to see a poorly-dressed, slightly-built man on whose arms and face clung particles of red sand, and whose worn shirt and trousers were stained red.

"Hullo!" returned Loveacre. "Where did you come from?"

Bony smiled. "I am just out for an afternoon ride. Who, may I ask, are you?"

The captain's brows rose a fraction. The voice and style of speech were singularly at variance with the appearance of this blackfellow—or half-caste, or whatever he was. The insurance assessor offered a shrewd guess.

"Are you, by any chance, Mr Napoleon Bonaparte?"

Bony bowed gravely. "I am. You gentlemen have the advantage, it seems."

"My name is Cartwright, and this is Captain Loveacre," announced the interested fire assessor. "I was hoping to meet you, as I believe you are in charge of this extraordinary matter. I have been sent by the Air Accidents Investigation Committee to ascertain if this fire was caused by incendiarism or by an act of God."

"Then, naturally, Captain Loveacre is even more interested in the wreckage."

"I am extremely interested, Inspector," Loveacre assured Bony with emphasis. "If ever you find out who did it, I would be eternally grateful if you just mention his name and give me a few minutes with him in private."

"Have you discovered any leads yet?" asked Cartwright.

"Tell me, first, what *you* have discovered," said Bony cautiously.

"Well—er, my report has, of course, to be submitted confidentially to the Air Accidents Committee. Doubtless, in due time——"

"You are, I presume, a civil servant?" suavely inquired Bony.

"No," replied Cartwright. "I am a fire insurance assessor employed by an insurance company."

"Pardon! My mistake is natural. I had no idea that red tape was so prominent a feature of the insurance world."

Cartwright chuckled. The dusty face and clothes, which seemed to indicate that Bony had been sleeping in a dog kennel, were so much at variance with the detective's keen, twinkling eyes and cultured accent that it was hard to imagine that they all belonged to the same man. Leaving the strewn wreckage, he stepped to Bony with extended hand.

"I am delighted to meet you, Inspector," he said. "Sergeant Cox told me I was to call you Bony."

"I am indebted to Sergeant Cox. I dislike being addressed either as Inspector or Mister, and I hate red tape, the god of the civil service, with all my soul. There is only one other man who hates that god more passionately than I, and that is my revered chief, Colonel Spendor. You were about to tell me how Captain Loveacre's machine was destroyed?"

"Actually, I was about to do nothing of the sort," Cartwright corrected, laughing frankly. "However, I will tell you that Captain Loveacre's aeroplane carried a high explosive when it was destroyed by fire. The explosion of petrol in the tanks could not have been of sufficient force so completely to disintegrate the structure. It could not have flung the heavy engine so far forward, the wings so far from the fuselage, and the fragments of both wings and fuselage so far outward from the central point."

"That is what occurred to me when I reviewed the wreck earlier to-day," Bony said in agreement. "Do you think that the machine was burned and wrecked by the explosive, or was the explosive detonated by the fire consuming the machine? Possibly I am abstruse."

"I understand your point. Yes, I think that the explosive was detonated by the heat of the fire consuming the aeroplane."

"Thank you." Bony pinched his nether lip with forefinger and thumb. Then: "Perhaps you could give the explosive a name?"

"Well—er——"

"Please answer me," Bony urged sharply. "*Could* you?"

Cartwright nodded.

"But," he said, "I would like you to understand that I have been instructed not to divulge the result of my examination outside my report to the Air Accidents Committee."

"I understand that quite well, Mr Cartwright," Bony responded earnestly. "In due time I shall have the gist of your report through my department—probably a fortnight hence. In two weeks' time your report will be quite valueless to me, because I shall know what I now want to know. At Coolibah homestead lies a young woman who is so helpless that she is unable even to raise or lower her eyelids. Dr Knowles says that if she cannot be cured of that strange paralysis she will shortly die from starved tissues. To me—and I think you, too, Mr Cartwright—the life of that young woman is of greater importance than the dignity of all the thousands of civil servants in this country. Until we know by clearing up the mystery of this burned aeroplane what has been done to that young woman she will be slowly dying. Again I ask you for the name of the explosive which shattered Captain Loveacre's monoplane."

The stubborn expression on the assessor's face slowly faded.

"Under the circumstances, I will tell you. The explosive was nitro-glycerine."

"Thank you, Mr Cartwright!" Bony said warmly. "You may be sure that I shall treat your confidence with great respect. In return, I will tell you what I know. Have you discovered how the aeroplane was fired?"

"No. I can obtain no definite proof. Have you that proof?"

"Yes, I have proof that a man walked through the bush, set fire to the machine here, and then walked back through the bush to the main Golden Dawn-St Albans road. Have you found anything that may be called a clue among the debris? Clothes buttons, for instance, or fragments of a woman's handbag?"

"Nothing. I cannot understand, or even imagine, the motive for destroying the aeroplane."

"I can."

"What?"

"Fingerprints. Either the man who stole the machine did not think he would have to abandon it, or he did not believe it possible to escape destruction when he did abandon it. The presence of nitro-glycerine in the machine points to the fact that he deliberately abandoned it so that it would crash with the passenger and be wiped out by the explosive. You cannot account for nitro-glycerine being in your red monoplane, Captain Loveacre?"

The captain shook his head.

"If he did what you say, then why? . . . Why should any man take that girl up in my machine and dump her with a wad of nitro-glycerine? Can you answer that question?"

"I feel cramped," Bony said provokingly.

Loveacre stared at him in blank surprise.

"Cramped? Well, what about a bottle of beer?" he suggested.

"Beer won't remove the cause," declared the detective. "Like Mr Cartwright, I am cramped with red tape."

Captain Loveacre looked startled. Then he grinned boyishly.

"I get you," he said. "Go on."

"Tell me," Bony urged persuasively. "How far, in your opinion, would your machine have flown after the pilot left it?"

"Now you're asking me. In still air it might have flown miles, or it might immediately have stalled."

"Well, being familiar with the machine, could you have fixed the controls with wire or something to make it self-flying until the petrol was used up?"

"I think that I might do that in still air, but when I jumped the sudden redistribution of weight would not be automatically countered without a human brain at the controls. On the other hand, the machine might not be disturbed by the pilot leaving it. It was an easy bus to fly, and it was possible for me to fly it at times 'hands off'—that is, without touching the controls."

"My last question. Assuming the thief fixed the controls, hoping that after he left the machine it would fly some considerable distance before crashing, and that he shut off the engine before he jumped, what most likely would have happened?"

"Anything—even what *did* happen. The bus at once began to lose height, but strangely enough did not lose flying speed. By a remarkable fluke it made a perfect landing on this lake when for miles around lies scrub and broken sand-plain country."

CHAPTER XIV

BONY DECLARES HIMSELF

CAPTAIN LOVEACRE had been flying for many years. The experience gained from several forced landings miles from any human habitation had fostered the habit of never going in the air outback without a small hamper, a billy-can, and a drum of water. When he announced that these things were in the grey biplane, the detective at once offered to fetch enough wood from the lake's shore with which to brew tea.

"Strange bird that," remarked Loveacre, when Bony had gone off for the firewood.

"Strange indeed!" agreed Cartwright. "The police sergeant was right about him, I wonder!"

"What?"

"I wonder, if given the same opportunities, how many Australian half-castes could reach the level of Bony's attainments."

The pilot frowned. "I have had dealings with a lot of them," he said thoughtfully. "In answer to your question, I'd say that quite a number could. Among the many I have met there are a lot of really smart fellows. Environment is against them, and so . . ."

"Well?" Cartwright pressed.

"The bush often gets 'em in the end. You take a black or a half-caste, and you put him to college or teach him a trade, but the time may come when he'll leave it all to bolt back to the bush. Some of them can't long resist the urge to go on walkabout."

"Perhaps they are happier on walkabout?"

"Of course," Loveacre instantly concurred. "They haven't got the curse of Adam laid on 'em like the white man. You can't tell me that it's natural for a man to slave in a factory, or on a road, or in an office. It is not natural for a man to work. That the white man does so is just because he's always been greedy for power over his fellows. Many blacks never have worked. They have never *had* to work and they can't see the *sense* of working. Blessed if I can see the sense of it, either. I know well enough that were I a half-caste I wouldn't work when I could go on walkabout and dig up a yam or catch a fish when I wanted to eat."

Ten minutes later they sat down with Bony on the ground and ate tinned sardines and biscuits and drank milkless tea.

After they had rested for some time, Loveacre jumped to his feet, and feeling for his watch, said: "Well, this won't do. We shall have to push off, for the sun is getting low,"

"It is ten minutes after five o'clock," announced Bony.

The airman had seen the detective glance at the sun, and when his watch proved that Bony was correct, he asked: "Did you guess the time?"

"I did not," replied Bony. "I have never found it necessary to carry a watch. When the sun is hidden by clouds I ask a policeman."

"Supposing you cannot find one?" inquired Cartwright.

"When that is so I do not worry about time. In fact, I seldom *do* worry about it." While they strolled over to the biplane, Bony said to Loveacre: "I am lamentably ignorant concerning aircraft. Assuming you were flying with your greatest enemy as a passenger, and assuming that you decided to murder him by jumping per parachute, leaving him to crash with the machine, would you switch off the engine or not?"

Loveacre regarded Bony with narrowed eyelids.

"Assuming that," he said slowly, "I think I would fix the stick and the rudder controls, and leave the engine running. To do that would give me a better chance of getting clear of the plane, although by first switching off the engine I would not be necessarily hindered from leaving the machine, nor would the parachute necessarily be fouled by the machine even if at once it went into a spin or stalled."

"Thank you! Might I ask both you gentlemen, as a personal favour, to accept in confidence what I have said about this matter?"

"Decidedly," the assessor promptly replied. When Loveacre added his assent, Bony smiled, saying:

"Until a few days ago I thought that I knew everything. It is a conceit due, I think, to my wife, to whom I am really a hero. I should have studied flying and all appertaining to it, for it was inevitable that an air crime would come my way. Where are you staying to-night?"

"Golden Dawn? You coming?"

"No, Captain, thank you. Well, kindly convey my regards to Sergeant Cox. And do, please, remember to be red-tapish. There are time when it is so convenient."

"So long, Bony. I'm damned glad to have met you, and I will look forward to meeting you again," Loveacre said warmly.

"Thank you, Captain. The pleasure, then, has been mutual."

"That goes for me, too," seconded Mr Cartwright. "We

will remember the god of the civil service when this aeroplane leaves the ground. Good-bye, and good luck!"

The two men climbed into the machine.

A quiet smile hovered about the finely-moulded mouth of Napoleon Bonaparte when, with his hands clasped behind him, he walked slowly to the timber, where his nervous horse was impatiently waiting.

Nitro-glycerine! Cartwright, he decided, was broad-minded and altogether a decent sort: a man, moreover, extremely clever. He would have liked to know how the fire assessor could, from the evidence at hand, determine that it had been nitro-glycerine which had partly destroyed the aeroplane, not gelignite, or dynamite, or gunpowder. The fact that some explosive had been used to assist destruction certainly pointed to one assumption. The man who walked through the bush to destroy the machine certainly did not carry the explosive with him. His object was to destroy any clues, and to do that it was sufficient to set fire to the plane. The explosive agent, therefore, must have been in the machine when it landed, and the inferences to be drawn from that were plain.

Mounting his horse, Bony turned it due north. He had to give the animal his attention, for it was thirsty and hungry and wanted to return to its home paddock. Reaching the boundary fence he found a place where the wires were slack, and, strapping them together, he coaxed the animal to step over them. Having released the wires he rode smartly north-eastward to Gurner's Hotel.

Dusk was falling when he reached the single-story, rambling, wooden building facing north across a three-chain road. The wayside hotel was set down in the centre of sparsely scrubbed land, and there were no other buildings within sight. On riding into the yard adjoining the building, he espied a horse-trough and dismounted beside it to allow the beast to drink. To him came a tall, lank, unprepossessing aboriginal, grotesquely attired in the tattered garments of a tramp.

"Are you the yardman?" Bony inquired.

"Too right, boss!" replied the black. "You stay here?"

"For an hour. I want a feed for my horse."

"Orl ri'! I feed him up goodo. You gibbit tchilling?"

"Here you are. Here's your shilling. Give him a good feed, mind."

Without haste, the detective strolled out of the yard and so to the door of the bar. The place was very quiet. East and west, the winding track snaked along the wide cleared road until masked by the falling night. Above, the stars hung like hurricane lamps beneath the roof of a shearing-shed. In the bar, Bony found a little rotund man with a round red face and dark appraising eyes.

"Good night!" said this individual, somewhat haughtily. "Travelling?"

"Are you Mr Gurner?"

"I am."

"Then I am glad to find you disengaged. I am Detective-Inspector Bonaparte. I want a drink first, then a confidential chat with you, and then dinner."

Mr Gurner's superior air had by now utterly vanished.

"The drinks will be on the house, Mr Bonaparte. I heard that you had come from Brisbane. Riding a hack? Staying the night?"

"Yes to the first; no to the second. I'll take a nobbler of port wine in a tumbler filled with soda water. See about dinner, will you? Then we can talk."

"Very well. It's been a hell of a day, hasn't it? That dust-storm was about the worst I've ever known."

When the little man returned his expression would have been jovial enough had his eyes been less hard. Bony called for another drink and opened the inquisition.

"I understand from Sergeant Cox that none of your people here heard an aeroplane passing overhead the night Captain Loveacre's monoplane was stolen at Golden Dawn. Who was here that night, and where did they sleep?"

"In the house. There was me and my sister, who does the cooking and housekeeping, the maid, and three guests. Jack Johnson, the yardman, slept in one of the sheds. No, no one here heard any aeroplane that night or any other. Extraordinary affair, don't you think? How is that young woman going along?"

"There is no change in her condition. Twelve miles north of here is a stockman's hut, occupied by a man called Larry the Lizard. What kind of a man is he?"

"To look at? Six feet or a bit over. Red hair and beard. Voice like a thunderstorm. He's neither better nor worse than the average bushman."

"And what waters are in the vicinity?"

"Well, there's Bore Fourteen, south of here and this side of Coolibah's boundary. There's another bore over at Larry the Lizard's place, and there's a surface dam seven miles along the road to St Albans on what is called Martell's Selection."

"Thanks. My thirst is still rather chronic."

While Mr Gurner attended to business, Bony noted the clean, scrubbed counter, the spotless shelves of bottles, the set of sporting prints high on the walls, and the petrol-lamp suspended above the bar. With the drinks set up between them, he leaned towards the publican and began to speak in a low, confidential tone.

"Think back to the night that aeroplane was stolen, Mr Gurner. Did you have a visit from the Coolibah boss stockman, Ted Sharp?"

"Yes!" replied Gurner without hesitation.

"What did he come for?"

Mr Gurner smiled knowingly. Affability itself, he seemed most anxious to assist the police in the investigation of a crime which had stirred the State.

"Ted Sharp came here to meet a man," he replied.

"Indeed!"

"Yes, rather a mysterious sort of fellow, too, if you ask me. I got a telephone message early that day from Yaraka from a person giving his name as Brown. Brown asked that a bedroom and a sitting-room be reserved for him that night. He got here about five in the afternoon. I put him in Room Four, and I let him have a spare room for a sitting-room. It was the first time I've ever been asked for one."

"What kind of a man was this Brown?"

"I certainly couldn't place him, Mr Bonaparte. He was a tall, thin, dried-up, miserable man about fifty or thereabouts. He arrived in a hired car, and he tells me that he and the driver may be stopping the night or they may not. He says he's expectin' a gentleman to call on him.

"Well, in they come. Mr Brown, he goes to his room carrying a suitcase in one hand and what they calls an attaché case in the other. The driver reckons he'll leave his gear in the car until he knows what's going to be done. Dinner-time comes round, and out comes Mr Brown to ask the way to the dining-room, and he's still carrying the attaché case. All through dinner he sits with that attaché case on his knees. After dinner he goes into the sitting-room I fixed up for him, and I'm told to take in a bottle of whisky, a jug of water, and two glasses. And there he stays all the evening."

It was evident that Mr Gurner was enjoying himself.

"Then," he went on, "a little after ten o'clock, who should arrive in his runabout truck but Ted Sharp. And what should he do when he comes in here, where I'm serving half a dozen customers, but whisper in me ear for this Mr Brown. Old Harry Wilson, the teamster, asks Ted to have a drink, and Ted puts him off, saying that he'll be glad to later on. So I shows Ted Sharp in to Mr Brown, and on the table I seen several papers with typewriting on them.

"They're in there as thick as thieves for more'n an hour. Anyway, it was well after eleven when Ted comes into the bar. I was tired and was trying to get Harry Wilson and Nutmeg Joe to clear off with another bloke called McNess, who was taking them to St Albans. Anyway, Ted shouts for all hands twice, and then he wants to know if he can use the telephone." Mr Gurner indicated the instrument on the wall between the bar counter and the rear door. "He rings through to Golden Dawn. Of course, the row is pretty bad. There was an argument going on between Nutmeg Joe and Peter Leroy, and I couldn't follow what Sharp was saying. I did hear him ask the night operator in the telephone exchange at Golden Dawn to take down a telegram and see that it was dispatched early the next morning."

"As you said, Mr Gurner, it sounds a little mysterious, but no doubt there is quite a simple explanation," Bony murmured. It was obvious that the publican did not feel any affection for the Coolibah boss stockman.

"Yes. Let's hope so, anyway," Gurner agreed. "I overheard a few words. '*Adelaide*' was one. '*Kane*' was another.

I heard him say: '*Be careful.*' And then: '*Nothing must ever leak out.*' That was all I did hear, and after Ted Sharp had shouted again out he goes to his runabout and drives off back to Coolibah. Oh, I forgot! He buys a bottle of whisky to take along with him."

"And when did Mr Brown leave?"

"Early next morning, heading back for Yaraka."

"Do you know the driver of the hired car?"

"No. He was a stranger to us. Like Mr Brown, he said nothing gratis."

"Hum!" murmured Bony reflectively. "Well, Mr Gurner, I am much obliged to you. Might I ask you to hold our conversation in strict confidence?"

Mr Gurner smiled.

"Of course. I am only too willing to assist the police. If you would slip a word to Sergeant Cox that I have helped you a little . . ."

The publican winked, and Bony winked back. Someone beyond the bar called that the dinner was ready, and Mr Gurner raised the counter flap invitingly.

CHAPTER XV

A RETURN TO COOLIBAH

THE date that Bony met Captain Loveacre and Mr Cartwright on Emu Lake was 6 November—nine days after the unknown girl had been found in the red monoplane. About eight o'clock on the following morning, Bony had rung through to Nettlefold asking him to transmit a message to Sergeant Cox, which was in effect a request to Headquarters to have the findings of the Air Accidents Investigation Committee kept out of the newspapers. Bony then said that he would be absent from Faraway Bore for a day or two, and as he would be returning to Coolibah by a devious route he would like his suitcase to be brought in.

Nettlefold had called at Faraway Bore for the suitcase, and there he gained the distinct impression that while Ned Hamlin knew nothing of any developments, the two blacks did, but would not speak of them.

On 8 November a car brought a newspaper reporter and a photographer. They went on to Emu Lake, and on their way back they bailed up Nettlefold for a story. Nettlefold cautiously told them something, though very little, about the finding of the aeroplane, but said nothing about the girl found in it. The natural result was that the reporter scented a hidden story, and stopped at Golden Dawn, apparently prepared to remain in the district indefinitely.

On the ninth, Cox rang up Coolibah Station four times asking for Bony, and that evening there arrived at Golden Dawn a dust-grimed and powerful car driven by a distinguished-looking man who asked to be directed to Dr Knowles's house.

Early the following morning Sergeant Cox again rang up, asking for the whereabouts of Bony and expressing some anxiety about him. An hour later Dr Knowles got through to inform Nettlefold that he was bringing a specialist, or rather the specialist was bringing him, as Stanisforth refused to risk his life in the air. Towards twelve o'clock they arrived, to be met by the genial cattleman.

"Welcome to Coolibah, Dr Stanisforth," Nettlefold greeted him. "I only regret that your visit is a professional one. We have so few visitors that we shall be delighted if you will consider yourself our guest for just as long as you please."

"I would like to stay a year," the great specialist returned. "I am wanting rest and quiet, but—" and he sighed. "Like a fool I have allowed my practice to become an old man of the sea."

"Well, come along in and have a refresher before lunch. My daughter is with the patient just now. On day duty, you know. Oh, here is Tilly! Tilly, please inform Miss Elizabeth that Dr Stanisforth and Dr Knowles have arrived."

He conducted his guests through the house to his study.

"I trust you did not find the long journey too wearisome?"

"On the contrary," said Stanisforth, "once beyond the settled areas, I could drive fast, and I find fast driving an excellent tonic."

"You would have found a better tonic had you consented to fly here with me," Knowles put in, smiling wryly.

"I fear not, my dear Knowles. Not after what a housekeeper told me when she brought the early morning tea. I hate heights, anyway. When a car stops through engine trouble one can get out and tinker with the machinery; when an aeroplane engine stops one can do nothing but regret that his executors will shortly be having a lot of worry. Ah——"

Elizabeth entered. Stanisforth bent over her hand and regarded her with interest.

"So you are the young lady who has taken it on herself to nurse a stranger found within the gates! You strengthen my faith in mankind, and it requires strengthening at times, believe me. How is your patient?"

"Just the same, Doctor. There is never any change in her," replied Elizabeth. "Sometimes, it seems like looking after a mummy—a living mummy! If you are ready I will show you your room before going back to her. Lunch can be served whenever it suits you."

"Excellent, Miss Nettlefold. I am really very hungry. Self before others is my motto. I will examine the patient immediately afterwards."

"Dr Stanisforth considers himself a humorist at times," Knowles hastened to explain when he saw a faint resentment in Elizabeth's eyes. She smiled then, and said:

"Of course! Come along. The roads are terribly dusty, but you are fortunate to have missed the sand cloud the other evening. It was one of the worst we have experienced."

She led the guests away, her father remaining to fill his pipe from the customary black plug tobacco.

"May I come in?" asked a low voice from the open french windows at his back. Swinging round, he blinked at the roughly-dressed man standing on the veranda. It was Detective-Inspector Napoleon Bonaparte.

"Why, it's Bony!" he exclaimed with pleasure. "Come in, of course. We have been wondering where you were."

"Be good enough to overlook my appearance," pleaded Bony. "With your permission I will close the door. Then, if I might so presume, will you give me a glass of soda water—with a dash of brandy?"

Without speaking, Nettlefold hurried to the wall cabinet.

"I noticed that you had visitors—ah, thank you!" Bony continued. "Not being very presentable, I concealed myself until the opportunity occurred to enter unobserved. Could I trespass on your kindness still further by asking you to smuggle me to a bedroom? As I know the situation of the bath-room, you could then leave me to gain its sanctuary."

"Yes, of course. Your room is ready for you at any time. But where have you been? Cox has been ringing up every day asking for you."

"I have been on a quiet little walkabout," Bony replied. "There were several matters I wished to clear up. How is the young woman?"

"There is no change in her. Knowles has just arrived with a specialist from the city, a Dr Stanisforth. They will be seeing her after lunch. And lunch is ready. You must be hungry."

"Not as much as you might expect, for I have been living on the country. Could you expand your generosity still further by putting up a fourth guest?"

"By all means. There's any amount of room."

"Then, when I am safely out of sight, please ring Sergeant Cox and ask him to spend the night here. Do not say I have returned. Just say you have had word from me."

"Very well. I'll see if the coast is clear."

They were at lunch when Bony entered the dining-room. Bathed and shaved, and dressed in a light-grey lounge suit, he had effected a complete metamorphosis. The ragged bushman had now become the polished inspector, more at ease with the company than Nettlefold himself.

"We were beginning to worry about you, Mr——er, I mean Bony," Elizabeth remarked.

"Indeed! Thank you for your solicitude, Miss Nettlefold," he told her gravely. "My business has been lightened by the addition of a little pleasure. How did you weather that sand cloud the other evening?"

"It was terrific, wasn't it? Fortunately we were warned of its coming by Ned Hamlin; yet, despite all our efforts to keep the dust out of the house, the place was in a shocking state when it had passed. We must have collected bucketfuls of sand."

Sand clouds provided a topic that lasted throughout lunch, and when the two doctors had been taken by Elizabeth to the patient, her father and Bony drifted to the study.

"Ah—it is nice to get into a comfortable chair again," Bony remarked. "I have been walking and sitting on my heels and lying on the ground o' nights, and I find that my body is less tough and supple than it was once."

Nettlefold chuckled. "When I was young," he said, "I gloried in camping out and sleeping on a waterproof sheet with one blanket over me and the saddle under my head. Now I look for a flock mattress and sheets and a feather pillow. Did you do any good outback?"

"Yes—and no. First, tell me how things have gone here."

"According to routine, excepting that I insisted on Elizabeth taking a turn off night duty. Ted Sharp continues to sit up on the veranda outside the sick-room, or prowl about close by. It seems improbable that that feller will make another attempt on the patient's life."

"It is not at all improbable," Bony contradicted. "We cannot expose either your daughter or the housekeeper—not to mention the patient—to the risk of another attempt. How many men do you employ?"

"Fourteen: including the men's cook, a groom, a Chinese gardener, and a tradesman."

"How many of them are usually about the homestead?"

"Two, with the Chinese gardener."

"Are there any new hands?"

"No. The last to be engaged is the tradesman. He's been here a year. Ted Sharp has been with me eleven years."

Bony's brows rose a mere fraction. He broke a little silence by asking:

"Where did he come from?"

"Candidly, I don't know. I never asked him. One doesn't ask such questions out here."

"I am aware of that. He has never volunteered the information, apparently. Good man?"

"Excellent in every way. He's a good man's boss, and a good boss's man. We—er—we rather like him."

"Does he know anything about sheep?"

The cattleman shook his head. "I don't think so."

"Do you know anything about sheep?" Bony persisted.

"Yes. As a matter of fact, when I was young I served

five years as a jackeroo on a sheep station. It was dow
in New South Wales."

"Is that so!" Bony sat bolt upright in his chair and re
garded his host with steady eyes. "I need your assistance,
he went on slowly. "To obtain it I must confide in yo
Usually no successful crime investigator confides in any one
I have in this case to be particularly cautious, because
am convinced that certain people command an excellent in
telligence service."

"Anything you tell me is in the strictest confidence."

"Thank you. I have established the fact that Captai
Loveacre's monoplane was destroyed by a man who walke
to it from the main St Albans-Golden Dawn track at a poin
some miles beyond Gurner's Hotel, and then walked bac
to the main track. That fact proves another—or goes a lon
way to prove it. In my opinion more than one perso
was engaged in the matter of this stolen aeroplane. Ther
is the man who piloted it, and there's the man who poisone
the brandy. The firing of the machine and the poisonin
of the brandy were done too closely together in time fo
one man to have done both.

"The man who destroyed the aeroplane—probably wit
the object of obliterating his fingerprints—did his work whe
wearing sheepskin boots having the wool on the outside
Out there we found no actual tracks of him, but we did fin
fibres of wool detached from his sheepskin boots. I under
stand that you have never run sheep on Emu Lake pad
dock?"

"There have never been any sheep running on Coolibah.

"There are, however, sheep on Tintanoo."

"Yes. Kane always has a few mutton sheep."

"What class of sheep are they, do you know?"

"Yes. They are Border Leicesters crossed with Merinos.

"Does he breed them, or does he buy them elsewhere?"

"I am not sure, but I think Kane purchases them from Olarie Downs. The Greysons run that cross. But Kane isn't the only man who buys killing sheep from them. The Olivers, of Windy Creek, do, too. So does the Golden Dawn butcher. You see, in this district we are cattle people, but some people run a few sheep to give us a change from the eternal beef. When I want mutton I always buy a carcass from the butcher, because the Coolibah fences are not sheep-proof."

"Hum! Well, that will widen the search." Bony produced a pocket wallet, and from it he took an envelope containing several cigarette papers, each containing a fibre of wool and each numbered in the order that the fibres were found. "Does this wool come from a cross-bred Leicester?"

Nettlefold looked closely at the several fibres.

"Yes, they are all from the same class of sheep, if not all from the same animal. You know, Bony, if that man walked through the bush from the main track to Emu Lake and then back again, he must know this country as well as I do."

"That's exactly what I think. He knew it so well that he could fly an aeroplane over it at night, and jump from the machine per parachute when he knew he was over fairly clear country. What puzzles me is how he did it without landmarks. He would be unable to follow a road, or distinguish any other landmark in the dark."

"I think he could," Nettlefold said thoughtfully. "Midway between this house and Tintanoo homestead there is a long sheet of water in one of the river channels. Once he picked that out on the dark ground, he could set his course for Bore Fourteen, which is north of Emu Lake paddock on Tintanoo. He would recognize those two waters by their shape: the long ribbon of it in the river channel, and the narrow channel of it, ending in a small lake, at Bore Fourteen."

"Ah! Thank you. Knowing the country so well, he would certainly recognize the shape of the waters you mention. Now, who *would* know the country as well as you do yourself?"

The manager considered.

"Kane, young Oliver, Ted Sharp, Ned Hamlin—oh, and a dozen others."

"Well, we are progressing, Mr Nettlefold," Bony said with satisfaction in his voice. "If I could obtain definite proof that when the aeroplane thief flew the machine he was guided by the water lying in that river channel, then I would be even more hopeful."

CHAPTER XVI

STANISFORTH PROVIDES AN IDEA

AT four o'clock, Tilly, the aboriginal maid, set the afternoon-tea table at the western end of the veranda outside the study windows, and when she had gone and Elizabeth had conducted the two doctors from the patient's bed, Bony and the cattleman rose and stepped out to join them.

At last Elizabeth asked the question that had been on the tip of her tongue for over an hour. "What do you think of the patient, Dr Stanisforth?"

"I will be candid," he told them, in a low voice. "Unless we can find the person who produced in her the condition of muscular paralysis, and he is made to disclose just what he did to produce that state, I fear that we cannot save her. Her condition is not due to brain injury, either physical or mental, and it is not the result of violence."

"You are, then, able to say that the paralysis was not caused by shock given by the landing of the aeroplane in which she was found?" Bony pressed.

"Yes, I can say that. And, while I am not positive, I incline to the opinion that the paralysis has been caused by some drug."

"Do you know the drug, or a likely drug?"

"There are several which could have produced the effect temporarily. The venom of certain snakes will create temporary paralysis, but I know of no drug that would produce such an apparently permanent effect."

"Have you knowledge of the method by which the drug was administered?" was Bony's following question.

"Dr Knowles and I are agreed that the drug was given through the mouth, probably with drink or food," the specialist answered. "Neither of us has seen a case exactly like it. We are like blind men. If the patient cannot be cured—if the antidote cannot be found and used—death inevitably will claim her."

"But surely we can keep her from dying, Doctor?" Elizabeth said desperately.

"Her pulse is weak, and growing weaker. Do not think I am making light of your nursing. I congratulate you on that. The cause of your patient's increasing weakness is the wastage of body tissues. She is unable to take normal nourishment. At present she is living on stimulants. Added to this is that, although the involuntarily controlled muscles are not completely affected by the drug, they are being seriously affected by the passiveness of the voluntarily controlled muscles which are paralysed. In short, the patient's condition is unnatural. I wish I could speak more cheerfully."

The ensuing silence was ended by Bony.

"If an antidote cannot be found," he asked, "how long do you think . . ."

"That is always a difficult question to answer," replied the specialist. "I can only guess it. In my opinion it would be from five to seven weeks. Certainly no longer than two months."

His verdict was followed by a much longer silence. Covertly, Bony watched those seated with him about the tea-table. Nettlefold stared through the fly-gauze towards the men's quarters. His daughter looked down at her hands now lying in her lap. Knowles at this moment defied analysis. He sat slumped into his chair, his head resting against its high back, his eyes closed, and the little trimmed black moustache quite unable to conceal the drawn lines about his mouth. The outward muscles of his left eye were throbbing, and the white hands resting on the chair-arms were never still.

"Do you think, Dr Stanisforth, that the patient would have a better chance if she were removed to a city hospital?"

Stanisforth leaned forward.

"Miss Nettlefold, her condition might react to radium or electrical treatment. I say only that it *might*. On the other hand, the journey to a city would be gravely dangerous. She might collapse, no matter how easy the trip was made for her. No, I think it better for her to remain here. Quite and careful attention are two factors that will help her, and while life remains there always is hope."

"She certainly shall have all the attention possible, I assure you."

Stanisforth smiled at her encouragingly. Then he turned to Bony.

"I suppose it is a case of foul play, Inspector?"

"I am convinced of it," asserted Bony. "Pardon my presumption, but might the patient react to hypnotism?"

Stanisforth shook his head.

"I have attempted it, but without success."

"When you hypnotize a person you gain control of the mind to the extent of making the subject do your bidding—am I right?"

"To a certain degree that is so."

"You cannot, however, project your mind into that of the subject?"

"No."

"Or be able to see into the subject's mind—read it, as it were?"

"No," Stanisforth repeated. "In an ordinary case I might be able to command a person to reveal by his tongue what is in his mind. I might make him write it. I cannot myself *see* it. Because I cannot overcome the girl's paralysis I cannot make her tell me or write down what we want to know. Why are you smiling, Inspector?"

"Doctor, you have placed me in your debt. You have given me an idea. I think I know how I might find out what is in the patient's mind."

"How!" demanded both doctors and Elizabeth.

"I am afraid I cannot explain myself just now," Bony said. "I cannot guarantee success, of course, but I believe there is an excellent chance—Ah! Here comes Sergeant Cox."

"But surely," said Stanisforth, "you can give us some idea——"

"I think it most unlikely that the patient would know the name of the drug," Bony pointed out. "She might not even know that she has been drugged, but she *does* know who took her up in Loveacre's red monoplane, and left her in it to crash to destruction. When I know who that is he will tell me the name of the drug given her, or what he did to her."

"If he chooses to tell you," Nettlefold argued.

"He will tell me," Bony repeated grimly.

It was five o'clock when Bony and Sergeant Cox left the

house to stroll down along the winding creek, which came from the east to skirt the men's quarters before going on to stop at a river channel. On the dead trunk of a fallen coolibah tree, they sat and waved back the flies with sprigs of leaves.

"Why were you so anxious to get in touch with me?" asked Bony. "Is there something important?"

"Yes. I found a swagman who heard an aeroplane fly over about two-fifty-five on the morning that Captain Loveacre's machine was stolen. It was flying west."

"Ah!" Bony sharply exclaimed. "Where was he when he heard it?"

"He was camped at the junction of the Coolibah track with the St Albans-Golden Dawn road."

"Indeed! Now that is most interesting. The stolen machine passed that road junction flying west at five minutes to three. Good! We can now roughly plot its course. At twenty minutes to two that night the machine is stolen from the rear of the hotel at Golden Dawn. It reaches and passes by the road junction at five minutes to three. At half-past three it passed above two aboriginal dog-trappers who were camped beside a small waterhole approximately two miles north of Emu Lake. Now, from the doggers' camp back here to the road junction is approximately seventy miles. The cruising speed of the machine is about one hundred and thirty miles an hour—about two miles a minute. From the junction to the doggers' camp the time and the mileage covered agree roughly with the known speed of the machine. Then from the junction to the hotel at Golden Dawn is eighty miles, covered by the machine—apparently—in ninety-five minutes, which is much less than one mile to the minute. You see, Sergeant, don't you? From Golden Dawn to the road junction the machine travels at less than one mile to the minute, but from the junction to the doggers' camp it travels at its normal speed of two miles to the minute. On the first stage it should have taken forty minutes, but it takes ninety-five minutes, giving a balance in time of fifty-five minutes. Now where did it go, and what did the pilot do during that fifty-five minutes?"

"Search me!" said Cox hopelessly. "Did you get any clues outback?"

"Quite a number. Listen carefully."

Graphically Bony related the finding of the wool fibres and then went on to describe how he had subsequently found two black dingo-trappers who were camped beside the small waterhole on Tintanoo on the night of 27-28 October.

"One of them owns a watch of which his is very proud," Bony went on. "He states that he and his companion were awakened at three-thirty by the sound of an aeroplane engine. The machine was flying high. Two days after that night one of them, when visiting his traps, found extraordinary markings on a low sand-dune. Extraordinary, because he could not understand them. They covered an area of several yards. At my request he drew on sandy ground marks something like them, and what he thought was to scale.

"I went with him to that place. The sand cloud, of course, had wiped out the markings, but after a long search I found two more fibres of wool. I am convinced that the markings were made by a man, wearing sheepskin boots, who landed there by parachute. Having gathered up the parachute, he walked with it northward to the main road, where he was met by an accomplice in a motor car. The following night one of them burned the machine, and the other poisoned the patient's brandy?"

"And he took the girl out over near Emu Lake and jumped from the machine, leaving her to crash in it?" said Cox.

"That is exactly what he did, Sergeant. Our man is cool and calm and without nerves. He must have strong reasons for so determinedly trying to get rid of Miss Double M. The machine landed somewhere out from or between Golden Dawn and the road junction to pick up the young woman. At least it appears so on the evidence at our disposal. Did you trace the swagman's movements?"

"Yes. He walked south along the east side of the river. He had been working up on Monkira, and he had money with him. Consequently, when he arrived at Golden Dawn, he at once went on the booze. He was quite orderly, and I could not get an excuse to lock him up for his own good until he had spent all his money and was kicked out of the pub. By that time he was in a bad state, and the information came out quite by chance after the wife and I had cured him of the ding-bats."

"Oh! So you take care of drunks, eh?"

"More or less," Cox replied carelessly. "Can't stop a man spending his cheque if he keeps peaceful and quiet, you know. But many of them drink all day and half the night and never eat, and then when their money is gone out they go on to the track in the horrors. Since one poor devil perished on the Common I have always locked up a man well the worse for drink, and my wife cures 'em with soups and things. On being ready for the road, I go along to the pub and demand to know how much he has spent. On the quiet, I make Allard, the licensee, give me back ten per cent of what the drunk has spent, and I buy tucker for him with it, and perhaps a pair of boots for the track."

"And this particular swagman? You have him still locked up?"

"No. He left for Yaraka the day before yesterday. I took his name, of course, and, because of what the wife did for him, he promised to report at every police-station he passed in case he should be wanted. I warned him to keep his mouth shut."

Bony warmed to this very human policeman and his wife. He had suspected the kind heart beneath the stiff exterior, but now suspicion had become fact.

"Make a note to get that man back again to Golden Dawn, and when you have him keep him locked up," he directed.

"But we have got nothing on him!" expostulated the sergeant.

"Never mind. Get him back. Frighten him with what might well be a real danger—that his having heard the aeroplane that night makes him dangerous to dangerous men. I want to see him. Feed him well. Supply him with a bottle of beer now and then, if necessary. Tick it up to me. It can go into my exes account. Now, who in your district would have nitro-glycerine in his possession?"

"No one that I know of. If I remember rightly it's very dangerous stuff to handle."

"Yes. It certainly is. We will discuss that again later on. Meanwhile I want you to telephone to Golden Dawn a telegram to be dispatched to the Commissioner. We will go back to the house now, and you can fix it."

"Very well," agreed the sergeant, producing note-book and pencil.

"Address it to: Colonel Spendor, Church Avenue, Nundah, Brisbane. Say:

Urgently require services of Illawalli, out from Burketown, North Queensland. He was of service in Windee case, you will recall. Have this aboriginal chief brought down by aeroplane and deliver Golden Dawn without delay. Personal felicitations. Bony."

Looking up after writing down the message, the sergeant regarded Bony with disapproving grey eyes.

"Do you often couch a request in such terms as these?" he asked sternly. "I thought the chief was a strict disciplinarian. And this telegram! You want it sent to the Commissioner's private residence?"

"I do, Sergeant. And the chief *is* a strict disciplinarian," Bony agreed, smiling. "I have found in my experience that the greater disciplinarian a commanding officer is the more ready is he to be himself subject to a little disciplining. Again, I have learned this simple lesson. If you want a thing, *demand* it. Never ask that it may be granted. Textbook knowledge of psychology is ever an asset. If I sent that request to the Commissioner at Headquarters it would be opened and first read by Clarke, his secretary, and Clarke would place it before the Commissioner with disapproval writ plain on his pasty face, and venting little grunts and snorts. Whereupon the colonel would pound his table and damn and blast me for being disrespectful.

"By sending the telegram to his private house this evening, and as his delightful lady will probably be with him, he will do the damning and blasting under his breath, and without doubt she will ask him what it is which so depresses him. He then will chuckle and give her the telegram to read, and tell her how that confounded Bony feller will never be cramped by rules and regulations. He'll say: 'No, madam. I tell you he won't be subdued by red tape. He's like *me*. Hates it like poison. Good man, Bony! Always gets there. Like *me*! He knows his own mind. Like *me*.' And he will be so pleased with himself that he will ring up Ross and order him to dispatch a plane to Burketown to fetch Illawalli here. And if Ross hums and haws about the expense he will be damned and blasted, too. Yes, a smattering of psychology is most useful. It enables one to know exactly how the other fellow will jump. The next time you ask for a transfer, my dear Cox, do not request it, *demand* it."

"I'd be demanding the sack," Cox pointed out with a chuckle.

Bony's eyes were twinkling when they rose to walk back to the house. . . .

After dinner, Bony excused himself and took his letters and the wad of foolscap reports written by Cox to his bedroom. Having made the usual pile of cigarettes and placed them on the bed table beside the slipper he proposed to use as an ash-tray, he settled to read both letters and reports.

There was a memo from Headquarters stating that no report had been received from other capital cities concerning a young woman whose initials were double M. The patient's photograph had been distributed all over the Commonwealth and had already appeared in the principal newspapers. Another official memo stated that inquiries in Queensland for a missing woman having initials double M had been so far without result.

Bony then began a perusal of Sergeant Cox's work, and quickly he understood how painstaking that work was, and how their superiors were right in their selection of Cox for this western post of administration. The man was a born administrator; and, because it was so, he was worthy of promotion to a district which would give him added responsibilities, and additional opportunities for his son.

The completeness of the concisely-written batch of dossiers delighted him. If the people to whom they referred knew what Cox knew about them, they would be truly astonished.

For instance: Nettlefold was stated to be part owner of Coolibah, holding 55 per cent of the shares in it. Ted Sharp came from pastoral people down on the Warrego. In 1928 he had inherited an uncle's estate sworn for probate at £3750. Owen Oliver, of Windy Creek Station, was paying the Queensland Child Welfare Department for the maintenance of a child born to a certain Berle Mannock. Dr Knowles spent on drink at the Golden Dawn Hotel the sum of £32 per month, and both Ned Hamlin and Larry Wentworth—known as Larry the Lizard—had served a sentence of three months at Winton for firing rifles in the bar of the Golden Dawn Hotel. Mr John Kane had done nothing reprehensible, but Sergeant Cox described him as "peculiar."

Having read all the dossiers, Bony possessed an excellent working knowledge of the history of almost every one permanently resident in the sergeant's wide district, and now with the letters and documents lying on the bed beside him, the detective pondered on the movements of the stolen aeroplane and the times at which it had been heard.

If the swagman's statement regarding the time that it had passed from east to west over his roadside camp was accurate it undermined the building of the theoretical structure on which he had been busy. The finger of accusation had pointed steadily at someone on Tintanoo. It had been maintained in that direction by the passage of the airman in the machine to a point on Tintanoo, and then from that point to the main road, as well as by the passage of the man who destroyed the machine sometime the following night. And now, if the swagman was correct in his time, the accusing finger wobbled from Tintanoo to someone living eastward of both Tintanoo and Coolibah.

Abruptly, Bony sat up and rang the electric bell. He was closing the windows when the maid knocked and was invited to enter.

"I regret to bother you, Tilly, but will you please ask Sergeant Cox to be kind enough to come here."

When Cox came in, Bony waved him to a seat on the bed and at once began in a low key.

"Those dossiers you have supplied are exceptionally good. Regarding that of Edward Sharp. You state that he came into a small fortune in 1928. That year he was employed here as boss stockman. He is still here in that capacity. Do you know why he stays after having inherited a fortune of nearly four thousand pounds?"

"I don't know. It has always been a mystery to me," Cox replied.

Bony slowly expelled cigarette smoke, forming perfectly-shaped rings. His eyes were nearly closed, and Cox watched him curiously. Then, in a flash, the eyes were wide open and he snapped:

"Do you think the postmaster would give you a copy of a certain telegram which was dispatched from his office early in the morning of 28 October?"

"I don't know. He might."

Bony sighed.

"This confounded red tape! We can, of course, waste a great deal of time by following the official river of red tape to its mouth in order to see that telegram. In this case time is of supreme importance in a race with death for the life of that helpless young woman. Perhaps if this were pointed out to the postmaster. . . ."

Bony related all that Mr Gurner had said about the mysterious guest on whom Sharp had called. Then:

"What is your personal opinion of Ted Sharp?"

"Favourable," replied the sergeant. "He is a little chummy with Owen Oliver, which is peculiar, because the two don't or shouldn't mix."

"Well, try to get a peep at that telegram. And then find out from Yaraka the man who drove the hired car to Gurner's Hotel, and from him all information about his passenger."

Cox noted it in his little pocket-book. Then, looking up, he surmised: "Funny Gurner never mentioned it to me."

"It's strange. I shall have to look into it. Now in Gurner's dossier you say he has been the licensee of the roadside hotel for forty-one years. He married in 1899, and his wife died last year. He employs an aboriginal as groom, a half-caste girl as maid, and his sister is the cook and housekeeper. What character has the black?"

"Neither good nor bad."

"Well, then, the maid?"

"She is a little loose."

"The sister?"

"Decent old sort and a good cook, although she's almost blind and hard of hearing."

"Oh! What about Gurner?"

"I've never had trouble with him," Cox admitted. "He and his sister run the place all right. Gurner drinks a little. He has never made a fortune out of his pub, but he's always made a fair living. Bit of a sportsman and runs a car as well as the truck with which he carts beer from Golden Dawn. He is always up to the minute with his fees, and he is the poll clerk on election days. Lovitt, the constable, takes a duty run out there once a week."

Bony added to the pile of cigarette-ash in his slipper lying on the table.

"I want you to go there and make inquiries," he said. "Say that you are after a car reported stolen from Winton and heading west. I want to know what traffic passed that hotel during the night that the aeroplane was stolen. The following night as well."

"Very well."

"Another dossier concerns the telephone exchange girl. You give her name as Berle Saunders. I suppose it is quite a coincidence that her Christian name is the same as that of the young woman whose child is being maintained by Owen Oliver?"

"Yes, I think so," Cox readily answered. "The girl Saunders and her brother, who is the night operator, are the daughter and son of Saunders who owns one of the stores and runs the butchery business."

"Well, my dear man, we have to make every horse a trier. Check up on that baby and this Berle Saunders."

"All right, I will. What's on your mind? Excuse my outward lack of respect, but hang it, I haven't forgotten what you said about the possibility of my getting promotion out of this part of the country."

"I know." Bony turned directly to face him. "I have not forgotten. These dossiers are a credit to any man. Make a note. Ask Headquarters to seek information of all importers and manufacturers of explosives concerning the delivery of nitro-glycerine to a person in this district."

"Right! But why . . . ?"

"I will tell you. Loveacre's red monoplane was destroyed by the explosion of nitro-glycerine in addition to fire."

"You don't say! But why? Fire was enough, wasn't it?"

"Fire would have been sufficient, my dear Cox, but fire was an uncertain agent. The man who stole the aeroplane, who took that young woman up in it and flew her out to Emu Lake, there to jump and leave her to crash in the machine, wanted to make it certain that she and it would be destroyed by fire. But an aeroplane can crash and yet not catch fire. So he placed a canister of nitro-glycerine in the plane, knowing that the impact with the ground would most certainly explode it."

"The swine!"

"I agree with your definition." It was one of the few occasions that Bony saw the sergeant's eyes opened widely. "Did you send the telegram to the Commissioner?"

"Yes. I got Lovitt in the office. Why are you sending for that aboriginal chief?"

When Bony smiled the sting of his refusal to impart further information was withdrawn.

"As the Emperor Napoleon used to say: 'The audience is finished.' "

CHAPTER XVII

TWO LITTLE MYSTERIES

WHEN the two policemen joined Nettlefold, Elizabeth and the two doctors in the study, Nettlefold suggested drinks.

"I vote we all attend to our own wants," the genial cattleman said. "You'll find everything in the wall cabinet. I used at one time to dream of occupying a large mansion containing a real bar and an attendant barman. Now I am satisfied with something much less ornate. A barman would give the place the air of a club."

"You are a member of the Apollo Club, are you not?" queried the specialist.

"Yes. I often spend time there when I'm in Brisbane."

"Thought I saw your name on the register."

Having brought his glass back to his chair, Dr Stanisforth and the cattleman began to talk personalities. Knowles remained seated, and Bony now knew positively that the man was fighting against the craving for whisky. Why? He recalled how the man's nerves twitched late that afternoon; and that since his return he had drunk nothing stronger than tea. Well, it was unwise to stop drinking so abruptly. Over thirty pounds a month, had it not been?

"Come along," he invited the doctor. "The sergeant finds the time too early, and the others are gossiping about people far above me."

Exhibiting no sign of haste, Knowles rose to his feet.

"Not a bad idea," he agreed, outwardly calm but unable to conceal from the detective's shrewd eyes signs of the terrible inward fight.

Bony would have preferred waiting for the inevitable tea to be served, but he felt genuine sympathy for this man. Despite his weakness, Knowles was a brave and cultured English gentleman, who, from the very beginning of their acquaintance, had evinced no sign of superiority, none of that mental snobbishness he had so often met and which so hurt him.

"I suppose you find this case taking a big bite out of your time," he asked.

"Soda water?"

"Please."

The siphon fizzed.

"I am thinking of throwing up my other work so that I can devote all my time to this one," Knowles said, after vainly trying to prevent the edge of his glass from tapping against his teeth.

"Then what about your other cases. How will they get along?"

"There are very few at present, and none of a serious nature." Knowles put down his empty glass. For a moment his iron will-power deserted him. His dark eyes widened and blazed at Bony. "Are you any nearer to identifying the devil who caused that paralysis of my patient?"

The mood passed, or was conquered. The cynic regained the mastery. He poured himself out another drink.

"It is usual for a detective to say that he is in possession of an important clue," Bony lightly declared. "He does that when he is completely baffled. So far, I am completely baffled with regard to the identity of the person who so determinedly tried to commit murder; but, to employ a childish phrase, I am getting warm. I now know much more than I did when I came here, a good deal more than I knew yesterday, and more than I knew an hour ago. Are you aware of the fact that I have never yet failed to finalize a case?"

"No, I didn't know it."

"I have been successful, Doctor, because I did not graduate from a beat, because I have always declined to permit red tape to control me, and because I overlook no apparently trivial side issues. Since I took over this case I have encountered no less than three little mysteries. They may have no connexion whatever with the major mystery. Yet, on the other hand, any one of them may be the very keystone of the arch supporting the big mystery."

"Indeed! Would it be presumptuous of me to ask what they are? Perhaps I could assist in clearing up at least one."

"Well, I think you could clear up one of them, but I hesitate to put it to you, fearing that the amicable relationship between us might be severely strained. You see, it concerns yourself."

Knowles stood quite still, the fingers of his left hand halted in the act of twisting the short ends of his moustache.

"The solution of the little mystery which concerns me would be of assistance in solving the major mystery?"

"I do not say that it would," Bony hastened to reply. "I will not say even that it would be likely. I mentioned the fact of these little mysteries because, in more than one case, a little mystery solved has enabled me to solve the big one."

"Very well. If I can clear up the mystery concerning myself I will be happy to do so on the off-chance that it will be of assistance to you in locating the devil who drugged that poor girl."

Bony leaned towards the doctor.

"Do not think that what I am about to ask is actuated by idle curiosity. The mystery concerning you is this: Why have you resolved to combat and to defeat the craving for spirits?"

In an instant the cloak of his national reserve fell about the doctor.

"I cannot see that that is any business of . . ."

"I agree, my dear Doctor," Bony interrupted. "It may be no business of mine, but it is just possible that it is. If you would rather not clear it up for me let us drop the subject at once. I have no desire to offend you or to intrude where I have no right. Shall we have another drink? I do not usually take more——"

Dr Knowles relaxed. There was a trace of eagerness in his voice when he said:

"Bony, I'll tell you. I'll tell you why I am struggling to cut out the whisky. Were I a criminal I would find pleasure in being arrested by you. A long time ago—years and years—I was in the third year of my medical course. That was in 1915. I was madly in love with a girl of my own age, and one night we were returning to her home at Ealing, outside London, having been to a theatre, when we were caught in an air raid. She was killed in my arms by a bomb splinter while we were taking shelter in a doorway.

"Her death profoundly shocked me, and I often doubt if since that night I have ever been really sane. I interrupted my medical course to join the Flying Corps. I began to drink, and I have drunk heavily since then because I have not the courage to commit suicide. I did well in the Air Force because the more I drank the better I could fly and fight. After the war I gained my medical degree, but I have only been playing at doctoring. Until now! Bony, the girl lying so still in that room is the exact double of the girl I loved and who died in my arms."

Seated in a wicker chair outside the door of the south veranda, Ted Sharp smoked and idly watched the red lightning flickering along the western horizon. Nettlefold strolled out.

"Storm coming up, Ted?" he asked the boss stockman.

"Yes, it looks like it, Mr Nettlefold. They'll be early this year. Might have one to-night—to be followed by two or three days of fine weather before the storms really set in."

"Humph! Well, we'll have to get the breeding cows out of the south river paddock into Emu Lake paddock. I've a mind, too, to put into Emu Lake the breeders now in Watson's. Think you could start the muster of the river paddock to-morrow?"

"Whenever you wish. There's Alec and Ned Story, and Harry and Syl here, and there's Ned Hamlin and the two blacks out at Faraway Bore. They could ride across and meet us."

"Very well. I'll telephone Ned Hamlin right away. You can take two of the blacks camped down the creek. They were asking to be put on only yesterday. I'd like to get all the breeders into Emu Lake, and I think we should delay no longer. We might get the storms at any time, and they might give us a local flood like we had in 1925."

"Yes, they might," Ted agreed.

"All right, then! You can get off to bed and have a real sleep. I will do guard duty to-night."

"Not a bit necessary. I slept all to-day. I couldn't sleep if I did go to bed. You still think it wise to maintain a guard? That feller isn't likely to make another attempt."

"Bony says that it's more than likely."

"Has he found out anything?"

"Quite a lot. I cannot tell you just what, because he told me in confidence. Bill Sikes is about the cleverest tracker I know, but this Bony can run rings round him. He was asking me about you a moment before I came out. Wants a word with you."

"Oh! What about?"

"That I don't know. I'll tell him you're here. Now I'll wake up Ned Hamlin about to-morrow's muster. Good night!"

"Good night, Mr Nettlefold."

The cattleman went inside, and presently Bony stepped out.

"Good evening, Mr Sharp!" he said in greeting.

"Ah, good evening, Mr Bonaparte! Looks like a storm coming."

"I earnestly hope that it does not rain. By the way, everyone calls me Bony."

Ted Sharp chuckled.

"And everyone calls me Ted," he countered. "I'll get another chair if you want to pitch for a while."

"Please do not trouble. I can sit on the ground here."

The detective made himself easy on the ground and proceeded to fashion the inevitable cigarette. He could not see the other's face, but he liked Sharp's voice.

"I understand that you come from the Warrego, down

in New South Wales. I know the Wyatts down there. Do you?"

"Who told you that I came from the Warrego?" Sharp asked with evident surprise.

"Oh! I really don't know. Someone. I was wondering if you know anything about sheep," Bony replied airily.

"A little," the other admitted cautiously. "Why?"

"Will you give me the benefit of your experience in this district?"

"There appears to be no reason why I shouldn't."

"Thank you! I felt sure that you would be willing to assist me. I want you to tell me why you did *not* go to Mitchell's Well on the night of 28 October, and why you *did* go to Gurner's Hotel."

The flickering lightning dulled by distance though it was, revealed to Bony the other's tense face and taut figure. When another investigator would have figuratively jumped in to follow up the advantage gained by surprise, Bony remained silent.

"I'll tell you," Sharp presently decided. "I slipped across to the hotel to get a bottle of whisky. It was a warm night, you understand, and I felt like a drink, but Mr Nettlefold has a strict rule against it."

"Was that why you rang up Ned Hamlin to back your story of having gone to Mitchell's Well?"

"Yes. You see, I wouldn't have Mr Nettlefold know about it for anything."

"So far as that is concerned, it is no affair of mine, but when you went to Gurner's Hotel expressly to interview an unknown stranger it becomes my concern."

"So you've found *that* out, too, have you?" Sharp exclaimed harshly.

"Of course!" assented Bony, as though it was but a perfectly natural sequence of events. "Who was that man, and what was your business with him?"

"I am not going to tell you."

"Oh, why not? I shall eventually find out what I want to know, but it will occupy valuable time."

"It will take you all your life," snapped the boss stockman.

"No, it won't," Bony said confidently, and then, when Sharp abruptly got to his feet: "Sit down, please! I have not finished with you, yet."

"I don't intend to answer your questions," the younger man burst out passionately. "My private affairs have nothing to do with your case, and therefore I am not going to discuss them with a confounded half-caste."

"Sit down, man, and don't be a fool," urged Bony politely. "You may be dealing with a half-caste, but you are also dealing now with an intelligence—an intelligence having the powers of a police officer."

"I don't care a damn about that."

"There are some detectives, I know, who do not respect confidences. I am not one of them. I take a pride in being an honourable man. What I wish you to tell me would be treated with strict confidence should it have no bearing on my investigations."

"Well, it has no bearing. Because it is so, I do not intend to say anything. The fact that you are a detective doesn't give you the right to pry into everyone's private affairs."

"Permit me to differ," Bony said, again politely. "In ordinary circumstances I would not attempt to pry into your private affairs, but the circumstances of the present case are far from ordinary. In this sparsely-populated district, a crime has been committed. Within fifty miles are about only a dozen men. It is absolutely essential that each one of those men is proved innocent of complicity. On the night that the crime was committed, you meet a stranger in mysterious circumstances—very mysterious circumstances. You trouble to lie to me about it, and you further trouble to ring up Ned Hamlin and ask him to back your lie that you visited Mitchell's Well.

"If your business with the mysterious stranger is perfectly innocent," continued the detective, "why hesitate, now that you know I know about the interview, to state the facts of it? Of far greater importance than the discovery and apprehension of the person who stole the aeroplane and destroyed it, as well as the person who poisoned the patient's brandy, is the acquisition of the knowledge of the drug given her and its antidote in order to save her life."

"My private affairs have nothing——" Sharp began again.

"I'm glad to hear that. You will, then, tell me who the man was who arrived at Gurner's Hotel and occupied a private sitting-room."

"I will not tell you. You can go to the devil!" Sharp almost shouted. "If you suspect me of being the criminal——"

"We can do nothing else but suspect you," came Elizabeth's voice from the doorway behind them. "I'm sorry, but I could not avoid overhearing what you were saying. Your voices were raised."

Bony was now on his feet, and side by side they faced the white-clad figure standing holding back the spring-hinged door. When she again spoke, her voice was cold.

"You should apologize to Mr Bonaparte for referring slightingly to his birth, Ted."

Beneath the coldness of her voice, Bony thought he detected soft entreaty.

"If Mr Sharp would only be open with me, my investigation would be materially assisted," he said slowly. "As for my being a half-caste—well, that is entirely a personal matter. As I pointed out, Mr Sharp's business at Gurner's Hotel may have no connexion with my present case, but there is the possibility that it may. I must know where every person in the vicinity of Emu Lake was on that vital night, and what he was doing. Come, Mr Sharp, do not make matters harder for me."

"I can assure you that my business that night had no connexion with the aeroplane and the drugged girl."

"In that case, be reasonable and give Mr Bonaparte the information he requires. Can't you see, Ted, that by refusing to speak you are forcing suspicion on yourself."

"I shall say nothing. Oh, can't you understand, Elizabeth?"

"I am afraid I cannot, Mr Sharp."

The formal address obviously stung. Lightning revealed the effect of the sting to the watchful Bony, and he thought he guessed another Coolibah secret.

"No, I cannot understand why you refuse to account for your actions that night when, as Bony says, everything—everyone's energies must be directed to discovering what is necessary to enable the doctors to save that helpless girl's life. If it is something digraceful . . ."

"Eliz'beth, please!"

"Miss Nettlefold!"

"Oh, all right! I . . . I can't say what my business was that night. To do so would ruin all my plans, smash my ambitions. It would drag in innocent people. No, I can say nothing."

When Elizabeth spoke again her voice was as brittle as thin ice.

"I must go in to my patient—good night, Bony."

The two men stood watching her dimly-white figure beyond the fly-gauze of the veranda door, a dainty figure outlined by the soft light within the patient's room.

"Damn you! Why the hell can't you mind your own affairs?" snarled Ted Sharp. He strode away into the darkness, leaving Bony to sigh:

"How like the Commissioner!"

CHAPTER XVIII

THE GUESTS DEPART

NEXT morning the gathering at Coolibah broke up. Dr Stanisforth again conferred with Dr Knowles, suggesting a certain course of treatment which might overcome the patient's condition. For the first time in years, the Golden Dawn doctor took his morning tea without a liberal addition of whisky and, in consequence, his nerves were visibly tormented.

The consultation took place in the morning-room and, at its close, the specialist scribbled on his prescription pad. Tearing off the leaf, he presented it to Knowles, saying:

"We will agree that it is not usual for a medical man to give unasked-for advice. I knew a man—an extraordinary case—who had sufficient mental power abruptly to stop taking morphia. He died. You will have to take care of yourself. Do not regard me as an interfering old fool, but make up the mixture I have prescribed for you and curtail the *other* mixture gradually, not suddenly. Now I must be off. I would like to keep in touch with this case, and I would consider it kind of you if you let me know how it goes. If I am able I will come out again in a fortnight's time."

"Good!" said Knowles, with a faint catch in his voice. "I will be following you to Golden Dawn with Sergeant Cox, and I will make up the prescription you have given me."

"Do. And have a drink now, old man. You must not shock your nervous system too severely. Good-bye—and good luck!"

While Elizabeth and her father were farewelling the specialist from the east veranda, Knowles was in his room measuring out a stiff dose of "that other mixture," and Bony was seated in the study in conference with Sergeant Cox.

"I would be pleased," he was saying, "if you would sound the Golden Dawn butcher to find out from whom he has purchased sheep and when, and to whom he has sold his skins over the last five weeks. You made notes relative to the nitro-glycerine and the examination of the people at Gurner's Hotel?"

"Yes. I will attend to that."

"Good! I may be away for several days on a walkabout undertaken with modern transport. Should anything of importance crop up do not call for me. I will communicate with you from time to time. Meanwhile keep your eye on that exchange girl and the night operator, her brother. I cannot lose sight of the fact that the destruction of the aeroplane, following so closely on its discovery by Nettlefold, may be due to some leakage in the telephone system. Either through the exchange operator, or by the line being tapped. Is there a policeman at St Albans?"

"A mounted man is stationed there."

"Perhaps, then, after dealing with Gurner about road traffic, you could run on into St Albans and ascertain if a strange car passed through there one week or two weeks prior to 28 October, when the plane was stolen. I would also like to know if there were any unusual visitors to the place."

"Right! I'll do that."

The door was opened to admit Dr Knowles.

"Hope I am not disturbing you, but I rather want to know the time you are leaving, Cox."

"By no means, Doctor. Come in," invited Bony, on his feet and beaming friendliness. "How is the patient this morning?"

Knowles crossed the room after closing the door and seated himself. His hands now were less palsied. Beneath his eyes, however, were patches of significant hue.

"The condition of the patient remains unchanged," he replied in tones that were almost harsh. Regarding Bony steadily, he added: "Yesterday afternoon you said you thought you knew some method by which we could know what is in the patient's mind."

"That is so," agreed Bony gravely.

"Then why the devil don't you out with it? If you can read her mind, why don't you?"

"I did not state that I could read her mind, Doctor. But I have sent for a man who I think is able to do so."

"Ah!" Knowles sighed, as though experiencing relief. "When will he be here?"

"That I am unable to say," Bony replied regretfully. "I will confide in you both when I really should confide in no one. The man for whom I have sent lives north-west of Burketown, on the southern tip of the Gulf of Carpentaria. His name is Illawalli, and he is a tribal chief of great importance and power. He is in possession of inherited secrets which are older than the Pyramids. By merely touching a man he is able to read that man's mind. I know this because he has demonstrated his power to me. I am glad to observe that neither of you are laughing. More than once he had offered to impart his secrets to me. In possession of them, I might easily become the world's greatest detective, but he imposes a condition I cannot accept.

"The date of his arrival will depend on whether he can be quickly located. He may be with his own tribe, or he may be with a distant tribe, not his own but of his nation."

"Every effort will be exerted to locate this extraordinary blackfellow?" Knowles pressed.

"We may depend on that being so."

"But could I not locate him and bring him here direct much more quickly?"

"By this time, Doctor, I feel sure an aeroplane already will have been dispatched for him. Meanwhile I may at any hour put my hands on the man responsible for the patient's condition. By the way, Mr Nettlefold, at my request, has relieved Sharp from night guard duty."

"Is it essential?" Cox asked.

"I believe it to be very much so. Do you know of any one who could be trusted to do it?"

Cox pondered. Then:

"My brother-in-law lives across at Yaraka," he said slowly. "He was once in the Force, and had to retire when one foot was permanently injured. He is still an active man, however."

"Ring him up and find out if he can leave for Coolibah to-day."

While the sergeant was busy with the telephone, the detective asked Knowles if he would be remaining long at Golden Dawn.

"No. I have to obtain certain drugs and stimulants proposed by Dr Stanisforth," Knowles explained. "It is my intention to fly back this afternoon. If Cox's brother-in-law is unable to come, I will do guard duty. What leads you to think that another attempt will be made on that girl's life?"

"Intuition. Probably you do not believe in intuition, but my wife does, and I am a firm believer, too. The purpose of the attempt to incinerate Miss Double M in Loveacre's red monoplane was to silence her for ever. While she lives there is the possibility that medical science will cure her of her paralysis, and her silence will then be terminated."

"My brother-in-law will leave Yaraka at once," Sergeant Cox interposed from the telephone. "I did not tell him what he is wanted for."

"That was as well." Bony rose. "I have to be off. I have borrowed Mr Nettlefold's spare car."

"And we must get on our way, too, Doctor," the sergeant said, heaving himself to his feet. "Your bag packed?"

"I am taking nothing but a dispatch bag. I am ready now," Knowles said like a man who finds inactivity unbearable.

The sergeant would have liked much to know how Bony intended to follow his planned walkabout, but by now he knew the uselessness of asking questions. He and the doctor having departed, Bony passed to his room to roll a swag, and his host went across to the store to set out rations and cooking utensils. Before leaving the house, the detective interviewed its mistress.

"I shall be away for a few days, Miss Nettlefold," he told her with smiling gravity. "You need have no uneasiness on the score of Mr Sharp's absence, because, later to-day, an ex-policeman will arrive to protect the house at night."

"But my father——"

"Your father has quite enough to do. Now I must be off. Hope with me that the seasonal thunderstorms will not come down from the north-west for at least another week. And do not relinquish hope regarding your patient. I have never yet failed to finalize a case. I see no reason why I should fail to finalize this one. *Au revoir!*"

"Good-bye!" she said slowly, returning his smile.

Five minutes later she saw him driving away along the track to Golden Dawn.

"I'd like to know what he's up to now," said her father, when he joined her from seeing Bony off. "Knowles is flying back this afternoon. An ex-policeman is coming to take Ted's place. They appear to think that another attack will be made on the girl's life."

"If it is, I will be ready," Elizabeth assured him. "I am going on night duty from to-night. Hetty has been unable to sleep properly these hot days."

"Humph! Anyway, this affair has made life interesting. I think, though, I would prefer the quietness of ordinary times."

"I do not. If only that poor girl was just ordinarily ill I would be enjoying it all."

For some hours, at least, John Nettleford experienced the quietness of ordinary times. He laboured in his office for the rest of the morning. About four o'clock, when he was alone at afternoon tea, Dr Knowles rang up to say that he was leaving Golden Dawn immediately in his aeroplane and unhurriedly the cattleman drove out to the natural landing ground to await his arrival.

Seated in the car, he smoked away the waiting minutes. He heard the engine before he spotted the black-varnished plane high against the colour-stained sky. It came dropping earthwards like a falling leaf, down and down to within a thousand feet, and then it rolled out in a zooming curve, shot skyward in a perfect loop, circled and approached the 'drome at speed. Its wheels tore up the grey ground in dusty clouds, and then it tipped forward; tried to bury itself with screaming protest. When finally it settled, the propeller was smashed and the under-carriage was wiped away.

Before Nettlefold could reach the wrecked machine, the doctor had climbed out and was awaiting him.

"Can you tell me, Nettlefold," he roared angrily, "why I can't fly when I'm sober?"

CHAPTER XIX

AT TINTANOO

THE motionless air vibrated with thunder which, to human ears, hardly sounded like thunder at all. The incessant vibration seemed to be less reality than a threat aimed at the soft peace of past nights. Here and there, on the arena of the sky, the aerial combatants were waiting for the order to join in battle array and begin the titanic struggle.

Napoleon Bonaparte was driving the Coolibah runabout car, and because he was alone he sang. Since leaving Coolibah a week before, he had done much driving and much singing, and now while crossing the endless river channels and their banks on his way to visit John Kane, his mood was a light one. Time had given him increased confidence in his ability to untangle the knots of this skein of drama precisely as time had shown to men the best course to follow across the extraordinary Diamantina River.

Approximately in the centre of the river, he stopped the car on the summit of a broad ribbon of ground dividing two channels, and there he rolled a cigarette. To the north and to the south the intertwining channels twisted beneath the coolibah trees.

A little to the north ranged the telephone poles connecting St Albans with Golden Dawn. They carried three wires: one terminating at Tintanoo; another ending at Gurner's Hotel; the third reaching the exchange at St

Albans. The poles withstood the onslaughts of many a vast, sliding, brown flood, but often the communications were destroyed by one or two of the poles succumbing to the torrent in alliance with the termites.

Driving a car across this river was a tiring job. Bony might have found it less fatiguing had the track been straight, but it twisted and turned incessantly, and demanded much braking and much gear-shifting. Presently, every time he was heaved above a channel bank, he could see ever more clearly the red-roofed homestead of Tintanoo sprawled beneath big bloodwoods growing on a spur of stony ground thrusting towards the river between the lower sand-dunes.

He was still on the switchback when the station dogs raced to meet and escort him up the sharp incline, past well-built stockyards, round the end of commodious men's quarters, and to the gate giving entry to the short path leading to the main veranda door of the rambling house.

Here was no litter, no untidiness, no decay. The supply of paint was obviously plentiful. Beyond the men's quarters two silent windmills were raising water into several large iron tanks set high on sturdy platforms.

The door in the fly-gauze protecting the veranda was swung outward by a young man who unhurriedly advanced to the fence gate, there to lean against it and to survey Bony. He was tall and well built, and he wore riding togs, which is not usual among bushmen. Bony noticed that his left eye was made of glass.

"Looking for any one?" he asked, in the tone often adopted towards people considered to be inferior.

"Ah—yes," assented the detective as though he now saw the young man for the first time. "I am looking for Mr John Kane."

The young man's right eye stared, and his head jerked towards the office building. One hand rested on the gate, revealing that the top of the second finger had been removed.

"You'll find him over there, I think," he said, and turned back to the house.

With a subdued smile playing about the corners of his mouth, Bony strolled to the white-painted, wood-and-iron building. Mounting the three steps, he crossed the veranda to enter a business-like office wherein a man in his shirt sleeves was working at a ledger.

"Well, what do *you* want?" he inquired without looking up.

"I wish to meet Mr John Kane."

"What for?"

"If you will kindly tell him that Detective-Inspector Bonaparte would——"

Brown eyes raised their gaze to survey the caller. Large teeth were revealed by a quick smile. The man rose with alacrity, and the left corner of his mouth twitched twice. When he advanced his right hand was outstretched.

"I am John Kane," he announced affably. "I am happy to meet you."

"Thank you! I have called hoping you may be able to assist me."

"Certainly. Come over here and take a pew," Kane urged, adding to the warmth of his welcome by whisking a chair to face his own beside the desk. "I heard that you had come west to go into the matter of Loveacre's aeroplane. Extraordinary affair, eh? Is that girl found in it by Nettlefold any better."

"I fear not. Her condition baffles both Dr Knowles and the specialist from the city. . . . How much longer will the weather keep dry, do you think?"

"It looks like breaking to-night," prophesied the squatter. "Have a cigar? No? I don't like this backing and filling of the weather. Generally the longer the seasonal storms delay the worse they are. You will be staying the night?"

"Thank you, but I rather wanted to take a run over to St Albans."

"Oh . . . you can go there to-morrow. You'd find it no joke to be caught in a thunderstorm on the flats this side of Gurner's Hotel. Better stay."

"It is kind of you to insist. I will accept your invitation with pleasure. Sometimes it is an advantage to be a police officer," Bony remarked.

"Indeed!"

"Yes. One receives invitations. Unexpected invitations."

The squatter's brows rose, and the permanent surprise in his brown eyes was emphasized still more. Smiling, he produced whisky and glasses, and he filled a glass jug with water from a canvas bag.

"I will be frank," he promised, when seated. "I have heard that you are a clever man, and clever people are always welcomed to Tintanoo. Cox sometimes stays overnight when he comes out this way, but I find him too much like my old O.C. in the army. He's intelligent, but only within the narrow limits of his profession. My bullock driver is also an intelligent man—on the subject of bullocks. In what way can I assist you?"

Bony occupied his eyes with the rolling of a cigarette. He tried, but failed to detect, a false note in the other's voice.

"I understand that a year or two ago one of your bores suddenly ceased to gush."

"Yes, that was so. The loss of the water was a serious matter."

Still no false note. John Kane spoke with perfect frankness.

"I understand, also, that all subsequent efforts to raise water at that bore failed."

The squatter nodded before saying:

"That's so, too. I had a contractor put the bore down another fifteen hundred feet. It was then that we decided to experiment. We smashed up the rock at the bottom of the bore with a couple of charges of nitro-glycerine. Even that failed to give us a new supply. It was all rather extraordinary, because, although all the Queensland bores are dwindling in output, we have never known one suddenly to cease producing water like that particular bore of mine."

Bony was carefully packing the tobacco into the ends of the paper tube.

"Nitro-glycerine!" he echoed.

"Yes, nitro-glycerine. It is unholy stuff to handle, but the boring contractor played with it as though it were treacle. It appears that he had on several occasions used that particular explosive with varying success. Is that what you wanted to see me about?"

Bony smiled. Looking up he saw a twinkle in the brown eyes. The left corner of Kane's mouth twitched rapidly. It was an oddity that one couldn't help noticing. Normally the twitch occurred about once every ten seconds.

"It is a subject that does interest me," admitted Bony. "I take it that a certain quantity of the explosive was brought here. Was the whole or only part of it used?"

"A part only. The remainder of what was brought is still here. It is kept in a specially-excavated cellar situated about a mile out. It is too confoundedly dangerous, you know, to have lying about. A slight jolt will send it off. Not for anything would I have been the truck driver who brought it here."

"Would not dynamite have done the job?"

"That's what I asked the contractor," Kane replied without hesitation and with perfect frankness. "He explained that dynamite is less satisfactory for the work required here, but the why and the wherefore I have forgotten. It appears that nitro-glycerine is largely used on the American oilfields. I do remember that after he had used up two charges I wanted him to take the balance away, but although I offered to give it to him for nothing he said he would leave it. The stuff is still in that cellar, and I have often considered hiring an expert to touch it off. It is quite useless to me now, and a possible danger to stock grazing near it."

"It is, I am given to understand, a thick, oily substance, faintly yellow in colour. Have you seen it?"

"Yes, I saw it when the contractor was here to handle it," Kane assented grimly. "It arrived in a carboy well packed in a crate with wood shavings. The contractor invited me to attend at the unloading. I really believe he wanted to see me get the wind up. I *was* windy, too. Having got the stuff down into the cellar without blowing us all to pieces the contractor poured some of the stuff into a tin canister of a size to fit within the bore casing. We then went out to the bore in the car. I went grey-haired on the trip. The contractor lowered the canister down the casing with copper wire, and, when it reached the bottom, he touched it off with a battery. There was a dull, muffled explosion, but no water came up. The bore casing was dry right down to the bottom."

"You have not used any of the balance of the explosive left over?"

"No, of course not! Why do you ask?"

"One moment. On examining the carboy in the cellar would it be possible for you to tell if any of the explosive has been removed since the contractor took the amount he wanted?"

"Well, I don't know," Kane answered slowly. "I would if a large quantity had been taken. I do not know how many gallons the carboy holds, but I can be sure in stating that the contractor took out about two gallons."

"I wonder!" Bony gazed pensively out through the open window to the cool white bungalow house. There was now no necessity to strain one's hearing to hear the muttering thunder. The black shadows of western Queensland's days were now no more, the piling clouds having at last defeated the sun.

Swiftly their gaze met. "I have reason to think, Mr Kane, that a quantity of nitro-glycerine may have been removed from your store," the detective said. "It is important to know for certain either way. Might I trespass further on your kindness by asking you to take me to the cellar to examine that nitro-glycerine?"

"If you wish to go, yes. But there is to-morrow."

"I hate to disturb you, but . . . well, we are certainly going to have an electrical storm, and should a lightning flash set off the explosive we should never know if any of it has or has not been taken, and it may happen, you know."

The squatter rose. He was smiling and chuckling.

"All right! I hate going near the damned stuff, but it doesn't do to fear fear. Come along. We'll slip out there in my car."

Outside, when they saw the western sky, he added: "We'll

have to hurry. That storm will break in another ten minutes, and I am not going to be down in that cellar when it does."

Within the corrugated-iron motor shed, Bony saw two trucks, two powerful motor-cycles, a Dodge car, and a single-seater Bentley. Kane took the wheel of the last mentioned, pressed down the starter button and, before the engine could warm up properly, they had shot out of the motor shed.

"Motor-cycles appear to be in general use on stations now," Bony remarked.

"Only one of those bikes is mine. The other belongs to young Oliver, of Windy Creek. You'll meet him at dinner. Hang on!"

The advice was sound. The seat-back hit Bony's shoulders when the car increased its speed. They were passing a blur of fence posts, and when Bony was wedging himself into his seat he noted that the speedo was registering sixty-four miles an hour.

"Thank heaven a man can travel at his own pace on his own roads," Kane shouted, swinging the car round a bend in the track. "We'll have a job beating that storm. This bus is a little sluggish as yet. You were wise to decide to stay the night."

Bony was flung against the door when the machine skidded round yet another bend, and then he was almost hurled against the dash when it was braked sharply to a halt.

"Here's the cellar!" Kane announced calmly. "Come on!"

Bony followed the squatter to a sunken pit, roofed with iron above ground level. Steps had been cut into the hard clay soil beneath the thin top layer of wind-blown sand, and down these Kane led the way to the stout wooden door which he unlatched.

"I dislike even breathing down here," he said. "There it is! If it went off we wouldn't know we were dead."

He directed the beam of an electric torch to the far end of the cellar, and Bony saw the packing-case. The side facing them had been removed, and there on its nest of wood shavings squatted the carboy.

"One moment, please! Your torch," requested Bony.

With the torch directed with apparent carelessless at the floor, he strode to the carboy. His eyes were gleaming when he came to crouch before the lethal monster imprisoned within the huge bottle. The glass was covered with fingerprints, oily prints first brought into sharp relief by the dust which subsequently had settled on them, and then dulled by successive layers of dust.

"Well!" he cried to the squatter who remained at the door. "The carboy is empty."

"Empty!" echoed John Kane. With greater confidence, he joined the detective, bending down to examine better the interior of the carboy. "Good Lord! So it is! Come on! Even that thunder might set off the smear of the stuff still on the inside of the glass."

"Yes, we'll go," Bony said gravely. "The storm is nearly above us. Like you, I fear to breathe."

With almost indecent haste for a grown man, Kane stepped to the door and ran up the steps. Bony remained two seconds longer. There was one particular fingerprint which aroused his interest. It was unlike the others. It was roughly circular, and across it were two distinct lines.

CHAPTER XX

THUNDER

THUNDER shook the Tintanoo house to its very foundations, and the lightning caused the lights to flicker, while Bony dressed with unusual care before dining. Beyond the open window of his bedroom, huge raindrops fell on the veranda roofing. Yet the worst of the storm was past, and, for all its commotion, remarkably little rain had fallen. Between the major thunder rolls of the nearer disturbance, his ears caught the rumblings of storms far to the west and north.

While dressing, Bony hummed a popular tune. The peculiar print on the carboy was an exceptionally fortunate and important discovery. It appeared to indicate that this stubborn mystery was at last giving way to his assault. In its dark fog, he thought he now could distinguish one personality among several half-formed figures. Owen Oliver!

The expert fire investigator had stated that Captain Loveacre's monoplane had been disintegrated by exploding nitro-glycerine. Then Cox had received and had passed on a report that nitro-glycerine had been sold to a man named Barton, a bore contractor, for use at Tintanoo Station, some considerable time before the aeroplane was stolen. Other explosives were used extensively for mining. They are reasonably safe to handle, and almost all western stores sell them. But nitro-glycerine is an entirely different proposition. No person would purchase and use it unless for some special purpose such as "bore shooting." Its sale, in consequence, is narrowly limited and restricted by stringent regulations. Excepting this Barton no person in western Queensland had sought permission to purchase this particular explosive since the year 1921.

John Kane now said that a quantity of nitro-glycerine down in his specially-constructed cellar had been removed without his knowledge and permission. It was reasonably certain that the nitro-glycerine which had assisted to destroy Captain Loveacre's aeroplane had come from that cellar. And then the print of the deformed finger! Only the keenness of his vision had enabled him to see it. One with ordinary eyesight would not have noticed it: more especially if he was particularly nervous of the monster chained within the bottle.

No one had visited the cellar after the sand cloud had passed by. Bony was assured of that by the ground at the head of the steps. All the fingerprints on the glass bottle had been registered prior to the sand cloud. Of that Bony was sure. The question presenting itself for answer was whether Owen Oliver had visited the cellar to steal the remaining portion of the explosive, or to take the remainder of it with the sanction of its owner. That he had visited the cellar was proved by the imprint of his partly-amputated finger on the carboy.

If he had not stolen it, then John Kane had sanctioned its removal. The object of its removal could be assumed with reasonable confidence. A further question arose, one that Bony found harder to answer. Without proof and without the aid of his uncanny intuition, he could not bring his mind to accept the fact—or even the theory—of John Kane's participation in the conspiracy against Miss Double

M. Not for many a year had a man's personality so baffled him.

When the recent storm was approaching Golden Dawn, and when another was far advanced from St Albans, the detective sat down to dine with three people. His host wore now a light black alpaca jacket. The elderly woman who acted as hostess had been introduced to him as Mrs MacNally, "who has been in the service of the family since before I was born," said Kane. She was eagle-eyed, and the years had caused her mouth to retreat and her nose and chin to advance. Her command of the aboriginal maids who brought in the dishes was firmly enthroned.

The last of the trio was Owen Oliver. He was dressed as he was when Bony first saw him, and his actions appeared to be a little too familiar for those of a rare guest at Tintanoo. Of medium height, his features were regular and finely moulded, but bore signs of dissipation. The brilliant hazel eye was well matched by the artificial one. After one swift glance at the shortened second finger of the right hand, Bony studiously refrained from exhibiting any interest in it.

Between twenty-four and twenty-seven, Bony thought him to be. His attitude to the detective was now less markedly superior, but still there was in it the almost unmasked hostility to his colour in the mind of one incapable of delving beneath the surface of things, whether of a man's skin or a problem of metaphysics.

The meal was plain but well cooked and well served. The table decorations were costly and tasteful. The large room was furnished with those sombre but solid period pieces associated with the reign of Queen Victoria; heavy, cumbersome furniture brought to this far-western outpost in the eighteen-seventies on bullock wagons. They were the years when furniture was furniture—furniture built to last for centuries, furniture prized as heirlooms.

The conversation began when Mrs MacNally inquired after the patient at Coolibah. Her voice was pleasingly soft —a voice trained in "a school for the daughters of gentlemen."

"Now the specialist has seen her, Dr Knowles is hopeful of saving her life," Bony lied. "The unfortunate young woman is so completely paralysed that she is unable to eat, unable even to open and close her eyes. Dr Stanisforth suggested a course of treatment which Dr Knowles is giving her."

"I've never heard anything like it," Mrs MacNally exclaimed. "Mark my words, there is something fishy behind it all. Mrs Greyson called in the other day, and she told me that it has created quite a stir in the district."

"Well, the circumstances are peculiar, to say the least," Kane reminded them. "No one knows her, where she comes from, what she was doing in the aeroplane, and how it got to Emu Lake."

"Wanted to steal it, I suppose," suggested Mrs MacNally placidly. "Young girls these days are always aping the men. This one learned to fly an aeroplane, and then she couldn't resist stealing one. Joy-riding, they call it. Plain theft, I say! Up she went in it, and then something happened to the machinery and she was injured when it came to ground. It is her spine, more than likely. The spine is the most delicate part of the body. I remember Mr Kane's father being thrown by a horse against a stockyard post, and he was laid up helpless for nearly a month."

"Was the specialist able to diagnose the cause of the paralysis?" asked John Kane, the perfect host.

"He gave it as his opinion that the young woman had been drugged," replied Bony.

"Drugged!" echoed Mrs McNally. "Well, well, to be sure! The young women these days are too fast, what with cocktails and cigarettes."

"Mr Bonaparte said that she had been drugged, not that she drugged herself," the squatter pointed out. "There is there a subtle distinction. You know, Mr Bonaparte, that is extraordinary. It implies that someone drugged her and put her into Captain Loveacre's aeroplane. Dashed if I can understand why."

"The whole affair is most baffling," admitted Bony. "There is no known motive, or even one on which speculation may be based. If the person responsible for drugging her wished to kill her, why take her up in an aeroplane containing a canister of your nitro-glycerine?"

"Yes, why?"

"I fear that my investigation has not proceeded as rapidly as I could have wished," Bony admitted gravely. "If the person responsible for her drugging wished to kill her, as I said just now, why not knock her on the head and bury her? Why stage such a spectacular drama? The Air Accidents Investigation Committee have reported that Loveacre's monoplane was destroyed by fire and by nitro-glycerine. I am now sure that a quantity of your stock of the explosive was placed in the machine to make it certain that it would be destroyed, and the young woman with it."

"Then it is a case of attempted murder?" offered Kane, astonishment plain upon his face.

"It appears to be. If only the young woman could speak my task would be made much easier. As it is, I am working completely in the dark. However, should Dr Knowles cure her—and he is hopeful of doing so—then we shall know all about her and what happened before she was found at Emu Lake."

"You think, then, that someone kidnapped her, put her into the machine he stole at Golden Dawn, put some of my explosive into the machine, too, flew her out to the vicinity of Emu Lake, and then jumped clear to let the machine crash?" Kane pressed.

Bony nodded his agreement.

"In that case, the thief must know this district pretty well?"

"Yes, he knows the country much better than I do. On the other hand, any person knowing the country so intimately would surely be known by other residents. They would know that he could fly an aeroplane. And I have been assured that the only people here able to fly an aeroplane are Dr Knowles and yourself."

John Kane regarded Bony with steady scrutiny. Owen Oliver was watching him with almost equal intensity.

"That is so!" Kane admitted. "And thank goodness both the doctor and I were in Golden Dawn the night the machine was stolen, and that we both were among those who rushed out to see—or rather to hear—the machine departing."

Bony smiled.

"I suppose it created quite a stir?"

"It did. The sound of the engine could not possibly be mistaken for a car engine. Everyone turned out in their night attire. I collided with Knowles, and we rushed round to the back of the hotel with about fifty other people." Kane sighed with mock relief. "And I could have been placed so awkwardly," he pointed out. "I could have been held up on a bush track by a faulty car, or I could have been away on a tour of inspection, when to have proved an alibi would have been next to impossible."

"Might not the airman, like the girl, have come into the district? The girl is a complete stranger here, by all accounts," interposed Owen Oliver, speaking for the first time.

"But that does not wipe out the fact that the pilot must have known this part of the country well," argued the squatter.

The approaching storm, heralded by its thunder rolls, was drawing near. Although the meal had not arrived at the coffee stage, Oliver pushed back his chair and rose.

"Please excuse me, Mrs MacNally, I must be off," he said. "I promised Dad I would be home to-night because of a muster to-morrow. There may be a lot of rain in this storm coming up."

"If you must go, Mr Oliver . . ."

"Yes, if you must," added Kane regretfully. "You'll have to ride like the dickens, though."

"Oh, I'll beat it all right," the younger man assured them.

Concerned for his departing guest, the squatter rose, too. Oliver shook hands with Mrs MacNally, but nodded coolly to Bony. Kane went out with him. When the door closed behind them, Bony turned to Mrs MacNally.

"How did Mr Oliver come to lose his eye?"

"Oh! He got it poked out when he was smashed up in a motor-cycle accident—hurt the part of one finger, too," she readily explained. "He's fast, that young man. Such a pity, too, for his old father is a fine gentleman, and his mother is one of the real Kennedys."

"The artificial eye is a good match for the real one, don't you think?"

"I haven't noticed it either way." Mrs MacNally leaned back in her chair, her dark eyes calmly observing the guest. She spoke with the forthright directness of her age. "He's a young man I do not like. He is too vain, too sarcastic, too sly. The last time he was here was on my birthday. No, I do not like him."

Bony smiled at the stiff old lady. "Might I ask how many birthdays you have spent at Tintanoo?"

"Now you are becoming personal, Mr Bonaparte," she told him archly. "You will be wanting to know my age next. Anyway, I'll tell you. I came here in 1884 to be a companion for Mrs Kane. It was the year that my husband died and the year before Mr John was born. Mr Charles was born on 28 October 1891. Oh me! A rampageous scamp was Mr Charles, but a nice boy notwithstanding. You would have liked the father. He was a great gentleman, even though his temper was so uncertain. And now he has gone, and his saintly wife, and poor Mr Charles and his wife. No, I shall not see many more October twenty-eights."

"Nonsense, Mrs MacNally," Bony assured her gallantly —even as his mind accepted the fact that Owen Oliver had been staying at Tintanoo the day prior to the night that the red monoplane was stolen. Had he taken a quantity of John Kane's nitro-glycerine on the occasion of that visit?"

Mrs MacNally certainly had strengthened concrete suspicions.

From without came the roar of a motor-cycle engine. Bony was listening politely to Mrs MacNally detailing the sins of the Kanes. A pounding of thunder submerged the noise of the motor-engine, and when again he heard it, distance had softened its harshness.

The storm arrived to shake the house and rattle the roof with raindrops. Still the heavy rain held off; the expected downpour did not materialize.

Later in the evening Bony sought permission to use the telephone. He raised Coolibah from the office. Kane heard all that he said to Mr Nettlefold, and what he did hear puzzled him. Bony asked that a spare tube be sent the next day to Faraway Bore for him to pick up.

CHAPTER XXI

THE CONFERENCE

THE humidity was uncomfortably high on 24 November, when Bony drove the utility into Golden Dawn from the direction of Windy Creek Station. It was a little before noon and the heavy clouds appeared undecided whether to coalesce and flood the world or to disperse for the day. The truck had barely halted outside the police-station when Sergeant Cox hurried out to greet the detective.

"They've found out who the girl is!" he exclaimed, his iron-grey eyes alight and his iron-grey moustache bristling more than was usual.

"That, my dear Cox, is very excellent—if excellent can be made superlative by the addition of very," Bony said gaily. "Now, into your office and let us gossip."

As soon as Bony was seated beside the sergeant's writing-table, his brown fingers became busy with tobacco and paper. Looking at them, the sergeant's brows drew together into a frown of disapproval.

"One moment!" pleaded Bony. "I have not smoked for at least half an hour. Before you begin, there are a few questions I wish to put. In your check-up of John Kane's action on the night of 28 October, what did he say he did at the time the plane was stolen?"

"That the sound of the aeroplane engine awoke him; that he then ran out of the hotel and joined others who ran to the place where the machine was moored; that he then stood with the little crowd of us until he returned to bed."

"Is that so? And what did Dr Knowles have to say about himself?"

"Dr Knowles stated that when he heard the aeroplane engine he ran out though the back of his own house to his hangar, thinking that someone was getting away with his machine. When he found that it was Captain Loveacre's monoplane which was being taken, he went back to his house and dressed. Then he came out to join the small crowd. He spoke to me."

"Very well." The cigarette now lit, the detective faced Cox squarely. "Now, please proceed."

Cox cleared his throat. Then:

"The licensee of the Masonic Hotel, Broken Hill, New South Wales, reported to the police there that the picture of the girl published in the *Barrier Miner* was recognized by his wife as that of a young woman who stayed at the hotel on the night of 20 October. She arrived by the Adelaide express, which reached the Silver City at eight-thirty that morning. During the afternoon she was visited by a young man. The following morning she paid her bill, and walked out carrying her suitcase. That was about ten o'clock. She gave her name as Muriel Markham."

Bony's eyes were gleaming. Since he offered no comment, the sergeant went on.

"A report has come through from C.I.B., Adelaide. A woman known as Muriel Markham lived with her mother at 29 Smith Street, Mitcham, up to 19 October. On 2 October her mother died, being buried on 3 October. On 19 October, all the furniture was removed to a city auction room. Character of both mother and daughter good. They were in comfortable circumstance, but did not entertain or mix with their neighbours.

"A later report from the same source says that a solicitor named Ormond had charge of the mother's estate. Everything was left to the daughter. The mother's income was derived from a pension, but from what financial institution or person, he does not know."

"Oh, yes, yes, yes!" Bony murmured. Then sharply he said: "Everything is coming out very well, if slowly. Before going on make a note. Ask C.I.B., Adelaide, to establish proof of birth of this Muriel Markham."

"Right! Anything else?"

"No. Proceed."

"Owen Oliver passed through St Albans on the track to Birdsville on 12 October. He was driving John Kane's Dodge. Kyle, the constable stationed at St Albans, is a methodical fellow. From habit, so he tells me, he notes down the numbers of all strange cars as well as those of cars owned by people not in his locality."

"Did he see this Dodge car on its return?"

"No. But then it could have passed through St Albans in the middle of the night. A policeman must sleep sometimes."

"Surely," Bony agreed. "Now let us get all this straight. A Mrs and Miss Markham live at 29 Smith Street, Mitcham. On 2 October, Mrs Markham dies, leaving the whole of her estate to her daughter. She is buried the next day. On 12 October, Owen Oliver is seen driving John Kane's Dodge car southward from St Albans. On 19 October, Miss Markham has her mother's furniture moved to an auction room, and in the evening of that day she boards the Broken Hill train. She arrives at the Masonic Hotel, Broken Hill, on 20 October, and that day is visited by a young man. The next day she leaves the hotel on foot and carrying her suitcase. And she is next seen in a red monoplane on Emu Lake on 29 October.

"The mother dies on 2 October, and on 12 October Owen Oliver leaves for Broken Hill. Ten days. Note, please. Ascertain if a letter could be sent from Mitcham to Golden Dawn, and a reply received, all within ten days. If not, then how many days it would take. When making inquiries at the post office—but no . . . What are you relations with the postmaster?"

"Friendly."

"When does he leave for lunch?"

"At one o'clock."

Since he could not see the sun, Bony asked the time. It was five minutes to twelve.

"Perhaps your son could deliver a note for the postmaster at his private residence," he suggested.

"Yes, he could on his way back to school."

"Then write a note asking him to be kind enough to drop in before returning to the office."

While the sergeant was writing, Bony rose to cross to the wall map, now back in its place, and with the point of his little finger connected the townships of Birdsville, Innamincka, Tibooburra and Tarrowangee with St Albans and Broken Hill. When Cox laid down the pen he asked him:

"If you were going to Broken Hill, would you not go via Eromanga and Thargomindah, Wanaaring and Wilcannia?"

"That track might be better, but the mileage would be higher," Cox pointed out. "I'll take this out to the wife to give to the boy. Will you stay and lunch with us?"

"On one condition," temporized Bony. "If your wife goes to no more trouble than setting an extra place."

"I'll mention the condition," conceded Cox, and tramped along to the kitchen.

Returning to his chair, Bony made yet another cigarette. Through the open, gauze-protected window drifted the low, menacing mutter of distant thunder. From much nearer came the hum of a motor car.

Cox returned to ease his bulk into his chair, and Bony asked:

"What kind of a man is this Owen Oliver?"

On the red face of the police sergeant spread an expression of disapproval.

"I never had any serious trouble with him," Cox replied. "I am glad of that on account of his people, who are thoroughly decent. Old pioneer family, you know. Young Oliver always has had more money that is good for him. He drinks a good deal, and he gambles. The girl, Mannock, he got into trouble, is not the girl Saunders. She lives in Brisbane. I never liked young Oliver, and there are few who do. Only son, and spoiled, with too much pocket-money from the beginning."

"You stress the point that he has always been used to having plenty of money," Bony cut in. "And yet, I understand, after the trouble with that Mannock girl, the father tightened his purse-strings. In fact, he has allowed his son only three pounds a week."

"Who told you that?" demanded Cox.

"The father himself. But I have met Mr Owen Oliver, and I agree with your estimate of him."

"Three pounds a week! I'll bet young Oliver spends more than three pounds a week over at the pub."

"Could he fly an aeroplane, do you think?"

"Never heard that he learned to fly," confessed Cox. "He once put in two years in a station agent's office down in

Adelaide. He might have learned to fly then, but if he had we should have heard about it. Why did you ask that?"

"Because after a long search occupying many days I discovered the wheel tracks of Loveacre's monoplane near an uninhabited hut on Windy Creek Station. The sand cloud had not blotted out the tracks. The time is accounted for —that ninety minutes it took the machine to reach the road junction from the Golden Dawn Hotel. The thief flew to that lonely hut on Windy Creek Station to pick up his passenger. Anyway, it appears so, although I found no evidence of her in the hut itself."

Silence fell. With tight lips, Sergeant Cox was staring at Bony, whom he had really suspected of joy-riding round the country instead of attending to his business. A youthful step sounded on the front veranda, and a figure flashed by the office door on its way to the kitchen. To them came a voice:

"Hullo, Mum! What's for lunch?"

The sergeant's wife replied too softly for her words to reach them.

"That, I assume, is James junior?"

"That is," agreed Cox. "What's for breakfast? What's for lunch? What's for dinner? They are his greetings."

"They are the best greetings that parents can possibly hear," affirmed Bony, his blue eyes twinkling. "Have you anything further for me?"

"Yes. I have a man in the lock-up. He has been there for two days and nights. But those aeroplane tracks out at Windy . . ."

"We will discuss them later. Is this man you have locked up the chap who camped at the road junction on the night of 28 October?"

"The same. He walked back to Golden Dawn because he had heard that a vacancy had occurred at Olarie Downs. As you instructed, I locked him up. He didn't mind when I hinted at things and promised to secure the job for him. Shall I bring him here?"

"Yes, do. By the way, is there no report regarding the coming of that aboriginal chief I sent for?"

"Only that Captain Loveacre has accepted the commission to go and get him."

"Then we should soon hear something definite. Yes, I'll see that man now."

Two minutes later, the sergeant ushered into the office a tall, shabbily-dressed man who stared at Bony with keen hazel eyes. His shabbiness was the more emphasized by the care he had bestowed with his razor and boot polish. He was invited to be seated at the table facing the detective.

"This is Edward Henry Joyce," stated Cox in his official manner. To the swagman he said: "This is Detective-Inspector Bonaparte."

"The sergeant informs me that you are now taking a short rest," Bony said, smiling.

"Well, it's a rest and a 'oliday," Joyce defined. "I 'as me three good meals a day, and a bottle of beer at eleven in the morning and seven at night. And no disturbances up to date by any blokes pinched by the sergeant. I ain't complainin'. And now that the sergeant 'as clicked that job for me—well, I'm in no 'urry to get to work."

"Ah! I am glad that you do not complain," said Bony.

"I would be a dorg to complain after wot the sergeant's wife done fer me last time I was 'ere."

"Would you consent to stay another week?"

"Two, if you like."

"Who knows that Mr Joyce is staying at the lock-up, Sergeant?"

"So far it's not general knowledge."

"Very well, then. If you will stay another week, I think you should. Now tell me. On the night of 28 October you camped at the junction of the Coolibah road with the main St Albans track. You say that about ten minutes to three o'clock you heard the noise of an aeroplane flying overhead. I have examined your camp site that night, and I know that you slept within fifty feet of the track. Please cast your mind back to that night. What time did you make camp?"

"Just after the sun went down."

"What time did you turn in, about?"

"About eight o'clock. It might have been a few minutes after."

"Well. Before you heard the aeroplane did a car or truck pass along the road?"

"Only a truck goin' from St Albans towards Golden Dawn," Joyce replied confidently. "It woke me up. I could make out the shape of the driver's cab. That was twenty minutes to eleven."

"You appear to be sure of your times."

"Too right! It was a clear night, and I've took an interest in the stars since I went to sea. No one can't fault me with the stars. There was two cars passed after the aeroplane went by. One passed towards Tintanoo about half-past three, and the other passed towards Golden Dawn about twenty minutes to five. Both of 'em was going all out."

"Much faster than usual at night time?"

"I should say," asserted Joyce. "They come on me like a roarin' willy-willy. They was gone by like a flash, as it was."

For a little space, Bony drummed his fingers on the table. Then:

"Since that night, Mr Joyce, you indulged in a beano of some importance. I hate doubting people, but, ask yourself, do you not appear to be remarkably sure of those times?"

"Sure! Of course I'm sure!" Joyce declared with pardonable vehemence. "I got a good memory wot no occasional bust interferes with. That night I gets waked up four times: one be the truck, two be the aeroplane, three and four be the two cars. Each time I looks at the stars, smokes a pipeful, and does a think. I got a good memory, I tell you. I can go back years and tell you where I was on a partic'lar day and the kind of weather it was. It'd take me some time to go back three years, for instance, 'cos I would 'ave to go back in me nut day be day. But I'd get there."

"Good! Well, Mr Joyce, I can assure you that by consenting to be Sergeant Cox's guest you have granted us a favour," Bony gravely said. "Tell me, now. Either before you spoke to the sergeant about hearing the aeroplane, or afterwards, have you spoken to any one else about it?"

"Now you're askin' me to recollect wot I did and said when I was under the influence," Joyce said reproachfully. "When I'm blotto me memory is as wonky as it's full of life when I'm sober. After I was sobered up 'ere, the sarge tells me to keep me mouth shut, and it 'as been kept shut."

"I am glad to hear that. Still, I think you had better remain here for another week. If there is anything you want—bar unlimited drink—you may ask for and get it. Listen to that thunder!"

"I'm 'appy enough. Was there some crook goin's on that night?" Joyce asked.

"There were," replied Bony, nodding. "I think it was

just as well for you that you did not attempt to bail up either of those car drivers to ask for a lift, or a match, or something."

"Ho!" snorted Mr Joyce, and his moustache trembled. "I've always been 'andy with me dooks."

"I do not doubt that. That, I think, will be all for the present."

"Then I'll get back to me cubby 'ole. Hooroo!" Joyce turned to the door, obviously pleased that his rest cure was to be extended for a full week. "Don't trouble, Sergeant. I know the way to the lock-up."

When he had gone, Bony turned to the sergeant.

"With reference to Ted Sharp. Have you found out anything about that man he visited at Gurner's Hotel?"

"Not a thing. He arrived at Yaraka by train, stayed there over-night, and the following day he hired a car to bring him across to Gurner's Hotel. On his arrival back again at Yaraka, as there was no train, he got the driver of the car to take him in to Winton. I got Watts, however, to give me a copy of the telegram Sharp sent in by telephone from Gurner's Hotel. Here is the copy."

Bony read slowly, and twice:

Telford, Box 1991Z, G.P.O., Brisbane. Have the money. My identity must not be disclosed on any account. Be careful of Kane. Proceed. Edward Sharp.

"Who is this Box 1991Z, Brisbane? Do you know?"

"Yes," Cox replied triumphantly. "The box is controlled by a firm of station agents. We have learned that the telegram was an instruction to them to purchase from John Kane a property he owns north of Tintanoo. On behalf of Ted Sharp they paid Kane forty-seven thousand pounds for it."

"Oh! That's a very large sum, Sergeant, for a boss stockman to possess," Bony murmured. "We know, of course, that he had a legacy amounting nearly to four thousand left him by an uncle. Now I wonder where he got the rest! And why all the secrecy about that man he met at Gurner's Hotel. That's the man we have to find. Ah! who is this?"

There entered a slight, bald and mild-looking man wearing rimless spectacles. He was presented to the detective as the local postmaster.

"I received your note, Sergeant, when I got home for lunch," he explained. "I had this telegram for you, and I intended sending it along by my little girl."

"It is considerate of you to come, Mr Watts," Bony said warmly. Cox opened the telegram, read it, and slid it across the table to Bony. "What I would like to know, Mr Watts, is this. Would it be possible to dispatch a letter in Adelaide addressed to Golden Dawn, take twenty-four hours to think of the terms of a reply, and to have the reply delivered in Adelaide within the space of ten days?"

After thought the postmaster shook his head. "No," he replied.

"Well, in that time could a letter dispatched from Adelaide be replied to by telegram and the telegram received in Adelaide within that time?"

"Yes. That, I think, could be done."

"Thank you! By the sound of the elements, we are in for a bad storm." Bony fell silent, again drumming with his fingers on the writing-table. Then he said deliberately: "Mr Watts, the urgency of a certain matter prohibits me from following the usual channels in gaining information from your department. Sergeant Cox here is a stickler for red tape. Red tape annoys me as a red cloth is said to annoy a bull. Could we not compromise? I will be frank. In strict confidence I want to know if a telegram of a private nature was dispatched from your office between 2 October and 20 October addressed to a person named Markham."

Mr Watts smiled before he said:

"I have been so long in this accursed place, Mr Bonaparte, that I sometimes think were I to defy regulations I might be transferred to another office in a place less dry and hot and dusty. In the circumstances I will go through the files and produce for your examination all telegrams dispatched to Adelaide during the period you mentioned."

"That, Mr Watts, is generous of you," Bony assured him. "You are a man after my own heart, but should you really wish for a transfer then dip into my wide experience of departmental heads and demand it with damns and blasts. Never proffer a request. Always make a demand."

When on his feet Mr Watts smiled happily at the detective.

"Now that seems sound advice, Mr Bonaparte. I wonder I never thought of it in that light after Brisbane's constant refusal. Well, I'll be off. I'll send those messages along some time this afternoon."

To this, Bony said hastily:

"Please don't, Mr Watts. I would like you to bring them yourself after the office is shut. Further, be sure that none of your staff, or the telephone exchange operator, sees what you are about. You know the advice about the right hand's relation to the left hand, eh?"

Mr Watts smiled again, and this time he winked. When he had passed out through the wicket-gate Bony picked up the opened telegram and read:

Delayed by bad storm at Cloncurry—Illawalli cheerful—Loveacre.

CHAPTER XXII

"MAN PROPOSES BUT——"

ANOTHER of the storm season's advance guard passed over Golden Dawn while Bony was lunching with the sergeant and Mrs Cox, the policeman estimating that from it forty points of rain fell. On returning to the office, Bony stepped out on to the veranda to see how the passing storm was painting the sky black to the north and east.

"It looks bad for Loveacre's chances of getting through to-day," Bony said with troubled voice. "Never before have I experienced such impatience to finalize a case. That poor young woman is getting very low. Dr Knowles is in despair."

"He appears to take more than a professional interest in her," was Cox's observation.

"Yes, he does. You see, he is in love with her. It must be terrible to be in love with a dying woman and have to watch her die."

The sergeant made no comment on this. For a moment the detective regarded again the temptuous sky. Now to the far west was growing a long ribbon of blue sky, and its promise of a fine afternoon lightened Bony's depression.

"Come! Let us take a walk to the post office," he suggested.

Together they sauntered along Golden Dawn's main street, breathing air freed of its dust, but warm and clammy. The scent of refreshed earth rose to meet them.

"I am glad to know that Captain Loveacre was commissioned to bring Illawalli," remarked the detective. "He is a good man. I understand that he possesses a fine reputation for sale flying, and is well familiar with outback conditions."

"Yes, he knows the country and its conditions all right," affirmed Cox.

Together they entered the post office building, and Bony's quick eyes noted the smartly-dressed, good-looking exchange girl seated before her switchboard, reading a novel while she waited for calls.

Mr Watts was dispatching a telegram, the clacking of his instrument coming sharply against the background of threatening thunder. Having finished, he rose with a smile to accept the message Bony had written on an official form and which was addressed to Captain Loveacre. It ran:

Do not incur unnecessary risks, but Illawalli urgently needed here. Notify me of your progress whenever possible. Bony.

"Going to clear up for a little while, Mr Bonaparte?" Watts said pleasantly.

"We are hoping so. How long will it take for that message to get through?"

"About twenty minutes. Urgent?"

"Yes. Mark it so, please."

"Very well. I will send it off at once."

Nodding affably, Bony led the way outside, and, there before the building, he said to Sergeant Cox:

"What is your private opinion of that young woman in there?"

"I've nothing against her, but. . . . She knows she's good-looking. Candidly, I don't like her."

"Hum! She doesn't produce in me that warm glow of

pleasure I always feel when in the presence of a good woman. I wonder, now!"

"What?" pressed Cox.

"I wonder if she is able to read the Morse code."

"I don't know. I've never heard her say she could. What if she can?"

Bony pinched his mouth with forefinger and thumb. He gazed skyward, and the sun being masked still by the clouds he looked at the clock above the entrance to the post office.

"Let us return," he decided.

Silent now, they retraced their steps, Bony obviously worried, the sergeant shrewd enough to know that but unable to guess the reason. The light was becoming quickly stronger. Westward the ribbon of blue sky was enlarged to a great field. On gaining the veranda steps of the police-station, the detective sat down on the topmost one and gazed across at the wooden store.

The minutes passed slowly, but presently a boy arrived on a bicycle and handed the detective a telegram. Bony tore open the envelope.

"Ah! Good news!" he cried. "Loveacre says that as the weather appears to be breaking in the west, and as all reports state that the weather is fine west of the Diamantina, he is leaving Cloncurry at once."

Then he was on his feet and running into the office. When Cox joined him, he was standing before the wall map.

"Look here, Cox. Look! The distance from Cloncurry is approximately three hundred miles. Loveacre handed in his message at two-twenty-four. He should be here in two hours and a half at most. Three hundred miles—two and a half hours! I wonder why he stated he would be flying direct? That implies that his originally-selected route was not straight."

"He probably intended to follow the air route to Winton, then on to Longreach before breaking away for Yaraka and Golden Dawn," Cox suggested. "A direct route from Cloncurry gives him no landing grounds, and a forced landing would be a bad business."

"That might explain it," Bony conceded. "Now listen carefully. When we sight his plane we will at once drive out to it and take over Illawalli. We will bring him here, where, perhaps, your wife would be kind enough to give him tea and sandwiches. While he is eating you fetch your car out. Then, when we are ready to leave for Coolibah, I will go first with Illawalli, and you will follow immediately after. When we are midway across the gibber plain I'll stop and you will draw up alongside. By that time I will have instructed Illawalli what to do. He will transfer to your car and lie down along the rear seat and out of sight for the remainder of the journey. Is that quite clear?"

"Perfectly. But why——?"

"I won't tell you, Sergeant, because I am a little uneasy. I have dark suspicions and fears that have no solid foundation. There is no other way of getting to Coolibah other than by following the road to St Albans and taking the side road?"

Cox shook his head. "It's a pity that storm the other day made the Coolibah landing ground unsafe," he said.

"It is a pity, too, that every one knows it, and that Captain Loveacre will land here when he comes. We shall have to run a possible gauntlet with the lightning. Ring up Coolibah, and ask for Dr Knowles, will you?"

A minute later Bony heard the doctor's voice.

"This is Bony speaking, Doctor," he said. "I wanted to

tell you that I will be arriving with my friend, Illawalli, early this evening. How is the patient?"

"Bad, bad, Bony! Respiration feeble. At times it is scarcely perceptible. Do you think he can do any good, your friend?"

"I hope earnestly that he will. Was that spare tube sent to Faraway Bore?"

"Yes. It was understood." A pause, then: "One has to guard against accidents. You will be coming across by car, of course."

"Certainly. Will you kindly inform Miss Nettlefold of my projected arrival? Is there anything I can bring out other than the mail?"

"No. Don't waste time, man. I am exceedingly anxious."

"No time will be wasted. Captain Loveacre, who is bringing my friend, is expected to arrive here at about five o'clock. It is unfortunate that he cannot land at Coolibah. Good-bye!"

When the detective replaced the receiver his eyes encountered those of Sergeant Cox.

"What's the little mystery about the spare tube?" questioned the big man.

"I wished to convey to your brother-in-law a request to increase his vigilance. Before I left Coolibah I made up with Mr Nettlefold a series of code messages. Is Constable Lovitt in town?"

When Cox replied in the affirmative Bony went on:

"Then have him ride his motor-cycle across the plain as far as the edge of the scrub, there to wait for us. Have him leave when the aeroplane is sighted. When he sees us he is then to ride on, like a pilot engine, ahead of us to Coolibah. Should he meet any motorist whose car is broken down, Lovitt will see to it that that motorist does not throw any—lightning."

"You expect opposition—a hold up?"

"I greatly fear being overwhelmed by a bad electrical storm."

Cox sighed. His expression was severe.

"I am afraid I don't get you," he said sharply.

"There have been many cases"—Bony prefaced a somewhat lengthy explanation—"when the police have been unable to bring a charge because of insufficient proof with which to convince a jury. They, the police, know a certain person to be guilty of a crime, but knowing is not proving it to others. I know who flew Captain Loveacre's red monoplane from Golden Dawn to Windy Creek Station, and then on to Emu Lake. I know who poisoned the brandy. I am practically certain who drugged Miss Double M, although, knowing these things, I have not sufficient proof to obtain warrants for two arrests. In this case I find much to annoy me. I am annoyed chiefly by the demand for haste dictated by the condition of Miss Double M. Nothing annoys me so much as having to hurry.

"So you see, I am compelled to use the powers possessed by my friend, Illawalli, in order that that young woman's life may be saved—if it is not already too late. Illawalli will finalize my case for me; he will cut in before I have reached the point where I can say: 'Here is how it all happened!' Being unable to prove who drugged the girl, I am unable to make him confess the name of the drug, and because the victim is dying I am unable to spend any further time drawing the net closer.

"In an effort to force the hands of the men who drugged and tried so hard to kill Miss Double M several days ago I let it be known that Dr Knowles was confident of curing her. I then warned your brother-in-law and Knowles to take every precaution against a determined attack on her life by asking that a tyre tube be sent to Faraway Bore. Nothing happened. I think now that nothing happened at Coolibah because certain persons feared that the risk would be too great when a safer chance could be taken to stop Illawalli from reaching the patient.

"At this moment it is possible that certain people know all about Captain Loveacre and his passenger, and of our hopes being centred in Illawalli. They do not know what I know and they do not know what I suspect. They think that if the girl dies they will be safe for ever. They believe that the drug they administered will not be conquered by any treatment Knowles or other doctors can give her. They know, further, all about Illawalli and his powers, and that Illawalli can and will read her mind to place in our hands all the proof we need. Knowing as much, knowing that Illawalli will have to be taken to Coolibah by road, I gravely fear that a serious effort will be made to stop him. Nitroglycerine was used in the aeroplane. A canister of it thrown against a car would certainly kill its occupants. With Lovitt ahead, and you behind with Illawalli, they will, I hope, recognize the danger—to themselves."

"Why not make the arrests and chance getting the proof," advised Cox.

Bony shook his head.

"It wouldn't do," he said. "No, it wouldn't do. We are not dealing with people with criminal records. If we made a mistake it would be finish for both of us. Come! I don't like the sound of that thunder."

He left the office, and walked quickly to the front gate where he gazed anxiously at the sky. To the west all was clear. The yellow sun was shining, and the wind was laden with strange and alluring scents. Directly above Golden Dawn rat tails of cloud were drawing swiftly eastward after the rear edge of the vast cloud mass that had passed over. The rear of the cloud mass lay roughly north and south, and moment by moment it was growing in depth, whitening in the sunlight. Here and there great plumes of cloud towered high above the edge of the mass, like snow-covered mountains, with flickering lightning in their hearts.

"Going to clear up," predicted Cox on joining Bony.

"I am sorry that I cannot agree with you."

"But all that is passing away eastward," Cox protested.

Bony continued to stare upward at the puffing, swelling cloud mass. Its base was darkening to ink-black, and the serrated top of the western edge, with the vast mountain peaks spaced along it, was being frozen here, gilded there by the sun. Icebergs floating on a sea of ink. . . .

Sergeant Cox gripped Bony by the arm. "That lot is going to come back on us," he growled savagely.

The detective nodded.

The gibber plain, sunlit to its eastern horizon, appeared as though a storm of wattle blossom had rained upon it. It was bright yellow in sharp contrast with the ink-black sky. The store, the hotel, and the houses north of the hotel stood out against the pall of sky like buildings floodlit against a dark night—night ripped and scarred by lightning.

"Yes, it will come back," Bony breathed. "And away to the north flies Captain Loveacre on a southerly course. He will now be flying southward in front of that aerial ice pack which will force him ever westward. He is too far away to be able to land at Golden Dawn in one hour's time, unless that storm again changes direction, and moves to the east."

"He will, then, have to make a forced landing somewhere," Cox pointed out.

"Without doubt, he will have to land many miles north or west of Golden Dawn. Then we will have to bring Illawalli many miles by car if the landing is made safely. The odds are that the landing will not be a safe one, because ground like this surrounding Golden Dawn is rare. Yes, a car will have to bring Illawalli over water-logged plains and swollen creeks. And perhaps the river will come down and stop us reaching Coolibah with him, preventing him from seeing the dying woman. And I will have failed! I'll not fail to produce her murderers, but I will have failed to save her life with my friend's aid. And I once told Dr Knowles that the Almighty holds the scales evenly between good and evil."

Bony's face was distorted with emotion. The tails of the storm now had been sucked into what had become the frontal ramparts. The air was clear before those ramparts of cloud, and now the cloud mountains were disappearing beyond the edge of the mass as it advanced over Golden Dawn. It began to rain before the sun was vanquished, huge, golden drops falling with seeming slowness to the ground, there to break into a multi-coloured mist.

Bony had just time to drive the runabout into Cox's garage and gain the station veranda before the deluge began.

CHAPTER XXIII

STORM HAVOC

AT the controls of a two-seater biplane, Captain Loveacre regarded with anxiety the writhing, twisting wall of snow-white cloud little more than a mile from the tip of his port wing. To maintain that distance from the perpendicular field of imitation ice and snow, he was forced to steer his ship several points west of south—several points westward of his course to Golden Dawn. He had flown a little more than half the distance from Cloncurry.

Bringing back the stick, he climbed quickly from five to twelve thousand feet, but still the summit of the cloud wall was above him. Unequipped for high altitude flying, he yet went up to fifteen thousand feet, at which height he was able to see another wall in the distance rising farther, thousands of feet over the first wall.

There was no getting over that storm with the ship he commanded, and to attempt to fly through it would be childish. He flashed a glance at the helmeted head of his passenger, who laughed and showed four wide-spaced teeth, and pointed at the wall before clapping his hands.

"Who says a black hasn't guts?" demanded the captain, who could not hear himself speak. He sent the machine in a long roaring slant down to three thousand feet.

There the engine continued the even tenor of its song of power. Now and then Loveacre could feel the concussions of the thunder, but he could not hear them. Now and then veins of deep orange were etched on the background of the stupendous wall of ice. The time by the dash clock was ten minutes after four.

Below, the world was pared neatly into a half-circle, a half-circle brilliantly floodlit with sunshine. The cloud foot appeared to be resting on the world—a world that was swiftly spinning into it as though it alone and not the storm and the tiny aeroplane were moving. Directly under them the ground was broken into several colours: grey and brown and bluish-green. Westward the colour was more evenly a uniform dark-green, denoting levelness in comparison with the low hills over which they were flying.

Already pushed far westward off his course, Loveacre decided that he must set down as near as possible to Golden Dawn. Two minutes after that he decided that he must land on the natural 'drome north of Coolibah, risking damage on the soft surface. To his knowledge there were neither 'dromes, or even natural landing grounds westward of that, save only Emu Lake. Here, of course, in this wide land there were no wheat-fields and meadows, no fallow paddocks and grazing lands. What appeared from the air as level ground might well be rough enough to wreck an army tank.

Now, below them, the earth appeared like a dark-green carpet on which a house painter carelessly had dropped splashes of light-brown paint, sand-dunes amid the scrub. The plane was edging towards a wide ribbon of country on which the trees grew in distinct lines. Loveacre knew it to be the Diamantina River, to which the storm was irresistibly pushing him.

He continued, hopeful of being able to land north of Coolibah, and hope lasted until he had been forced to the east side of the river channels, and could not then see either Tintanoo or Coolibah homestead. He followed the eastern channels for some time, but at last the storm pressed him gradually across the river to its western side.

Hope of landing at Coolibah vanished. On his scribbling-pad he made some rapid calculations, checked them, estimated his position at forty miles north of Tintanoo homestead. Forty miles—twenty minutes in this hundred-and-twenty-miles-an-hour machine.

It was singular how the trees below grew in defined lines. The paint splashes along the eastern border of the river were being swiftly blotted from sight by the foot of the cloud wall. It seemed that it was the earth which was moving, as though the lines of trees were slipping eastward to be devoured by the storm.

He was now flying above the sandhills bordering the western edge of the river, and grimly he steered along them, his eyes searching ahead for Tintanoo homestead. Five minutes after that he distinguished the red roofs of Tintanoo. He was then half a mile from the storm face. Tenaciously he drove southward, defying the storm, ever narrowing the space between itself and him. The homestead ahead had become the judge's box on the course, on which he and the storm fought out a hard race.

The vast wall of cloud was rearing above him when, with accelerated speed, he swooped down in a steep slant towards the red squares and oblongs. A minute, and he was only six hundred feet above them, circling, peering downward on either side of the cockpit. There was a narrow strip of ground east of the homestead on which he might effect a landing, but already he was flying in the golden rain which outran the deluge joining earth and sky together.

He was too late. Lightning flickered with blinding brilliance, and the plane rocked in the vibrations set up by the thunderclap. The narrow strip of land below faded. Then from his sight the homestead faded, and he was forced to race the storm into the clear and sunlit air in front.

Winding westward, lying like a sleeping snake, stretched the track to St Albans. Where it passed through the green-black scrub its brownness was emphasized, but where it crossed broken sand country and grey flats it was difficult to follow even when only five hundred feet above it.

Loveacre unrolled the map. He had never been above this particular section of country before. Finding Tintanoo homestead on the map, he then saw that he was heading for St Albans. Was there not a hotel along this road—a hotel called Gurner's Hotel? Of course there was. It was supposed to be north of Emu Lake. Emu Lake was a safe landing ground, but . . . .

The country ahead was clearing of trees. Loveacre decided to keep on along the track. If he found no possibility of landing within a few miles past Gurner's Hotel he would turn south and seek Emu Lake. . . .

On the roofs of Coolibah the rain roared with a persistent drumming. In the pitch-black, lightning-shattered night the weight of falling water could be almost felt. The reverberating thunder never ceased.

Slowly pacing to and fro outside the patient's room, softly tramped the guard. He was keeping to the shelter of the veranda this stormy night, and he was mentally alert, knowing that the celestial uproar would mask the sound of an arriving car or the footsteps of an enemy.

Within the room he was guarding, Dr Knowles was sitting beside the bed gazing at the white, thin face of the helpless Muriel Markham. Behind him stood Elizabeth, her hands clasped, her expression one of profound anxiety.

The doctor was holding with his fingers one inert wrist, feeling the pulse, his dark eyes concentrating their gaze on the twin semi-circles of dark lashes lying against the alabaster skin. The girl was breathing so gently that, allied with the expressionless face, at first glance one would have supposed her dead.

Knowles was a beaten man, and he knew it. He had done everything known to medical science to restore animation to the patient's paralysed muscles, but he was vanquished. He had spared neither Elizabeth nor himself, but without avail.

With the abrupt action of a nerve-racked man, he bent over his patient and lifted first one and then the other of her eyelids. For a full second he gazed into the expressionless eyes. For the first time they did not register a greeting. Always before they had smiled at him, but now they were vacant of intelligence. With infinite tenderness he closed them, and stood back, to contemplate this woman who might have been created from rough-hewn, flawless marble. Elizabeth saw the agony in his face when he turned to her.

"Even the elements have conspired against us," he cried softly. "I came in to tell you that Bony rang up just now. Loveacre and his passenger failed to reach Golden Dawn. Nothing is known of what has happened to them."

"We must not abandon hope yet, Doctor," Elizabeth pleaded. "You are all to pieces. What are you doing to yourself? You must not worry so."

His smile was mirthless and terrible. He motioned to the large table, and beside it they sat, the shaded reading-lamp pitilessly revealing their worn faces.

"I'll tell you now what I am doing to myself," he said,

a fierce note of triumph in his voice. "For the first time since 1917 I have lived a full forty-eight hours without whisky. You cannot possibly understand what it has meant to achieve that. You cannot grasp what I have borne to secure forty-eight hours of freedom from the toils of John Barleycorn."

Knowles drew in his breath sharply. In rapid speech he told her what he had told Bony regarding the loss of the woman who had taken shelter with him in a London doorway.

"This bush castaway is the image of the girl who died in my arms," he explained to a wide-eyed Elizabeth. "That night most of me died, too. I wanted to die, but I was a coward. I could not commit suicide. I adopted John Barleycorn as a friend, seeking in his friendship forgetfulness. Sometimes I found it, but the more I clung to John Barleycorn the farther death drew back from me to take my enemies in the air. And then . . . and then, here in this room in the form of our patient I see again that woman I loved. To me the resemblance is unearthly. I saw then that I must be keen enough, clever enough to save her, and that to do it I had to strike off the chains my friend, John Barleycorn, had wrapped about me. And I have done it—freed myself. I have conquered alcohol, for I know now I need never seek it again. Through these long weeks I have fought a thousand devils—real devils, devils I could see—and I have won. Because of her I have won."

Elizabeth's eyes were streaming tears, but they never faltered in their gaze.

"Yes, I have won," he went on. "For what? For what have I fought, if we fail to save her? I love her, do you hear? I'm thirty-eight. She is about twenty-three. She could never love me—if we saved her—but that is of much less importance than the fact that I love her and would be paid for all the terrors I have faced by one smile. I ask nothing. I tell you, I ask nothing of her, and nothing of God except that her life may be granted to me . . . and now . . . now this storm."

He fell silent after that outburst, and for a little while Elizabeth was unable to speak.

"I have guessed you cared, Doctor," she whispered at last. "But she won't die! She cannot die after all we have done together! Not after what she has unconsciously done for you. If Inspector Bonaparte's black friend comes. . . ."

"It might have been possible, Miss Nettlefold, if he had arrived last week," Knowles told her. "It promised hope when we needed it. But now—how could any man read a patient's mind when that mind is not functioning? She is beyond the help of any magic, black or white."

It was eleven o'clock at Golden Dawn and the rain had stopped. Over the plain to the east the stars were beginning to show, but to the far west lightning still split open the sky.

Within the police office, Bony sat before the telephone and the large-scale map spread over Sergeant Cox's table. The detective picked up the instrument and called the exchange.

"Have you yet been able to get through to Tintanoo or Gurner's Hotel?"

"No. The lines are still out of order," replied the night operator.

"Well, ask Mr Watts to speak, please."

A moment. Two. Then came the postmaster's voice.

"I am sorry to have kept you on duty to so late an hour,

Mr Watts," Bony said regretfully. "It seems that all those western lines are down. You haven't been able to raise the St Albans exchange?"

"No, we have failed to raise any one west of us," Watts replied. "As you say, all the western lines must be down. Most likely a pole has been shattered by lightning."

"That is what has happened, no doubt. It is kind of you to stay on duty, but there appears to be no reason to ask you to stay longer."

"That's quite all right, Mr Bonaparte," Watts said quickly. "I am trying to raise St Albans by a roundabout route. I have got round to Springvale to the north."

"Good! We have plotted Loveacre as far south as four miles east of Monkira Station. We have worked out the speed of the storm and Loveacre's speed—of course sheer guesswork—and it places the captain somewhere west of a line drawn from the river's western channels a little north of Tintanoo homestead to a range of sandhills on Coolibah called the Rockies. When will you be sending out a linesman to repair the break in the western lines?"

"First thing to-morrow morning."

"Do the poles closely follow the road?"

"In some places, no. But my man uses a truck for the work, and it should not be long before he discovers and mends the breaks. I'll ring immediately I can get St Albans."

"Thank you."

Replacing the receiver, Bony pushed away the instrument, and fell again to studying the map. At his side Cox sat bolt upright in his chair, smoking his pipe with savage energy. Presently Bony said:

"If it were not for that Markham girl I would be enjoying all this. I do not so greatly fear for the safety of Captain

Loveacre and Illawalli as I fear that it will be too late for Illawalli to do anything after all. Loveacre is too good a man to court death in that storm. He was south of Rosebrook when the storm turned back, and he was still west of the storm when he got as far south as Monkira. I incline to the belief that when he found himself unable to reach Golden Dawn he made for the temporary dry-weather landing ground north of Coolibah, and that when he could not reach there he flew west across the river to land somewhere near Gurner's Hotel, where the country is fairly open, or to Emu Lake, which he knows . . . .

"We'll ring Coolibah."

Within a few minutes he heard John Nettlefold's voice.

"We have had one hundred and thirty-five points of rain here," Bony opened. "How much has fallen at Coolibah?"

"One hundred and forty. I was on the point of ringing you up when your call came through. For some unknown reason I have got through to Tintanoo on the river line when all previous efforts to do so failed. Kane informs me that Loveacre's machine passed overhead at the same time as the storm arrived. It looked to him as though the captain intended to effect a landing on the strip of clear ground between the river and the homestead. It was just as well that he didn't, because it is a steep incline. Loveacre then flew west. Kane got through to Gurner's and told him to keep a look-out and be ready with his car to go after the machine while it was in sight in case it landed, but Gurner had left on a trip to St Albans. Later Gurner rang up from St Albans, reporting that the machine passed over him soon after he left the hotel and landed off the road ahead of him. It was smashed badly in the landing. He rescued Loveacre, who is badly injured, and took him to the doctor at St Albans, but he did not mention anything about

Illawalli. When I asked Kane about the passenger he said that Gurner said nothing to him about there being a passenger at all."

"Ah! That's strange," said Bony, his calm voice concealing his nervous tension. "Will you again ring Kane and get him to make contact with Gurner for information about Illawalli? Good! I'll be here. Then would you get through to Ned Hamlin and ask him to be sure that both Shuteye and Bill Sikes are at the hotel by seven in the morning? I'll be there then to meet and pick them up. Illawalli was with the captain. Of that there is no doubt."

When Bony had repeated the information to Cox he looked at the time. "Loveacre's down," he said harshly, "but no Illawalli! Between Gurner's and St Albans. I leave at daybreak for Gurner's."

CHAPTER XXIV

BONY IS AGAIN SUBMERGED

TWO days and nights had passed, and Bony was exceedingly weary. A dozen times during this period of incessant labour, with the assistance of Bill Sikes and Shuteye, he had had to dig the runabout from rain-soaked road bogs.

Captain Loveacre had elected to put his plane down on flat claypan country not far from the western end of Tintanoo and on a small selection owned by people named Martell. What had from the air appeared to be a good landing place was made traitorous by low banks of sand enclosing the claypans, and the machine had turned right over on its back, smashing the propeller, its broken body forming an arch that had prevented a fatality.

Loveacre had received a severe blow to his head and another to his face. He came round to reality to find himself lying on wet ground with heavy rain beating down on his upturned face. In his throat was the fire of raw whisky. Quite oblivious to the elements was a little, round-faced man standing beside him.

"Do you think you could walk across to the road where I was obliged to leave my car?" this man had asked. "You're too heavy for me to carry, but you certainly require surgical attention."

"I'll try," Loveacre assented. "How's my passenger?"

"Passenger? I've seen no passenger!"

With the assistance of Mr Gurner, Captain Loveacre had looked for but had failed to find Illawalli. The storm was intense. Gurner was anxious to reach St Albans before the heavy rain sank far into the ground and produced bogs on the road, and the captain was really too ill to be much concerned about the disappearance of the old chief. He fainted once before the car was reached, thereafter suffering periods of unconsciousness while being taken to the bush nurse stationed at St Albans. Not only was St Albans Gurner's destination: it was nearer to the scene of the crash than Coolibah and Dr Knowles.

Gurner stated that he had left his hotel two miles behind when the biplane flew over him. He did not actually see it land, but, having passed through the Tintanoo boundary, he saw the tail showing above a line of tobacco bush right off the road. Gurner had crossed to the disabled machine to find Captain Loveacre hanging head downward from his seat. He had not seen a second man. The storm broke while he was getting the unconscious airman clear of the machine, and only after a considerable time had he been successful in bringing Loveacre to his senses.

Gurner and the St Albans constable had been met by Bony the next morning at the scene of the unfortunate landing. The detective had with him both Shuteye and Bill Sikes. The storm had obliterated all possibility of tracking Illawalli, and no signs of him had been found then or subsequently. Having learned who the passenger was, the constable offered what Bony had to accept as a sound theory. The flight and the crash had so frightened Illawalli that he had run away, and, doubtless, even now was making his way back to his own country.

All night through Bony had crouched over a little camp fire, now and then pushing together the ends of four or five sticks in order to maintain a low flame. Near by stood the utility, and beside it slept the two blacks. He had spared neither them nor himself. Tintanoo, the Martells and Coolibah had contributed horsemen to muster miles of surrounding country for Illawalli. All effort had been without result.

It was supremely urgent to finalize this case, to secure one, if not more, vital links of the chain he was forging. The evening before he had learned from Dr Knowles that Muriel Markham now was rapidly sinking. Dr Stanisforth had arrived to join forces in the fight to prolong her life. It was the physical condition of Muriel Markham that placed the detective in a dreadful quandary. Should he order the arrest of John Kane without having the proof that Kane was at the head of the conspiracy?

If he ordered the arrest of John Kane, and despite luck and bluff failed to obtain a confession of complicity, his fine reputation would be blasted. People like John Kane cannot be arrested on flimsy evidence. Morally certain that Kane had been behind the whole matter of the stolen aeroplane, Bony toyed with an idea this early morning—an idea that was nothing less than conscripting his two aboriginal companions, kidnapping the squatter and taking him deep into the bush where means might be found to force a confession from him.

It was, however, only an idea—an idea he knew to be beyond possibility of being put into practice. It was not that the execution of such an idea would ruin him, but rather that it might prove to be fruitless. Without proof he could not move against the squatter.

The sun slipped above the horizon, and still Bony crouched and pondered what his next move was to be. Shuteye awoke and called Bill Sikes, and presently they crossed to the fire, their coming arousing Bony to the reality of the new day and the desire for food.

"You bin sit here orl night, eh?" Shuteye exclaimed with wide eyes. "Now, you buck up, Bony. All thing goodo bimeby."

His brain aching, Bony looked up into the big, round, jovial, black face, and then at the other, ugly and scarred, that came into his vision beside the fat one. When he did not speak, Shuteye did.

"Me, I don't reckon ole Illawalli run off back home at all. Suppose he was frightened blackfeller when aeroplane came down smasho! At first he run and run, and then bimeby he remember good feller Bony and he stop runnin'. He say: 'Bony, he fix me up goodo. He gimme plenty tucker and tobaccer.' Then ole Illawalli, him come look-see ole Bony. P'haps he see homestead, and he tell people he look-see Bony and they telephone."

"Well, he has not returned, nor has he got any station people to communicate with us," Bony pointed out, adding: "And this is the beginning of the third day since he vanished."

"P'haps he not run away any time," Bill Sikes put in. "P'haps he's hid up somewhere. That Jack Johnson look like he know something. When we were there I talked to him about Illawalli and he keep lookin' on the ground. Jack Johnson no good feller. He's crook."

"You mean the yardman at Gurner's Hotel?"

"Too right! I bet that that Jack Johnson know where ole Illawalli is."

"We go find out, eh?" suggested Shuteye. "P'haps Jack Johnson he pretty fine feller and know nothing, but we grab 'im and take 'im away into bush and make him talk, eh?"

Black eyes no longer reflected a humorous soul.

"Hum! There lies a possibility I have not considered. You should have spoken like this the day before yesterday," Bony said slowly. Gradually his lack-lustre eyes regained their old keen brightness. He expelled his breath, breathed deeply. He felt as though he was emerging from a dark cavern into brilliant sunlight.

Self! He had thought only of himself, of his career, of his unblemished reputation. What was all that weighed in the balance against that young woman's life? It was as air. The fact was that he was becoming old, too cautious, too prone to follow the civil service gutter marked out by red tape. Red tape had never been any assistance to him. Daring and the contempt of established authority, on the other hand, had more than once enabled him to bring to a brilliant close a difficult investigation.

Still crouched over the fire, he offered no assistance to his companions, who now were preparing the breakfast of johnny-cakes and grilled kangaroo steak. The depression that had enchained his mind was giving way to the growing strength of a clear resolution.

Bluff! That was it, bluff! He had to bluff! Bluff offered a chance to dig from the ground of obscurity a nugget of fact. Time was on the side of the opposing force, and this was the first of his cases in which it had been. Formerly time had been on his side. Patience had been the chief factor of his success. Patience! He had been too patient!

The investigation was like a machine he was laboriously building—a machine that would never work until he possessed all the component parts. Well, he would heave a crowbar into the machine, smash it, and then see what parts he had with which to begin again. He would order the arrest of Owen Oliver on suspicion of having destroyed

Captain Loveacre's aeroplane. Oliver might talk, and, if he did not, then he would have to be made to talk. In addition to this move he would search Gurner's Hotel for Illawalli without the formality of a search warrant. Bluff! It would be a gigantic bluff. He would either smash his career or discover the person who drugged Miss Double M. Into his world of thought entered the pleasing voice of Shuteye.

"What you do now, Bony?" he asked softly.

"Throw a seven if you don't eat your breakfast, Bony, that's what you'll be doing," warned Bill Sikes. "You smoke and smoke and not eat. That no good."

Bony looked at them. They were squatting over the small fire eating a johnny-cake held in one hand and a wedge of grilled steak held in the other. His meat and johnny-cake they had placed on a plate together with a knife and fork, and into a tin pannikin had been poured strong tea.

"You are a pair of good lads," he told them smilingly, and at once their faces brightened. "This day will determine whether I go back to Brisbane as a senior police officer, or I wire to Marie, my wife, to join me and go bush for ever. First we will go to Gurner's Hotel. Then we will call in at Tintanoo."

It was a few minutes after six when they set off for the main road and Gurner's Hotel. They were bogged four times before getting off the little-used track beside which they had made camp, and it was, therefore, nearly eleven when Bony pulled up outside the wayside hostelry.

"You two come with me," directed Bony. "I want you to do just what I tell you, and do it without asking questions."

Within the bar they found Gurner alone. He was seated behind the counter, engaged by a newspaper.

"Hullo, Inspector! Found that nig yet?" Gurner demanded with sarcasm in his throaty voice.

"Not yet, Mr Gurner. I wish to use your telephone. May I?"

Mr Gurner slipped off his high-legged chair to raise a counter flap, permitting Bony to reach the wall telephone at that end of the bar.

"Serve each of my friends with a bottle of lemonade, and draw me a glass of beer," Bony ordered.

"It's against the law to serve aborigines here. Still—lemonade's all right, I suppose."

"I am not respecting the law to-day," said Bony. "It may be that after to-day you may not be troubled to serve aborigines with anything, Mr Gurner."

"What's that?"

"One moment, please." Bony rang, and Miss Saunders's cool voice replied.

"Kindly put me through to the police-station," requested the detective, watching Gurner attending to the drinks. Then, with a palm pressed against the mouthpiece, he said to Bill Sikes: "Go out and bring Jack Johnson here."

Wordlessly the aboriginal obeyed. Mr Gurner stared at Bony. Miss Saunders said: "Here you are," and then Mrs Cox spoke.

"He is up the street somewhere," she said in reply to Bony's inquiry after her husband. "Is it important? Who is speaking?"

Bony informed her and stressed his wish to speak with the sergeant, whereupon Mrs Cox volunteered to go after him.

Replacing the telephone receiver, the detective passed to the front of the counter and picked up the glass of beer after pushing lemonade towards Shuteye. Mr Gurner pretended to be interested in his paper—until Bill Sikes returned pushing a reluctant blackfellow before him.

"You Jack Johnson?" sharply demanded Bony.

"Too ri'!" assented the yardman. Bony went on:

"I wanted to tell you a little story, Jack Johnson. There was, not far way, a station homestead where the cat always was having a rough time. It appeared that when the missus nagged the boss he roared at the boss stockman, and the boss stockman snarled at the stockmen, and the stockmen kicked their dogs, and the dogs chased the unfortunate cat. As there was a drought, the cat could not stalk the birds and take it out of them. Now, Jack Johnson, you are the cat. You are going to get all the kicks and no ha'-pence. I am going to arrest you and take you off to jail."

"Whaffor! Whaffor, Bony, boss, Mister Bonaparte? Me done nuthin'. Whaffor me go jail?"

"Because you are a bad-feller blackfeller," Bony said mercilessly. "You are the cat, remember. In jail all blackfeller get one big walloping. Do you want me to arrest you and take you to jail?"

"No, no! Me no wantum!" cried poor Jack Johnson.

"All right, then. Now you tell me where that blackfeller chief, Illawalli, is."

"How in hell does he know that?" interposed Mr Gurner.

"You are one of the dogs that chased the cat," Bony told him. "Kindly be silent. Now, Jack Johnson!"

"He doesn't know where——"

"Yes, I do Mister Bony Bonaparte," yelled Jack Johnson. "I no go jail. I tell you. Ole Illawalli, him down in store cellar."

The telephone bell rang sharply.

"He—he's lying," shouted Gurner, pointing at the quaking yardman. "The missing nigger isn't on my premises, I tell you. If he is, then that black devil sneaked him into my cellar."

"Quiet, Mr Gurner. One moment, please," entreated the detective. "Ah! That you, Sergeant? You know who is speaking? Right! The time has come to act. I want you to go along to the post office and request Mr Watts immediately to relieve Miss Saunders from duty. I understand that Mrs Watts was at one time a telephone operator, so she may be prevailed to take over from Miss Saunders. Please do that. I want Miss Saunders out of that post office in ten minutes. Ring me when she has been relieved."

Turning away from the instrument, Bony regarded Gurner with gleaming eyes peering beneath knit brows. Gurner looked most uncomfortable. It was evident that he had no idea why Bony was demanding the removal of the telephone operator at Golden Dawn. Then Bony said softly:

"You, Bill Sikes, take Shuteye and make Jack Johnson show you where Illawalli is. Bring him here."

"I won't have it," shouted Mr Gurner violently. "Where's your warrant?"

"Permit me to remind you, Mr Gurner, that your premises are open to the police at any time. Permit me also to remind you that your best future policy is to confess all you know about the kidnapping of Illawalli, and of several other matters about which I intend to ask you."

The discovery of Illawalli now spurred Bony to the edge of recklessness. In the bar Gurner's breathing was the only sound. The publican was watching Bony with his little eyes. The detective could see the man's brain working at high pressure. To them presently came the sound of shuffling feet approaching the bar along the house passage, and then into the bar came Shuteye and Bill Sikes carrying by feet and shoulders the inert figure of an ancient, white-haired aboriginal, who still wore on his head an airman's flying helmet.

It was Illawalli.

"Is he dead?" inquired Bony with icy calm.

Shuteye laughed. "Ole Illawalli, him drunk."

"He was down there in the booze cellar all free to drink what he liked," supplemented Bill Sikes. "And he liked, too right!"

"I know nothing about him!" shouted Gurner, springing off his chair to peer over the counter at the figure now lying on the bar-room floor.

"Jack Johnson, he says Gurner and Mr Kane took ole Illawalli down into the cellar," Sikes explained. "Jack Johnson say Mr Kane brought Illawalli in his car. They took Illawalli down the cellar, and Mr Kane himself say to drink up and stay there before Bony come for him."

"Lies! All lies!" cried Gurner violently. "If it ain't lies—if Mr Kane did put him down my cellar—then he'll pay for all the grog that nig has swamped! I didn't know he was down there. I ain't been there for a week."

"Jack Johnson says you and Mr Kane took tucker down to ole Illawalli, and las' night when ole Illawalli wanted to come up you took him a few Pink-eye gins to keep him drunk," Bill Sikes continued. "Ain't that all correct, Jack Johnson?"

The yardman admitted it with surprising cheerfulness.

Again the telephone bell rang shrilly.

"Cox here, Bony. Mr Watts wants to speak."

"Very well."

"Ah, Mr Bonaparte! W-what's all this regarding Miss Saunders?" stuttered the postmaster. "Sergeant Cox asks me to suspend from duty the telephone exchange operator, Miss Saunders, but he gives me no grounds for such action.

I don't understand it. Without grounds for action I could not do that. Miss Saunders has always given me satisfaction."

"Mr Watts," Bony said calmly, "I thought it better to ask you to suspend Miss Saunders from duty than to instruct Sergeant Cox to arrest her. You see, the local lock-up has only two cells. One of them is already occupied, and I want to fill the other with another person. However, if you decline to suspend her from duty——"

"Good God!" Watts exclaimed in a lowered voice. "All right. I'll do it. I can send for my wife to take over *pro tem.* All the same, I fear there will be departmental trouble."

"In which case you will receive promotion and a transfer to a more pleasant locality," Bony reminded him, chuckling. "Please ask Sergeant Cox to speak."

When Cox spoke Bony asked him if Miss Saunders had left the exchange.

"Yes, she is just passing out through the post office door," Cox stated grimly. "What's she done?"

Bony looked at Gurner, and Gurner was staring blankly at him.

"As Miss Saunders has been suspended from duty, Sergeant, get a warrant and arrest Owen Oliver on a charge of having destroyed an aeroplane, the property of Captain Loveacre."

Cox wanted to bark a dozen questions, but all he said was. "Very well."

"And, Sergeant, use care in this matter," Bony urged. "Better go prepared for violence. Now, please put me through to Coolibah."

In two minutes he was in touch with John Nettlefold.

"Tell me, Mr Nettlefold, which is the better track to

Coolibah from Gurner's Hotel—that via Tintanoo, or that via Faraway Bore?"

"Via Tintanoo, Bony. The track from Faraway Bore is impassable between the river and the Rockies. Have you had any success?"

"I am leaving at once for Coolibah. *Au revoir.*"

Sikes was ordered to go out to the utility and arrange the gear so that Illawalli might be placed on it for the journey to Coolibah. Insensible though he was, the patriarch's face was a noble one. The incongruous airman's helmet was removed, and Shuteye was sent with it to the car, Bony knowing how that helmet would be prized in the days to come. When his assistants returned the detective was taking a statement from Gurner, who now had decided to tell all he knew. Which, outside the kidnapping of Illawalli, was not much.

Illawalli was removed to the utility. Gurner was requested to sign the statement and to initial every page of it. Then Bony asked for a screw-driver. He took the telephone instrument bodily from the wall and carried it out to the car.

"Just so that you can't ring up Mr Kane and talk about the weather," he told Gurner.

CHAPTER XXV

COOLIBAHS IN WATER

THE day turned out to be brilliantly fine. Small and fluffy clouds hung suspended against the turquoise sky while a light southerly wind tempered the sun's heat. Bony, with Bill Sikes beside him and Shuteye looking after Illawalli in the truck body of the car, drove towards Tintanoo at a steady thirty miles an hour. Eventually they saw the red-roofed buildings marching to meet them from out the sparse scrub.

The main road passed five hundred yards south of the homestead. For traffic destined to call at Tintanoo there was a branch turn-off from the main road on both sides before coming opposite the homestead, and when Bony and his companions reached the western turn-off, a blue-coloured single-seater shot out of the eastern turn-off and on the main road, and in a moment had disappeared over the lip of the incline leading down to the river channels. For just one instant they had been able to see the driver. It was John Kane, driving his Bentley in his usual reckless manner. Bony felt sure that he was heading for either Golden Dawn or Coolibah.

He was sure, too, that John Kane had recognized the Coolibah utility if not its driver. At the moment Bony had seen him, the man was smiling. The detective wrenched at the steering wheel and shot off the main road and up the east turn-off. A few seconds later they stopped before the office. Ordering Sikes to follow him, Bony jumped for the veranda, found the office door locked, and then shouted to his companion to join him in the assault on it.

The door crashed inward at the impact of their combined weight, and the detective sprang to the government telephone. He rang, waited. He rang again, and waited another quarter-minute. Then he opened the box of the machine and found that the batteries had been removed.

"Bring in Gurner's telephone," he ordered sharply. "Hurry, and take care not to upset the batteries in it. Understand?"

"Too right!" shouted Sikes, and leaped for the door.

It was quicker to transfer the wires from one instrument to another than to change the batteries, and within three minutes, with Sikes holding the hotel instrument in his arms, Bony heard the cool voice of the postmaster's wife, who had taken over the duties of Miss Saunders.

"Police-station, please," he requested quickly.

A further thirty seconds of anxious waiting followed, and then came the voice of Constable Lovitt.

"Ah, Lovitt! This is Inspector Bonaparte. Where is Sergeant Cox?"

"He's gone out to Windy Creek, Inspector."

"Listen carefully then. I want you to act immediately. Get astride that motor-cycle of yours and take the track to Tintanoo. Ride like the devil. You will meet John Kane on the road, for he has just left Tintanoo. If you do not meet him before you reach the Coolibah junction track make sure that he has not turned and gone to Coolibah. If he has, get after him! If he has not, then you must block the road with fallen timber in order to stop him. You are to arrest him. Have you got all that clearly?"

"Yes, sir. On what charge is he to be arrested?"

"On the charge of having stolen Captain Loveacre's aeroplane."

Lovitt whistled. Then he said:

"Special precautions, Inspector?"

"Yes, certainly! Hold him until I reach you. Don't waste a moment! It is vital that you reach the road junction before he does."

Bony rang off. His blue eyes were gleaming. The time for action had come, and he was thrilling like a racehorse going to the starting-post. The removal of the telephone batteries had been the grounds for his present action, and before he looked inside the second telephone instrument, that communicating with the river homesteads, he knew that the batteries in it would be missing, too. Above this second machine was a card bearing the names of homesteads, and opposite that of Coolibah was printed: "*Three short rings.*"

Within half a minute Gurner's instrument was attached to the wires of the second telephone, and within thirty more seconds the detective sighed with relief on hearing Elizabeth's voice.

"Ask Dr Knowles to speak to me, please, Miss Nettlefold. Hurry. The matter is urgent. Yes, yes! No questions now. Dr Knowles, please."

Then Knowles was asking the reason for the summons.

"Where is Nettlefold?" demanded Bony, and, on being told that the cattleman was out on the run, he groaned. "Listen, Doctor! I have reason to believe that John Kane is making for Coolibah to do that patient of yours a mischief. I have just got in touch with Lovitt. I have ordered him to ride his motor-cycle to meet Kane, who has just left Tintanoo, and to arrest him. I hope that Lovitt will reach the road junction before Kane does, but there is the possibility of Kane's getting there first. Nettlefold being away with the car complicates matters. What's that? Ted Sharp is there with his runabout! Now let me think. Wait a moment. Yes! I'll take a chance with Ted Sharp. Drive with him towards the road junction, say about two miles, and there block the road with trees to stop Kane's car. If he gets ahead of Lovitt, bail him up and hold him until Lovitt arrives. *On no account let him pass!* I am uneasy about Ted Sharp. I hope unjustifiably; but you must use your discretion. Take a gun. Kane might attempt to use one. Will you go at once?"

"You can depend on us, Bony. And you can depend on Sharp, too, I think," Knowles said quietly and without bothering to ask time-wasting questions. "We will go at once. We'll take care of Kane."

"Good man! Kane is in his Bentley, and I have not a ghost of a chance of overhauling him. Now get away. And' thank you!"

Without troubling to remove Gurner's telephone instrument, Bony shouted to Bill' Sikes, and together they ran out to the utility. Crying to Shuteye to get aboard, Bony started the engine, and they were away, roaring down the steep incline to the river channels.

"Shuteye!" he shouted, and then when Shuteye replied: "Open my suitcase and give me my pistol."

The utility roared up the first of the channel banks, and Shuteye handed the pistol round the hood to Bill Sikes, who passed it to Bony. Bony put the weapon on the seat beside him, and shouted to Shuteye to stand up and keep a look-out forward above the hood for Kane's Bentley. There was the possibility that beyond one of the river channel banks, lying concealed, John Kane awaited them to fire a fusillade of bullets. He could do that easily enough; he could destroy them and yet remain safe himself behind an earth-work.

Suddenly Bony jammed brakes, bringing the utility to a screaming halt on the narrow summit of a bank. Down in the channel beyond them was slipping southward a body of brown water. It was the beginning of a great flood of water that had fallen over the Diamantina water-shed from the recent storm.

"Go back! Turn round, Bony! It's a flood!" cried Bill Sikes.

Actuated by the same impulse, they left the car and were joined by the excited Shuteye. They saw the water stretching north and south in that channel that was, perhaps, fifty feet in width, water cutting them off from the eastern side of the Diamantina. It came sweeping round a northern bend, carrying sticks and rubbish, rippleless, in aspect solid, probably as yet only a foot deep.

Beyond them the coolibah trees shut from sight the distant sand-dunes bordering the east side of the river. Bony turned to the runabout, jumped up into the truck body and then climbed to the hood top. From this position he could see the eastern sand-dunes, and he estimated them to be one and a half miles distant at the nearest.

One and a half miles of channels rapidly flooding to bar them from the eastern sand-dunes, and some eight miles of them lying westward to the high ground at Tintanoo! Why had not the doctor reported the coming of this flood? Had he known? Had Kane, for some reason, deliberately kept the Coolibah people ignorant of its coming? But now was no time to cogitate. Soon they would be like mice floating on a wood chip in a bucket of water. Already in the deeper channel they had crossed, the flood water must be increasing.

It was too late to turn back—even were he so minded. Were they west of the river the flood would cut them off from Coolibah for weeks. Even minus the urgency of getting Illawalli to Coolibah, their only chance of life was to push forward to the nearest side of the river—east—push on on foot, because the utility would certainly be stopped in that deepening channel.

"Come on, Bony!" the blacks shouted in unison. "Quick! Water coming down behind!"

The detective glanced to his rear. A line of debris was being rolled over and over down the channel last crossed, and beyond it the sunlight gleamed on runnelled water. The debris line passed them, travelling faster than a man could run.

Bony shook his head, and jumped to the ground.

"We would never get back to the west side," he advised his companions. "We have to get Illawalli and ourselves to the east side, which roughly is a mile and a half distant. Bill, unstrap the water-bag."

Shuteye laughed, faintly hysterical.

"Wot for we want water?" he asked. "Plenty water in the ole Diamantina now."

"We must try to revive Illawalli. We cannot carry him far," Bony said sharply.

Shuteye and he dragged the inert form from the utility, and Bony, snatching the water-bag from Bill Sikes, poured a stream of cold water on the face of the heavily-breathing aboriginal chief. A bony black hand feebly attempted to ward off the stream. Black eyes opened—to be blinded with water. The sunken mouth opened—to be filled with water. The gaunt figure then struggled to rise, and was assisted by the detective and Sikes.

"Who you?" Illawalli asked the latter.

On turning to see who held him on his other side, his narrowed, lethargic eyes opened to their fullest extent.

"Bony!" he gasped. "Goo' ole Bony! Ough! I bin feel crook. Plenty too much booze."

"Listen, Illawalli," Bony urged earnestly. "We are caught by a big flood. We have to wade and swim to reach high land, do you understand? Wake up! Do you hear me! *Wake up!*"

"Too right! Ough! I'm crook."

Illawalli was violently sick, while they dragged him down the channel bank to the edge of the shallow water. The water was flowing swiftly, but did not reach their knees when they splashed across to the farther dry bank. The old man's legs were so useless to him that it was necessary almost to carry him up the bank, with Shuteye pushing him behind.

The next channel was dry as yet, but it was their last dry crossing.

Strength slowly returned to Illawalli's skinny legs. The flying helmet was jammed hard down on his white head, the chin-straps flapping on his thin shoulders. The head sagged pitifully. He cried constantly to be allowed to lie down. When crossing a channel in which the water reached their waists, Bony splashed it up into the chief's face, and this assisted to revive him.

"Goo' ole Bony! My father and my mother! My friend! My son!" Between gulps for air he ejaculated these expressions of affection. "That there little white feller, he give me booze, plenty booze. He say you come soon, Bony. He say me drink up, and I ole fool. I drink up plenty. I ole fool to drink and drink, but little feller white feller; he don' want no money, he don' want nothing. He good feller white feller, and I was ole fool. Ough! This feller plenty crook."

"You will get better as we go along," Bony said cheerfully. "Ah—here is where we swim."

Wading now was no longer possible. To cross a fifty-yards-wide channel meant being swept down several yards. To cross a channel two hundred yards wide in which the current was stronger meant a crossing at a sharp angle. Fortunately, Coolibah homestead lay many miles to the south, but the farther south the flood swept them so much wider was the crossing.

The sun poured its heat on them, and to each man was attached a cloud of flies and mosquitoes. To touch a stick on the water was to be bitten or stung by a venomous insect. The banks were giving up their countless insect inhabitants, and these were swarming into the coolibah trees.

Gradually the effects of alcohol were lifting from Illawalli. Forced exertion and contact with water were lightening the lethargy from the old aboriginal's brain. That was just as well, for all were rapidly tiring. They could not linger on a dry bank before taking the water of each channel. Before and behind them ranged the coolibahs—strange, shapeless trees of which not one inch of wood was straight. Already the low-lying channel banks were submerged, bringing two channels together to form a wide, swiftly-moving, brown flood, the submerged channel banks marked only by the line of trees rooted in them. Dry banks became ever more widely separated, and those yet above water were rapidly sinking into the flood like bars of sugar in hot tea.

"Look, Bony! There's a car!" shouted Bill Sikes, as they stood in a group on a dry bank, Illawalli now needing but little assistance. On the far side, apparently floating on the water, was the black top of a car hood. Its passengers were not to be seen. They were not sheltering on the opposite bank or clinging to coolibah trees beyond it.

Whose car? About a mile of water channels and bank islands lay between it and the distant sand-dunes now to be observed beyond the trees and supporting the turquoise rim of the sky. Bony knew, of course, that there they must be at least a mile south of the road crossing. The car would not have floated down to its present position, and the only inference to be drawn was that its driver had been following a little-used track, or no track at all, to reach the eastern side of the river near Coolibah. Was it John Kane's Bentley? While his assistants were helping Illawalli, Bony ran along the bank and took to the water above the submerged vehicle. Reaching the hood, he gripped it and worked his way round it. He found that it was facing the east. Not without difficulty, he felt with his feet into the driving seat, discovering nothing to prove that the body of the driver was there. Farther round the hood he managed to stand on the engine bonnet, and again feeling with his feet he established that the radiator mascot was the figure of a swan. It was Kane's Bentley.

Experiencing infinite relief, Bony swam on after the others. So Kane had been caught by the flood water just as they had been. He had been going to Coolibah by a short cut, avoiding the mileage via the road junction, and had he reached Coolibah this way he would have been unopposed, because the doctor and Ted Sharp would be two miles away on the road to Golden Dawn.

The flood was rising with astonishing rapidity. The channel banks were noticeably sinking into the brown water, sliding in vast volume southward to the arid desert of north-eastern South Australia, there to vanish into the earth or to be evaporated by the sun.

The race for life continued. Illawalli had so far recovered from the effects of his debauch as to be able to manage for himself. The four kept together, the first to climb out on to a channel bank waiting to assist the others. No man showed signs of panic; no man swam ahead in a frantic effort to reach dry land, to save his own life, careless of the fate of his companions.

Being the oldest, Illawalli was the first to tire. Then Bony began to feel the effects of the swim. Shuteye maintained his vigour, while Bill Sikes was to prove a tower of strength.

At last they reached a narrow ribbon of dry channel bank. The water could be seen eating into it like ink into blotting paper. Bebind them no ground was visible at the foot of the lines of coolibah trees.

Bony was panting for air. Illawalli crouched on the narrowing ribbon of ground. The others turned anxious eyes to the old man and Bony. After a moment or two Bony squared himself and gravely addressed Bill Sikes and Shuteye.

"We have a long swim yet. I want you to understand that Illawalli must be taken to Coolibah as quickly as possible. You have to help him and not bother with me. You have to take him to the white feller doctors at Coolibah. Illawalli, my old friend, you have to put up a big fight. When you reach Coolibah tell them who you are. Tell them that you have come to read the mind of the sick white woman. They will take you to her. You will touch her and read out her mind to the white feller doctors what you see there."

The old and marked face melted into a smile.

"You funny feller, Bony. We go where you go," Illawalli said.

"Too right!" agreed Shuteye.

"Me, too!" added Bill Sikes. "You blow out, Shuteye he help you. Ole Illawalli blow out, me help him. Too right!"

"Neither of you alone can help Illawalli to reach dry ground. If you don't do as I say we may all be drowned. No, you both must help Illawalli."

"Too much talk," Illawalli pointed out impressively. "Like white feller, we throw 'way too much time. Water—she get higher and highest and she run fast and fastest. Plenty time corroboree talk afterwards, eh?"

"Confound you for staunch fellers," Bony shouted.

Together they stepped into the water and swam. Careful not to expend energy through fighting the current, they swam steadily.

There was no cease from effort, no respite during which strength might be recuperated. Bony's arms now were filled with lead. His thighs were aching with cramp. He was being swept into a tree-top by a strength greater than his own, a tree-top rushing at him with traps set beneath and above the water, fashioned by its gnarled branches.

He felt a body beside his own—a body that pushed vigorously. Shuteye cried out:

"Swim, Bony! Swim, Bony! Go on, swim, Bony!"

With the low measure of his failing strength, Bony struck out. Cramp! He was getting cramp in his legs. They felt dreadful. If only he could stop movement and rest. What the devil was Shuteye punching him for?

"Take 'er easy, Bony," shouted the fat man from beside him. "Clear water now. On your back! On your back! Ole John Kane, he war perched in tree like a fowl. You hear him screech?"

Bony obeyed. The clear dome of the restful sky met his weary eyes. His mind was dominated by a strange lethargy.

He found that existence was quite pleasant: this drifting, this gentle drifting. . . .

"Come on, Bony! Give 'er a go! Kickum feet!" implored Shuteye. "Go on! You sleep? *Kickum feet!*"

Bony obeyed, finding that the pain had gone from his legs, but that still the molten lead remained in his bones. Time went on and on. Kick, kick, kick! Always kicking. Why was he always kicking? It was so senseless. He wanted just to rest.

Quite without a period of transition, his mind became clear. He could hear Shuteye's rasping breathing, and he felt the swirl of water about him created by Shuteye's legs. And he knew that Shuteye would not abandon him even to save himself.

"Let go!" he shouted weakly.

Turning like an eel, he was swimming beside the gasping Shuteye. Now, so near that their whaleback summits towered above them, a range of sand-dunes, clean of herbage and light red of colour, was sliding northward. Desperately he swam. Someone was yelling, and because it was not Shuteye, he wondered who it could be. Now Shuteye was trying to shout, a gurgle in his voice. Bony was spent. It was now impossible for him to swim. Why swim, anyway? There was neither sense nor reason in swimming when he did not want to. The light went out in a red glare which quickly faded to complete darkness. Someone was still holding him, still punching him. It was not unpleasant, this surcease from action. Then the daylight burst into his open eyes, and he saw the ugly face of Bill Sikes. He smiled at Bill Sikes, and then closed his eyes.

CHAPTER XXVI

THE MIRACLE

IT was like waking in the warm sunlight of early morning. The harsh cries of cockatoos came across the summits of the dunes from a line of bloodwoods behind them. But when Bony stirred and sat up he was violently sick. Beside him was old Illawalli, who took one of his hands.

"I wait, Bony. I know you sleep. Bimeby you be all ri'. You jus' tired, but bimeby you all ri'."

A peculiarly exquisite sensation was running up his arm above the hand held by the chief, a feeling that quickly banished the terrible lethargy of all his muscles. It crept all through his body and swept out of his mind the desire to sleep, like a fresh breeze off the ocean. Now, without assistance, he sat up straight. Illawalli continued to hold his hand.

The westering sun hung above the distant lines of coolibah trees ranged beyond the wide stretch of water visibly running past them—water which the circular line of dunes pressed back to the west. Bony and his companion sat within a few feet of the brown flood, while farther along the "shore" Shuteye was working a pointed stick with his hands, and Bill Sikes was determinedly blowing into a little pile of dead and powdered speargrass among which the stick point was buried. Smoke was rising from the grass pile, and the fat man was urging the other to blow harder.

"That Bill Sikes, he fine feller," Illawalli said with conviction. "He grab me and he pull me out of the water. Then he run alonga sand range and in he go for you and Shuteye. Shuteye he not let you go till he pretty near dead drowned, and Bill Sikes he have to get Shuteye and you out together. No Bill Sikes, Bony, you dead now, all ri'!"

"I can believe that, Illawalli. How do you feel?"

The old man's black eyes twinkled. The white stubble of beard and the fringe of scant white hair, to be seen below the flying helmet, emphasized the colour of his skin.

"We rode the emu that flies, the white captain and me," he said. "We see the clouds of the beeg storm ri' close. Then we go look over top of them. Cripes, I was cold, Bony! I shiver. I want little fires all round, but I don' mind. The emu that flies couldn't get over that storm. She thunder and she lightning. Funny, I want to puff and puff, and puffin' no good. Then the white feller captain—him good feller all ri'—him send that emu down closer to ground and I stop puff puffing and don't want little fires no more. Then we get closer to the storm and presently we fly over station homestead. But it ain't no plurry good. We're too late for the emu to stop and have shuteye. We fly along above track. Then we see house. Then we come down, and the emu begins to run alonga ground. *Woof! Bang!* Som'it hit me wallop, and I go shuteye.

"I wake up with little white feller looking at me, and tall white feller clost. He had beeg eyes and a devil in his mouth, and he say: 'You Chief Illawalli?' I say, yes, too right! He say: 'You come see Bony?' I say, yes, too right. He say: 'I take you see ole Bony. This white feller, he take care of white feller captain.'

"So off we go in motee car. She rain and she thunder and lightning, and the tall white feller he drive motee like hell. Presently we stop at a pub like that one up in Burketown. Then white feller with devil in his mouth, he say: 'You gotta stop here and wait for Bony. Bony come bimeby. Then he take me down steps. He go away and come back with pannikins and a little devil you take off shiney things from bottles. Him not too bad. We drink up goodo. I have a shuteye long time, wake up, and a drink up goodo, go shuteye some more. Bimeby little feller white feller he came down and he say: 'How you do, Illawalli? You have good drink up. All yours. You no pay. So I drink up like an ole fool. Now ole Illawalli him pretty crook."

"Did the devil in the white feller's mouth go like this?" asked Bony, imitating John Kane's peculiar mouth twitch.

"Too ri'!" assented Illawalli. "Now whaffor you want me, Bony?"

"You 'member long time ago I sent an emu that flies to bring you to a station called Windee, and there you met old Moongalliti and told me all that was in his mind?"

"'Course! I don' forget. You 'member I wantum to be beeg feller blackfeller with ole Moongalliti and I gave him white feller dope and then when he plenty sick we go look-see him and I give him blackfeller dope make him well. Me, I beeg blackfeller after that. Too right!"

Bony told all he knew concerning the condition of Muriel Markham, and of his hopes that, by the aid of his remarkable powers, Illawalli would read the young woman's mind and tell them many things.

"Goodo! I see what she thinks." Then the ancient chief leaned towards Bony, his keen eyes studying the detective, in them a look of entreaty. "An' you 'member me say one, two, three times me say, I give you the secrets my father give me and his father give him and so 'way back before

Ara waded through the sea to come and drop spirit babies in the bush to wait for blackfeller lubras to come by?"

"Yes, I 'member," assented Bony wistfully. "But the price you ask I cannot pay. Do not tempt me again, Illawalli. I cannot pay it. I cannot give up my whitefeller life to rule your tribe after you dead." Then, as though to put temptation behind him, he called to Shuteye. "Hi, you Shuteye! That tobacco dry yet?"

The two blacks had kindled the fire and were drying tobacco and cigarette papers. At Bony's voice they turned about to grin delightedly at him, and Bill Sikes called out:

"You good, Bony! You wanta smoke?"

Bony stood up.

"I do," he replied. "How far are we from Coolibah?"

" 'Bout ten mile," replied Shuteye.

"Then, when that tobacco is dry, we will be getting along. I'm hungry. We all must be hungry."

"Too right, we're hungry," agreed the fat Shuteye. And Bill Sikes asked:

"Hey! Wot are we gonna do with Mr Kane? He's roostin' like a fowl in a tree out there."

"Where?" demanded the astonished detective.

"Out there!" shouted Shuteye mirthfully. "We come along pass him, 'member, when I lug you alonga."

They pointed to the nearest line of coolibah trees, fully a third of a mile across the brown flood, and, knowing the aborigines as he did, the detective was astounded by the casual manner in which John Kane's dangerous position was made known to him. Illawalli had recited his adventures; the others had laboured at making a fire with primitive methods: all while a white man was in grave danger of drowning.

Faintly from the north the soft chug-chugging of a motor-cycle engine reached them, and above the relief that Kane had not reached Coolibah was now the satisfaction that Constable Lovitt was approaching. The aborigines—their philosophy in many respects was delightful—thought to do nothing until their leader Bony, should recover sufficiently to continue to give directions with regard to the rescue of a man whom they knew was to be arrested.

Lovitt came in sight, riding his machine with practised facility along the foot of the sandhills. His progress was necessarily slow, and it was some few minutes before he arrived.

"Glad to find that you got over all right, sir."

"Yes," admitted Bony. "We have had a long and arduous swim. I would have been drowned had it not been for Shuteye and Bill Sikes. I shall make it a point to see that they are suitably rewarded."

"I did not meet John Kane, sir," Lovitt explained. "When I came to the flood I knew that if either you or he did escape it that you would land far south of the road crossing. Have you seen anything of him?"

"Oh, yes. Like us, he was caught," Bony replied. "Only a minute ago my attention was drawn to the fact that he is now roosting like a fowl in one of the nearest line of coolibah trees. How we are going to rescue him I do not rightly know. I am afraid I could never manage it."

Lovitt gazed out to the trees and vainly tried to pick out John Kane, despite the eager assistance of the two blacks. They could see him, they asserted, but the constable could not make him out until he used the field-glasses he carried in his kit-bag.

"Yes, there he is," he said. "He's in that largest tree towards the end of the line. Well, sir, I think I'll go out for him."

"The current is very strong, Lovitt," Bony pointed out. "There is no possibility of obtaining a boat, I suppose?"

" 'Fraid not, sir. No, I'll have to swim. Will you come with me, Sikes?"

"Too right!" replied the ugly but tough aboriginal.

"Me too," chipped in Shuteye. "We go up river about a mile, swim down to Mr Kane, and then fetch him out alonga that sandhill down there."

"That's sound," agreed Lovitt. He eyed Illawalli and said: "You can come with us up river and take charge of our clothes. Bring them down to where we'll get ashore."

They all walked northward along the edge of the river for nearly a mile until Lovitt decided, after a searching study of the flotsam, on the place to take off. White man and blacks stripped, and with dawning comprehension Bony watched the constable strap his pair of handcuffs to his naked waist.

"I may have to knock him out, sir," Lovitt said casually.

"You may," Bony gravely agreed. "If he refuses to leave his perch there will be nothing else for it. Good luck!"

Illawalli and he picked up the constable's uniform and the blacks' clothes, and slowly walked downstream watching the bobbing heads. Wisely, Lovitt allowed Sikes to lead, and the watchers saw how Sikes craftily swam with the current and yet edged constantly farther from the shore. Presently, when the three were being swept swiftly downstream, Bony and the old chief were forced to walk rapidly.

They could just see the three heads reach the tallest tree of the line, and after that they could not follow what happened. It was Illawalli who first saw the three rescuers far below the tip of the tree line, and they left to walk on round the great natural bay created by the sand-dunes that turned the flood westward.

They were standing waiting and watching Lovitt and Bill Sikes bringing ashore the inert figure of the Tintanoo squatter. They waded into the flood to assist them, and Kane was dragged to dry land.

"Half-drowned?" Bony inquired.

"No, he is all right," Lovitt panted. "As I expected, he wouldn't leave the tree. I had to go after him, and got badly scratched. Was compelled to knock him out; but we got him, and that's the main thing."

Dr Stanisforth straightened up from his bent attitude over the patient at Coolibah, removed the earpieces of the stethoscope, and looked at Dr Knowles with eyes from which hope had vanished.

"She is very low," he said, "but her vitality is extraordinary, and she may live yet another week. At the moment she is not asleep; she is insensible. She may never regain consciousness."

"Then we may no longer hope to save her?" whispered Elizabeth.

"Her condition has failed to react to all our treatment. We have done everything that medical science has made possible."

Knowles turned his anguished face to the wall. The specialist looked pityingly at him. Elizabeth Nettlefold stepped swiftly to the younger man's side and was about to say something when the door opened.

Bony stood surveying them. He glanced across at the white figure on the bed. Knowles leapt across the room so that they stood face to face, the doctor's eyes desperate, the eyes of the detective without expression. Then, into the tense hush broke the soft voice of the half-caste.

"Will you permit my friend, Illawalli, to visit your patient, Doctor?" he asked quietly.

"What! You have found that aboriginal witch doctor? You have come through the flood?"

"Yes. Illawalli is outside, awaiting your permission to enter."

The hope blazing from Knowles's eyes subsided.

"You are too late," he said bitterly.

"Then Miss Double M is dead?"

"No, Mr Bonaparte, but she is close to death," Stanisforth answered. "She is no longer conscious."

"Even so, you will allow my friend to see her?"

The specialist shrugged. "Your friend can do no harm," he grudgingly conceded.

"Very well, then. Kindly do not interfere with Illawalli."

Opening the door, Bony beckoned, and there entered the tall, gaunt figure of the old chief still wearing the flying helmet.

"Illawalli," Bony said softly, "the white woman is dying. Can you read the mind of a dying woman?"

The incongruously-dressed ancient swiftly appraised the others.

"I have been thinking," he said. "Maybe it is as I have thought. Give me light."

Bony switched on the ceiling light. Illawalli passed to the bed, and gazed down at the wasted, expressionless face. The silence within and without the room was profound. The specialist was visibly sceptical, but on Elizabeth's vivid face shone the dawn of a great hope.

With the ball of a little finger, Illawalli raised the patient's eyelids and gazed long and keenly into the vacant dark-blue eyes turned slightly upward. For fully half a minute he looked down into those vacant eyes, and then gently closed the eyelids. Taking up one of the waxen hands, he pressed the point of a finger into the flesh of the forearm, and Bony saw that the little pit in the flesh made by the forefinger remained clearly indented after the finger point had been removed. Gently the old man put down the nerveless hand and arm on the coverlet. Turning, he addressed Bony:

"Come!"

Then Dr Knowles was standing before them, his eyes glassy, his mouth trembling.

"You can do nothing? You cannot read her mind and tell us who drugged her?" he cried savagely.

"No. Ole Illawalli cannot read the shuteye mind," Illawalli replied with regal dignity. "You wait. Bimeby me and Bony come back. Bimeby sick white woman no shuteye. She get up! She talk! She laugh. Come, Bony!"

Together they passed out of the room, and when in the corridor the old man said sharply:

"Light, Bony! Bring beeg feller light."

The detective found Mr Nettlefold in the study, and the cattleman produced a lamp which gave a brilliant light. Illawalli took it and, with Bony at his heels, hurried from the house. The chief led the way past the men's quarters, on down the creek now filled with the flood water, and then, like a gnome of vast proportions, he set to work gathering the leaves of certain plants brought up by the recent thunderstorms.

"You beeg feller fool this time," he said, chuckling. "You no 'member how blackfeller dope waterholes to make fish all stiff and come to top of water, eh? White woman, she bin doped like blackfeller fish. Now I gibbet her dope to kill the other dope. Me fine feller blackfeller, all ri'! Bimeby that white woman, she goodo. She no die, Bony. No fear! Bimeby she open her eyes and she smile at ole

Illawalli, and then bimeby still she laugh at ole Illawalli and tell him plurry fine blackfeller doctor. Better'n whitefeller doctor, any'ow!"

Bony drew in a long breath.

"Oh, that's it, is it? What a fool I am! What a blind idiot! Why did I not guess that?"

"Don' you lash yourself, Bony," Illawalli pleaded. "You don' look for blackfeller dope in white woman for sure."

"No, I did not look for an aboriginal poison. I saw no aboriginal influence at work in this case. Fool—blind fool! I see it all now. I recall something to which I should have given much greater attention. I was told that John Kane had been living for some time with the aborigines of York Peninsula. Of course! When he learned that you had been sent for he knew for what purpose."

"Don' you lash yourself," again cried old Illawalli. "No man he know all. You worry too much over white woman dying and you don' think properly. Now we go to homestead. I got what I want. We get fire going and we boil up med'cine, eh?"

"Come along, then."

Back again at the big house, Bony called on Hetty, and she took them along to the detached kitchen.

An hour later they slipped into the patient's room. Elizabeth and the two doctors were still there, and to Dr Knowles Bony handed a china basin and a spoon.

"Give her as much of this as it is possible for her to swallow," he instructed.

Stanisforth came forward to gaze disapprovingly at the dark-green liquid in the bowl.

"What is that stuff?" he demanded. "We must know what it is before we can permit it to be given to the patient. We are responsible for her."

"I do not know the ingredients," Bony confessed. "And I do not think Illawalli will tell us. You may, however, have no fear that it will harm her."

"But—but——"

"What is it?" Knowles asked the chief.

"Med'cine make white woman better," came the evasive answer.

Knowles flashed a doubtful look at Stanisforth.

"Tush!" the specialist burst out. "An aboriginal mess like that! It is impossible! It is unheard of! It is an outrage on the ethics of our profession."

"Not long ago hypnotism and psycho-analysis were regarded by medical men as outrages on the ethics of your profession, Doctor," Bony said quietly. "I know the type or class of drug which was given the patient, and this is the antidote."

"It cannot make the patient worse," Knowles cut in impatiently. "I'll give it her."

"The responsibility will be yours, Knowles," Stanisforth said stiffly.

"And mine," Bony added. "And mine. Don't forget that!"

Illawalli was standing apart with arms folded, his majestic face calm in repose. Elizabeth and Hetty gazed from the doctors to him and back again. Abruptly Knowles turned to the bed.

For several minutes he endeavoured to induce the unconscious girl to swallow, and presently he looked up, defeat written in his eyes. Then Illawalli strode round the bed to reach the opposite side of the patient, whose head was cradled in the doctor's right arm. Taking her hands into his, he said softly:

"Drink! Drink! Drink! You hear ole Illawalli talkin'?

He say drink. You drink, white woman! You wake! You hear ole Illawalli talk. You do what ole Illawalli tell you."

For ten minutes they watched and waited, Knowles giving the liquid in the basin drop by drop, keeping her mouth slightly open with the tip of a little finger.

"How much, Illawalli?" he presently asked.

"All, whitefeller doctor."

The minutes passed. The empty basin was taken away by Hetty. They now stood about the foot of the bed. The silence was absolute. Illawalli continued to sit crouchingly, holding the girl's hands, and then he cried softly, triumphantly:

"She comes. White lubra she comes back from the darkness. My hands know it."

"*What!*" Knowles exclaimed in hissing whisper.

"*Hist! Wait!*"

The tension grew: became unbearable and yet had to be borne. Illawalli turned partly round to smile at the watchers. Now they found no incongruity in the tweed trousers and the cheap cotton dress shirt and the flying helmet. In Illawalli's triumphant smile they saw the personality of a man they were never to forget. From him they stared at the marble face still cradled in Knowles's right arm.

"My hands talk. Put her down, whitefeller doctor," Illawalli requested.

Knowles obeyed. Dark lay the hair, and dark lay the lashes on the marble face, so dreadfully devoid of expression. Then Elizabeth bent forward over the bed-rail, and Knowles drew in his breath with a sharp hiss. Elizabeth thought then that the lashes were trembling, and it was the first time she had seen them move. A moment later the miracle happened.

The face of the girl seemed to dissolve. The cold whiteness and the soullessness of it sank away, to be replaced with life and an expression of calm peace. It was as though a statue was coming to life, was alive and sleeping. About the tender mouth hovered the ghost of a sweet smile.

"You wake, white lubra!" cried old Illawalli. "You open your eyes. You see all whitefeller friends and ole Bony and ole Illawalli. You wake, wake, wake! *Open your eyes, your eyes, your eyes!*"

Quite abruptly the girl's eyes were wide open. The smile became more emphatic. The large blue eyes slowly moved their gaze from one to another, taking them all into their orbit.

"You better now, eh?" Illawalli said. "Now you eat plenty tucker, eh? Then you sleep long and wake up strong and goodo, eh?" To Knowles he said: "Quick! Give her tucker. She hungry. She eat. She sleep. Bimeby she goodo."

He continued to hold her hands, and Knowles held a consultation with the specialist.

"All goodo, eh?" queried Illawalli. "Me fine feller blackfeller doctor, eh? Bimeby you eat plenty tucker. You get strong as buffalo."

He continued to hold her hands and to murmur about eating and sleeping, and presently Dr Knowles came with a bowl of beef tea and a little toast. And the patient willingly opened her mouth and swallowed.

"Now you sleep," suggested Illawalli. "You sleep, eh? Sleep is good! Sleep is good!"

And lo! The girl lay sleeping, on her warm face still the sweet smile.

CHAPTER XXVII

KNOTS UNTIED

FOR the first time for weeks a cheerful atmosphere brightened the sunlight falling on Coolibah. Two parties were gathered on the wide south veranda of the spacious house, two parties of happy people taking afternoon tea. One party consisted of the perfect number—two—the patient and Dr Knowles; the other was larger, comprising Elizabeth and her father, Sergeant Cox and Bony, Ted Sharp and Captain Loveacre.

"Bony, before you go, you really must tell us everything," urged Elizabeth. "I've tried the pump-handle on Sergeant Cox, but he clamps that stubborn jaw of his and simply won't speak."

Bony regarded her fresh beauty with twinkling eyes. Then he said solemnly:

"I am almost as tongue-tied as Sergeant Cox."

"Go on, Bony, there's a decent sort," urged the airman, one eye still hidden by the bandage covering his nose.

"Very well, then!" assented Bony. "As a preface, I have to assure you that this case has given my vanity a severe shock. Sergeant Cox has done infinitely more important work than I. In this matter I have been a mere amateur, and the only credit I can take is that I guessed the reason for the conspiracy against the patient's life. Sergeant Cox gathered the proofs.

"Well, the beginning dates back before the war. At the close of 1913 old Mrs Kane was dead, her husband still ruling at Tintanoo. Beside that station he owned considerable property, which he then intended to leave equally to his two sons, John and Charles. That was the year when Golden Dawn was a town ten times larger than it is to-day, when a Miss Piggot was teaching at the school, and a Mr Markham, a solicitor, was living there with his wife.

"Early in 1914 Charles eloped with Miss Piggot, and they went to Sydney. Old man Kane called for Mr Markham, and he made a new will, leaving the whole of his estate to John. Then came the war, and, defying the old man, John joined the A.I.F., went overseas, and eventually obtained a transfer to the Royal Flying Corps. That caused the old man to send for Mr Markham again, and to make a fresh will, leaving everything to his four nephews.

"The old gentleman appeared to have a mania for will-making. In 1920 he made yet another will, in which his two sons were made equal beneficiaries, to the total exclusion of the nephews. Shortly after that John, the son, again quarrelled with his father and went off with a missionary into York Peninsula. He was, strangely enough, keenly interested in anthropology, and when north he heard of Illawalli and his remarkable powers. Once again the old man cut him out of his will, leaving everything to Charles and his heirs.

"Towards the end of this year, 1920, both Charles and his wife were killed in a motor accident, and their tragic deaths materially hastened the death of the old man. Shortly afterwards, Mrs Markham left Golden Dawn to live in Sydney—and to care for Muriel, a daughter born to Charles and his wife, and of whom neither old Kane nor his son John Kane knew anything.

"Old Kane being dead, the son returned to Tintanoo, and it was then made manifest that the old man had been extremely remiss in not himself destroying the wills he had made when each new one was signed. Markham coolly produced the last will, making Charles and his heirs the beneficiaries. Charles was dead, but Charles's daughter was still living. Markham produced the birth certificate. He then produced the previous will, leaving everything to John, and he suggested that in return for a pension of a thousand a year he would put that will forward for probate and withhold the last one. Having obtained an official copy of the birth certificate of Muriel Kane, John Kane surrendered to the blackmail, or rather concurred in the conspiracy.

"Unlike nearly all blackmailers, Markham was satisfied with his thousand a year. He died in 1927, and the pension was paid thereafter to his wife—who held the transferred power. She was not by any means a bad woman. Between her adopted daughter and herself a strong affection had arisen, and on her deathbed, knowing that the pension would cease with her life, she confessed all to Muriel Kane and produced the wills, the last of which left all old man Kane's property to her as heiress of the dead Charles, her father.

"Muriel then wrote to John Kane, her uncle. The letter was typewritten, for the girl had fallen into the modern habit of typing her correspondence. The more easily, as she was a free-lance journalist, and habitually used a machine. Generously, she offered to take but half of the estate, permitting him to retain the other half. He replied, expressing his gratitude and his contrition, and he suggested that as he was in poor health she should visit him at Tintanoo. He would send a neighbour in his car to meet her at Broken Hill. She received that communication the day before Mrs Markham died, and almost at once Owen Oliver left to meet her and to bring her north. It is quite a long story, you see.

"The arrival of Muriel Kane at Tintanoo was arranged. In Golden Dawn was Captain Loveacre and his air circus, and early that day Mrs MacNally, the jackeroo, and all the men at the homestead were sent off to Golden Dawn. They knew nothing of her arrival. At breakfast she was given the poison used by a tribe of aborigines of Northern Australia to poison fish in waterholes and make them rise to the surface. As a student of aboriginal life, Kane knew it well. She was then taken to an uninhabited hut on the boundary of Windy Creek Station.

"Owen Oliver has always been a wild spendthrift, and to curb his vicious habits his father curtailed a once too-generous allowance. Young Oliver began to borrow, and when his creditors threatened to go to his father he applied to John Kane for temporary assistance. It was a debt that made Owen Oliver a tool. Kane promised to wipe out the debt and to give him five thousand pounds for his assistance.

"The night following her arrival at Tintanoo, Muriel Kane found herself paralysed, lying on the floor of the empty hut on Windy Creek. That night John Kane stole the red monoplane and flew there, to land on a narrow ribbon of level ground in the near vicinity and aided only by Oliver's torch. He must have had extraordinary nerve.

"Into the aeroplane they packed a large canister of nitro-glycerine and strapped the helpless girl to the passenger's seat. Kane took enormous risks that night, the chief of which was taking off from unlighted, and almost unknown ground, with that terrible explosive in the plane. He flew straight for the junction of the Coolibah track with the St Albans road. Flying westward, he flew between the homesteads of Coolibah and Tintanoo, picked out his position by a long strip of water lying in one of the river channels, then flew north of west, and so passed north of Gurner's Hotel. He circled southward until he saw below him the bore stream and lake, known as Bore Fourteen, which is but a mile or so north of Emu Lake paddock. There he fixed the controls of the machine, and then he made his only mistake. Before jumping he switched off the engine. With sheepskin boots on his feet he landed by parachute, gathered up the parachute and walked with it to the main road, where Owen Oliver soon arrived to pick him up.

"With extraordinary good fortune the machine landed perfectly on an area of ground, which, compared with the surrounding scrub and broken country, was no larger than a grain of sand. This was something neither Kane nor any one else could have foreseen—something that scarcely any one in the world would have believed possible. But it has happened before.

"Together, Kane and Oliver drove at breakneck to Golden Dawn, where, one mile out, the car was stopped. Kane then walked to the town and to his bed at the hotel, reaching it a little before day broke. Oliver turned the car and drove back to Tintanoo.

"Kane's statement that he was at Golden Dawn immediately after the aeroplane was stolen was false. He certainly was in his bed at the hotel in the morning, but when he claimed to have collided with Dr Knowles in the rush to see the stolen plane fly off, he relied on the doctor being, as was then too often the case, in no condition to deny it.

"Now into this affair entered the telephone exchange operator. She hoped to marry John Kane. He, indeed, had promised to marry her. At his request, she reported to him everything which passed along the telephone wires through her exchange and everything which passed along the telegraph wires through the post office, she being an expert telegraphist and able to hear and read the clacking of the instruments. That is, she told him everything which could, even remotely, bear on the theft of the aeroplane.

"When John Kane learned of the discovery of the monoplane and the young woman in it he communicated with Owen Oliver, and Oliver, wearing his master's sheepskin boots, went out to Emu Lake and fired the machine in order to destroy all fingerprints. The nitro-glycerine, of course, exploded. Knowing that medical men might achieve a cure—knowing that most probably the young woman would be taken away to a town or city hospital—John Kane himself came to the house that same night and attempted to poison Miss Kane by putting strychnine in the brandy. It was his last chance, because that telephone girl informed him of the watch being kept. She informed him of my sending for Illawalli, and without doubt, had Captain Loveacre landed my friend at Golden Dawn, we should have met opposition when bringing him here. I have told you how Kane did deal with Illawalli.

"He knew that I had ordered the suspension of the telephone operator and the arrest of Oliver. He knew, too, I was on my way in from Gurner's Hotel, and he removed and concealed the batteries working the two telephone instruments in his office. Fortunately I had with me the telephone instrument I had removed from Gurner's Hotel. I believe he then planned two objectives. He knew that the flood was nearing Tintanoo, and he decided to lure us in our much slower car across the front of it and then, when he was half-way over, to take a seldom-used branch track leading direct to Coolibah. Had he achieved the first objective he would have been safe, knowing that Oliver would stubbornly refuse to talk. And now Oliver has talked, and John Kane is destined for a long term of imprisonment.

"Kane is somewhat an abnormal type. He has revealed courage of a high order—proved when he took to the air that night with enough nitro-glycerine to blow up a town hall. His plan to remove Miss Kane without trace—that is, without leaving any clue to her identity—was original and well executed. But, like all clever men, he made mistakes—mistakes which a less clever man would not have made! He was clever enough to deny the fact that he held a quantity of nitro-glycerine down in the cellar. Not knowing just what I knew, he played well the card of perfect frankness. That was a good card, and it might have been the winning card if only he had remembered to wipe away Owen Oliver's fingerprints on the empty carboy.

"That, I think, is about all. With Muriel Kane alive he was practically a pauper. She offered him half of her grandfather's estate, but he was not satisfied with that. Having lured her to Tintanoo, having assured himself that the vital wills were lying in a safe-deposit vault in Adelaide, he conceived the idea of stealing the aeroplane, and making certain that his niece's remains would be found among the debris and taken for those of the thief. After all the astonishing risks he took, he should have succeeded, but the more perfectly the crime is conceived and executed so, strangely enough, the more likely is fate or chance or a higher Power to step in."

"But what about Gurner?" protested Cox.

Bony smiled. "Mr Gurner is more fool than knave. He likes, evidently, to oblige powerful squatters. No doubt, in future, my dear Cox, you will keep your eyes on him. As John Kane did not, and now never can, pay him for the drink consumed by Illawalli, I vote that we leave him to gather enough rope for his next masterly crime. When your successor arrives you might——"

"What! You are not leaving us, Sergeant?" exclaimed Nettlefold.

"I did not know——"

"Possibly I have been a little premature," Bony cheerfully cut in, "but I'm afraid that Sergeant Cox will be leaving the district for a more important post as soon as I can arrange matters." He rose, his blue eyes twinkling with good humour. "And now we must be off. I will leave Illawalli to your kind care, Miss Nettlefold. The captain tells me that he will be ready to fly him back to his own people at the end of next week. It was, my dear Captain, both generous and wise of Dr Knowles to make you a gift of his now repaired aeroplane. He will never fly again. He told me that when sober he is a perfect fool in the air, and that, as he has forsworn John Barleycorn, he always will be sober in future. As for your utility, Mr Nettlefold, I will see to it that the loss is made good. Where, I wonder, is my old friend, Illawalli?"

"He is over there playing with a pup," Loveacre replied, pointing out through the fly-gauze to the ancient chief sitting in the shade cast by the office and fondling an energetic cattle pup.

"I will return in a moment. Pardon me," Bony murmured. He left the group and walked along the veranda to the white bed screens. Outside them he coughed loudly, and then with a happy smile stepped round them to see Miss Kane sitting propped with pillows on the bed, with her medical attendant standing beside her. Her face was flushed either with returning health or some mental excitement. Bony had been a constant visitor since that dramatic night when Illawalli thawed the ice freezing all her muscles, the ice that had kept her prisoner in her own body . . .

"I have come to say good-bye, Miss Kane," the detective said softly.

"Oh, not good-bye, Bony! Let it be only *au revoir*," the girl cried, her eyes becoming abruptly misty. "You will come again some time to see us, won't you?"

"Thank you! I would like to return to stay with you and Dr Knowles, say late next year. You will not, I trust, fail to send me at least one crumb of the wedding cake?"

"Oh, Bony! How did you guess?"

He smiled. "To Bony all things are known."

Stepping forward, he gallantly kissed the warm hand held out to him. The doctor's hand he clasped and shook vigorously, and then, wishing them all good luck, he left them.

The others were waiting for him outside the veranda door. Bony noticed how Ted Sharp kept in the background, as had become his habit. He had observed, too, that Elizabeth's attitude to the boss stockman was distinctly cold.

"Give me another minute, Sergeant," he pleaded. "Miss Nettlefold, I wish you to come with me. You, too, Ted."

Taking the girl's arm he urged her across to the perplexed Ted Sharp, and then with his other hand gripping Ted's arm he took them both across to the lounging Illawalli. On seeing them approach, the chief stood up to receive them with dignity.

"I am about to leave you, Illawalli," Bony told him regretfully. "Before I go I want you, as a favour, to read me this white feller's mind."

"Give your hand," requested the ancient, his expression stern.

Ted Sharp hesitated.

"Give him your hand, there's a good fellow," urged Bony genially. The boss stockman complied then, hostility yet in his mind against the detective. For thirty seconds his strong brown hand was gripped by the skinny black one before Illawalli said:

"You come to Coolibah many years ago. You find here nice young white girl. Bimeby you tell her you love her, and she say no; she no un'erstand her own heart. Then your father's brother he die and say you have two-three thousand quid. All them quids they very nice, but they no good you buy beeg station and plenty cattle! So you say nothin'. P'haps you tell white girl again you love her and again she no tell her own heart.

"And then letter come and you told your father him die and him say you have *orl* his money. The law man him write you go Brisbane and sign papers and then you get orl beeg money. You say: 'No. I stay here and your offsider him brings papers to Gurner's Hotel. I sign 'em there.' So law man's offsider him come to Gurner's pub that night the fine feller captain's plane him stolen. You go there and sign 'em papers and law feller's offsider him say orl them quids belonga you in bank.

"Now you say yourself, I buy Garth Station. You know old John Kane he own Garth. Way back long time, Mr Nettlefold and John Kane they have row, and bimeby Mr Nettlefold he tell Kane him buy Garth. And John Kane him laugh and him say: 'No, never you buy Garth, I watch that.' You know if you go Kane and say you buy Garth, Kane him say: 'You want Garth for Mr Nettlefold and I say plenty times I no sell Garth to Mr Nettlefold.'

"You cunning feller, orl right! You send letter to station fellers down in Brisbane. You tell them ask Kane how much he want for Garth. You tell them go careful or Kane him find out you after buy Garth. They say so much. You say wait. Then d'rectly you sign papers belonga law man's offsider, you send wire message to station fellers in Brisbane tell them they buy Garth quick you got plenty money. You reckon you have Garth and seven thousand cattle you say to white girl you love her, she marry you, you got plenty cash, plenty cattle. You cunning feller, too right! You nearly go jail 'cos you cunning feller, too."

The old man released the brown hand, and, looking into Sharp's astonished face, chuckled grimly. Then, before the boss stockman could say a word, Illawalli took Elizabeth's hand.

"The white lubra is joyful,'" he said. "She knows that the sick white lubra soon be better, that she soon go away with doctor feller. One time Miss Eliz'beth she lonely and sad. She not know what make her sad and lonely. Then she know, then she know when she take sick white lubra and nurse her. She think she know what she want, so that no more she will be lonely and sad. Then some whitefeller, he play the fool with my friend Bony. He no talk when he should. He think him cunning feller and he don't say nothing when Bony put him questions. Now she know white feller him not crook and she joyful. She know she marry Ted Sharp when he ask her. She know she want to look after him and bimeby . . ."

"Oh, Illawalli!" the blushing Elizabeth exclaimed reproachfully. Ted Sharp straightened his shoulders and looked from her to Bony, who was bidding Illawalli an affectionate farewell.

Bony smile at them in turn and hurried back to the house where the others were gathered about Cox's car. The goodbyes were prolonged. Nettlefold was hearty. Loveacre was dashing despite the disfiguring bandages. Elizabeth came hurrying with Ted Sharp from the direction of the office. Her eyes were like stars. Cox climbed in behind the wheel, and Bony joined him in the front seat. Bony waved to Illawalli, and then, just when the car was about to move off, Ted Sharp sprang to Bony's side to whisper:

"I apologize, Mr Bonaparte, for being such a stupid cad."

"Not a cad, Ted; merely too cautious."

"You are generous. Tell me this: Did that old chap really read our minds? He guessed a lot of things about me . . . and . . . in the office, Elizabeth told me that he read her mind all right."

Bony chuckled and pinched the boss stockman's arm.

"No," he confessed. "I am afraid I told Illawalli what to say."

EPILOGUE

"So you see, sir, that I fell down on the job," Bony pointed out to the white-haired, fierce-eyed gentleman sitting in a lounge chair within a comfortably-furnished study. "Had I used my brain properly I could have finalized the case weeks ago and have saved the State the expense of sending that aeroplane for Illawalli, and the expense of sending another back with him. To Sergeant Cox is due the entire credit for clearing up a nice little puzzle."

"H'rumph!" snorted Colonel Spendor. "Now tell me why you had the effrontery to telegraph me here at my private residence concerning an official matter? And why the devil do you come here to make your report? The office is the place, sir, for all official business."

"But are you not pleased to see me, sir?" asked Bony with innocent astonishment.

"Of course, but what's that to . . ."

"And, sir, have you not been entertained by my story of the stolen aeroplane?"

"I do not deny it," shouted the colonel. "Bring two of those glasses from the sideboard—and the damned whisky. Hi! We must have that Illawalli feller attached to us for duty."

"Would you kill an old man, sir?" Bony inquired, setting glasses and decanter on the small table beside the Chief of the Queensland Police Force.

"Why, no! Of course not!"

"Then permit him to return to his own people. He would die soon in a white man's city. In return for his services, I told him that you would be pleased to present him with a gold watch and chain."

"A gold . . . . A gold watch and chain! Where the devil am I to get gold watches and chains to present to aboriginal chiefs? Tell me that."

"I thought, sir, that you might like to buy him one. The Chief Secretary . . . a special grant, sir. Illawalli would be so proud to have a watch presented by you, sir."

The colonel glared. He was about to suggest a toast, remembered himself, and glared again at the well-dressed and debonair half-caste.

"Well, remind me about it in the morning. What next?"

"Er . . . with reference to Sergeant Cox, sir. I hear that a sub-inspectorship will shortly become vacant. The Red Tape Worshippers are backing Miller. Now Sergeant Cox . . ."

Colonel Spendor banged the table, his face growing deeply scarlet, and through the open french windows from the veranda came a cool, sweet voice which said:

"Now, Father! Keep your temper."

"Er . . . h'rumph. Yes, of course, my dear," the colonel stuttered. "But this damned Bony feller . . ."

"Please, Father, vary your expletives. The one becomes so monotonous," pleaded the sweet voice.

"Your pardon, my dear. I forgot you were there."

Colonel Spendor glared at Bony. He was very angry. And then slowly anger melted before the sun of a big and generous heart.

"There is a vacancy here and now, of which you know nothing," he said. "If your report, to reach me to-morrow, coincides with your verbal report this evening, Sergeant Cox shall receive the promotion and a transfer."

"I will keep the Colonel to his word, Bony," promised the sweet voice.

"Sir, I know a good policeman when I meet him," added Bony, referring to Sergeant Cox.

"And I know a damned bad one when I look at him, and I am looking at one this moment," the colonel flashed.

"Your opinion of me, sir, exactly coincides with my own," Bony instantly agreed.

The colonel chuckled, and rose to his feet to stand with military stiffness. Together they passed through the windows to the veranda where a little woman sat in the falling twilight.

"Madam," Bony murmured, bowing, "I thank you for your support this evening."

"You deserved it, Bony, in return for your most interesting story, well told," replied Mrs Spendor. "And you need not remind the Colonel of his promise to send to that wonderful aboriginal chief the gold watch and chain. I will see to that, too."

And when the sound of Bony's departing taxi died away, Colonel Spendor lit a cigar.

"My worst policeman," he said. "My best detective!"

ARTHUR W. UPFIELD

WINDS OF EVIL

When Detective-Inspector Napoleon Bonaparte sets out to investigate two bizarre murders at Wirragatta Station all the odds are against him. The crimes were committed a year before and the scent is now cold, and any clues that have survived have been confused by a bumbling policeman.

As Bony follows the trail, he is first threatened and then attacked by the mysterious murderer. It's a case which taxes his ingenuity to the limit.

DEATH OF A SWAGMAN

"Our distinctive student of violence arrives incognito at Merino, in western New South Wales, and, as a first move, provokes the local sergeant to lock him up. The method in Bony's madness is that while serving a semi-detention sentence and being made to paint the police station, he wears the best of all disguises . . . Here again is a first-rate Upfield mystery, made warm by humour, by the background characters and his portrayal of the natural background scene."

— The Age, Melbourne.

ARTHUR W. UPFIELD

AN AUTHOR BITES THE DUST

Though used to dealing in character assassination and verbal back-stabbing, the literary clique gathered at the house-party of Mervyn Blake, famous author and critic, is shocked when their host is found dead in his writing room. Detective-Inspector Napoleon Bonaparte, forgoing a holiday to assist the Victorian police in the investigation, quickly adapts himself to the world of literary hates and jealousies. With little to go on, Bony gradually pieces together the mystery. A cat, a ping-pong ball, an alcoholic gardener — these unlikely clues suggest the lines of investigation, but it is Bony's observation of human nature and some shrewd literary sleuthing that finally uncover the murder method, and the murderer.

BUSHRANGER OF THE SKIES

An extraordinary case for Detective-Inspector Napoleon Bonaparte opens when a police car is bombed from the air on a lonely outback road by a mysterious pilot who plans to conquer a nation. The trail through the Land of Burning Water tests Bony's endurance to the limit and takes the detective as close to death as he has ever been.

ARTHUR W. UPFIELD

THE NEW SHOE

On March 1st an engineer began his tour of inspection of the Split Point Lighthouse. He found the Light in perfect operation, and saw nothing to indicate anything unusual . . . nothing, that is, until he discovered the naked body of a man entombed in the thick wall.

Who was he? And who had fired the shot that had killed him? Nine weeks later the police were no closer to answering these questions. They had no clues to the identity of either victim or murderer, and the case was beginning to look like the perfect crime . . . perfect for Bony.

MURDER MUST WAIT

In the little town of Mitford, New South Wales, four babies have mysteriously disappeared — all boys, all under three months old, and all apparently neglected by their mothers. The local police have given up, the trail is cold — the only hope is Bony. And when Inspector Napoleon Bonaparte arrives on the scene a new dimension has been added to the puzzle. A fifth child has vanished and his mother has been found lying beside the empty cot . . . dead.

But Bony's brief is to find those babies and, for once, murder must wait . . .

ARTHUR W. UPFIELD

BONY AND THE WHITE SAVAGE

By a lonely roadside in the south-west corner of Western Australia, old-timer Karl Mueller is roused from his drink-sodden sleep by approaching footsteps and the sound of whistling. What he sees on waking (or thinks he sees) is enough to make him stiffen with fear, and more than enough to worry the police into calling for Inspector Napoleon Bonaparte.

The disturber of Mueller's rest is Marvin Rhudder — once an upstanding theological student, now a convicted rapist and basher, a bloody savage whose recapture will put all of Bony's sleuthing and tracking skills to the test.

THE LAKE FROME MONSTER

When Eric Maidstone was found dead near Bore Ten, just west of the Dingo-proof Fence, the first thought of those who discovered his body was that he might have been attacked by the rogue camel known as "The Lake Frome Monster". But camels don't carry guns . . . and Maidstone had a bullet-hole in his chest which put the Monster in the clear.

So who **did** kill this young man? It was up to Bony, disguised as a worker on the Fence, to find out.